Almost Midnight

Almost Midnight

Paul Doiron

MINOTAUR BOOKS
NEW YORK

First published in the United States by Minotaur Books, an imprint of St. Martin's Publishing Group

ALMOST MIDNIGHT. Copyright © 2019 by Paul Doiron. All rights reserved. Printed in the United States of America. For information, address St. Martin's Publishing Group, 120 Broadway, New York, NY 10271.

www.minotaurbooks.com

Library of Congress Cataloging-in-Publication Data

Names: Doiron, Paul, author.
Title: Almost midnight / Paul Doiron.
Description: First Edition:. | New York : Minotaur Books, 2019.
Identifiers: LCCN 2019005587| ISBN 9781250102416 (hardcover) | ISBN 9781250102430 (ebook)
Subjects: | GSAFD: Suspense fiction.
Classification: LCC PS3604.O37 A46 2019 | DDC 813/.6—dc23
LC record available at https://lccn.loc.gov/2019005587

ISBN 978-1-250-10241-6 (hardcover)
ISBN 978-1-250-10243-0 (ebook)

Our books may be purchased in bulk for promotional, educational, or business use. Please contact your local bookseller or the Macmillan Corporate and Premium Sales Department at 1-800-221-7945, extension 5442, or by email at MacmillanSpecialMarkets@macmillan.com.

First Edition: July 2019

10 9 8 7 6 5 4 3 2 1

For Charles Spicer

PART I

A Civil Death

I

I passed the morgue's meat wagon on my way up the hill to the prison.

Another inmate overdose, I figured. Maybe a suicide. If it had been a homicide, I would've heard about it. Natural causes were always a possibility. So many prisoners, especially those condemned to life behind bars, seemed to give up the ghost prematurely, dying being their only real chance at escape.

I wondered if the corpse belonged to one of the men I'd arrested.

The sun had broken through the clouds, but the American and the Maine state flags hung damp and dripping from a steel pole before the complex of whitewashed buildings. The architect had done a good job disguising the essentially retributive nature of the penitentiary. From the parking lot you could barely see the three sets of razor-wire fences or the guard towers with riflemen in them watching the distant tree line. At night it was different. The misty glow of the klieg lights radiated so high into the sky it illuminated the bellies of the clouds.

I locked my service weapon and automatic knife in the steel box I kept under the seat of my personal vehicle, an International Harvester Scout. Then I made my way across the lot to the gleaming façade, still wet with rain.

"My name is Mike Bowditch," I told the guard behind the desk, showing him my badge and identification card. "I'm an investigator with the Maine Warden Service. I should be on your list."

The correctional officer, or CO, was a paunchy, pouch-eyed man I didn't recognize and whose name tag was obscured by a nonregulation fleece vest. Over the past four years, most of the guards I'd gotten to know had quit or been fired. Prisons never make those best-places-to-work lists. He half rose from his chair to appraise my outfit: waxed-cotton jacket, thermal tee, damp jeans, and muddy Bean boots.

"You been working undercover?" he asked.

"More like underwater."

"Huh?"

"I've just come from fishing."

"Catch anything?" he asked with utter disinterest.

"Some decent-sized salmon. What happened to CO Tolman?"

"Never heard of him." He squinted through a pair of thumb-printed reading glasses at his computer. "You're here to see inmate Cronk?"

"That's right."

"You need to leave keys, coat, spare change, in one of those lockers. Anything that might set off the detectors or conceal contraband." He slid a pamphlet at me. "Here's a list of prohibited items."

"I have it memorized. Look, I drove four hours from Grand Lake Stream to get here before visiting time was over. That's fifteen minutes from now if I'm not mistaken."

The guard put down his readers and studied my windburned face. The lobby of the Maine State Prison was this man's personal fiefdom. He didn't know me. He could have made me wait.

"Is this visit business or personal?"

"A bit of both."

He hadn't anticipated that answer. Or maybe he didn't care one way or another. He waved me through with the back of his hand.

The two guards manning the body scanners had high-and-tight haircuts and muscles you only get from pushing and pulling barbells. Like the CO at the desk, they wore midnight-blue uniforms with gold badges pinned to their shirts and portable radios fastened at the top buttons.

"How're you doing today, Warden?" the lighter skinned of the two asked. He was one of those pale-eyed, white-haired, pinkish people who'd missed being born an albino by a flip of the genetic coin. According to the tag on his chest, his name was Pegg.

"How am I doing? That depends if you let me out of here at the end of my visit."

"I hear *that*, bro. I ain't even claustrophobic but sometimes this place makes me feel like I'm in a trash compactor—and I got a motherfucking key."

Pegg was so white he was translucent, yet he talked as if he'd come straight out of Compton. I sensed he must be a recent hire since he still had a gloss on him that hadn't been worn off or fouled by the existential filth of his workplace.

"The warden's good to go, Pegg," said the other guard, who was as dusky and dark eyed as his counterpart was colorless. He had the permanent scowl of a veteran CO. His ID gave his surname as Rancic.

But Pegg, I had already surmised, was a talker. "You're here to see Killer Cronk, right?"

"Is that what you're calling Billy now?"

But Pegg was too busy performing for his older colleague to listen to me. "So maybe you can settle a bet for us, dog. Rumor around B-Block is that Billy was a supersoldier back in the 'Stan. Is it for real he cut out a Taliban dude's heart after the raghead shot up a school?"

"Sounds like a tall tale to me."

Not that my friend was incapable of such an act.

Pegg winked at me through pallid lashes. "That means it's the truth, yo! What did I tell you, Rancic?"

The protocol was for the two COs to take turns guiding in a visitor or group of visitors.

"How about taking the warden in before he runs out of clock?" Rancic sounded eager to be rid of both of us.

Chastened, the white shadow escorted me down the cinder-block hall to the visiting room. He instructed me to have a seat in a gray plastic chair while he went to fetch Billy from his cellblock.

Weak sunlight from the prison atrium shimmered through a window onto the pressed-wood table. It reflected off a teal-blue backdrop in the corner against which inmates could take photographs with their loved ones. It was the only spot where visitors were allowed to take pictures.

Every time I reflected upon this place, a Latin term resurfaced from deep in my memory: *civiliter mortuus*. The words translate to "civil death." In common law, the phrase applies to the loss of almost all of a person's rights and privileges after having been convicted of a felony. By this definition, prisoners could be numbered along with vampires, zombies, and ghosts as members of the undead. No wonder the Puritans had referred to the first jail they'd built in Boston as "a grave for the living."

I tried to relax, but my lungs were having trouble processing the stuffy air, as if the afternoon's previous visitors had sucked all of the oxygen from it. I still couldn't believe that I had been persuaded to leave my vacation to return to this bell jar—and all on the thinnest of pretexts.

Several hours earlier, I'd been standing in icy, waist-deep water casting Barnes Special streamers to salmon that wouldn't bite unless you bounced your flies off their noses. That was where Aimee Cronk had reached me. I had tucked the six-weight under my arm to dig the vibrating phone out of my waders.

"Billy needs to see you. He says it's a matter of life and death."

"He's said that before, Aimee."

"Not like this he hasn't."

"Still."

I could imagine her on the other end: a short, pretty, ginger-haired woman who was plump in all the right places. It sounded as if she was standing in the open air: the parking lot of a Dollar Store, Family Dollar, Dollar General. One of those places. I heard big-engined vehicles downshifting as they passed.

"Admit it, Mike. You're worried Billy's going to waste your time with one of his crackpot theories."

"That's not true."

"Bullcrap."

Aimee tended to dress in flannel shirts, elastic-waist jeans, and Keds. More than once I'd seen people literally look down their noses at the mother of five as she pushed her loaded shopping cart up to the register and paid for the groceries with a SNAP card. *Isn't this overweight, uneducated woman ashamed to be living off everyone else's tax dollars?*

I could have told those snobs a few things about Aimee Cronk, starting with how her cart wasn't full of the processed food they imagined but fresh vegetables, lean meats, and unsweetened cereals—she had no higher priority than feeding her children the best meals she could afford.

I could have told them that Aimee hated taking assistance and only did so to supplement the two jobs she worked, as a part-time receptionist and a part-time waitress, neither of which offered benefits.

I could have told them that the Cronks had been compelled to sell their house to cover Billy's legal bills and were then forced into bankruptcy when Aimee was diagnosed with a uterine cyst. The treatment would have been covered by Medicaid in most other states but not in Maine, where the governor had opposed the expansion of the program. As a result they were living in a rented apartment in Lubec above a rat-infested warehouse that shipped clams by truck along the Eastern Seaboard.

I could also have warned the snobs that Aimee had read their hateful minds—just as she'd noticed the half-gallon Tanqueray bottles they'd hidden in their carts under bags of quinoa and cases of coconut water. Despite never having graduated from high school, let alone college, Aimee Cronk was the most gifted natural psychologist I'd met. The woman had a bullshit detector so sensitive it registered a lie before it took shape in the back of your throat.

"Whatever Billy's worked up about, it's for real this time," she continued. "Now, what do you have planned that's more important than helping your best friend in the world?"

"That's kind of manipulative, Aimee."

"Darn tootin', it is."

And so I had unstrung my fly rod and packed up my wet waders and driven through a snow squall that had become a rainstorm that had become a partly sunny afternoon by the time I reached the Midcoast. Such was the month of April in Maine.

* * *

The security door opened with a click, and in strode Billy Cronk.

Pegg, for all his hours in the gym, looked like a Munchkin by comparison.

I always forgot what a scary son of a bitch my friend was. Six feet five and all muscle. Irises the color of a glacial pool. He wore his blond hair long, occasionally in a braid; his beard was woven of red and gold. Even women who were terrified of him found him sexually compelling—maybe especially the women who were terrified.

"Make it fast, guys," said Pegg. "You got to be outta here by three-thirty, yo."

Billy folded his long body into the chair across from me. He wore jeans and a blue cotton shirt, rolled up above his forearms to reveal the war ink tattooed there.

"Thanks for coming." His voice had always been more of a growl. Imagine a bear with a Down East accent.

"I know it's been a while."

"You're busy with your new job. I get it."

"That's no excuse."

"You don't need to apologize."

I found myself in no hurry to get to the reason he'd called me here. I feared it would confirm my suspicions that this latest crisis was as bogus as the previous ones.

"The medical examiner was leaving as I was entering the prison. Was it another overdose?"

"Yeah, I didn't think it could get worse, but six guys have OD'd since the New Year, all fatals. Drugs are easier to score in here than candy bars."

He began to tap his foot under the table.

I had delayed as long as I could. "Aimee said you have something important to talk with me about."

He lowered his voice as if a microphone might have been hidden under the table. "There's a new CO here. A female sergeant. Her name is Dawn Richie. She got transferred over from the Downeast Correctional Facility after the governor closed it."

"She was lucky. Most of the guards at that prison lost their jobs."

"She was lucky all right." He cast a stealthy glance at Pegg, who was standing against the wall, nibbling his nails. "I need you to do something for me, Mike. It's a matter of life and death."

"You know I'd do anything for you, Billy."

"I need you to look into Richie for me."

"Look into . . . ?"

"Investigate her. Learn as much as you can about her past. No one can know you're doing it. You can't tell a soul. Not even your new girlfriend. Especially not Dani. If word gets out, I'm a dead man."

My heart had become a dead weight inside my chest. "You want me to secretly investigate a Maine State Prison sergeant?"

"You've got to do it fast, too."

"Why?"

He folded his powerful arms across his chest, showcasing the green dagger tattooed along his ulna. "I can't tell you that."

It wasn't the request that gave me pause. Nobody who knew me—certainly none of my superiors—would have accused me of being a stickler for protocol. The problem was Billy's overactive imagination. The man saw conspiracies everywhere. More than once he had sent me on a chase for a nonexistent wild goose. At what point are you hurting, not helping, a friend by indulging his make-believe suppositions?

"You need to give me a reason."

"You want a reason? How about you do it because you owe me."

For the past four years he had never once uttered those words. I realized now that my reluctance in coming to the prison today was because I had sensed my long-unpaid bill had finally come due.

Billy Cronk was behind bars, separated from his wife and children, because of me.

Four years earlier, two lowlifes had tried to murder Billy and me in a gravel pit in the woods of easternmost Maine. They had almost succeeded. They *would* have succeeded if Billy, the veteran of Iraq and Afghanistan, hadn't gone into berserker mode. What started as self-defense ended with bloodshed of a kind I'd never before witnessed. When Billy had blown apart a helpless man's skull with a burst of .223 rounds, he had, in his blind fury, unquestionably crossed a line that I couldn't ignore and remain a law-enforcement officer.

It was the hardest decision of my life. But I chose to uphold my oath and testified truthfully to what I'd witnessed in the gravel pit. The judge sentenced Billy to seven to ten years in prison for manslaughter.

The searing memory of Aimee Cronk's sobs in the courtroom made it harder to say what I had to say now. "Billy, there's no way I can do what you're asking me to do. I'm a warden investigator, not a PI."

My refusal—after his having called me on my debt—seemed to catch him off guard. "But you know all the tricks."

"You know I'd do anything for you, Billy."

His nostrils flared. "Except this."

"The last time I was here you accused the infirmary staff of having trustees sneak olanzapine into your food because you refused to take it. Only the symptoms you described—hyperactivity, insomnia, paranoia—are the *opposite* of the effects produced by that drug. Before that was the incident of the 'stolen' wedding ring that you forgot you'd hidden. And the time someone was supposedly embezzling funds from your canteen account that turned out to be a math error. Do you want me to go on?"

"You think I'm crazy."

"I don't think you're crazy."

"I'm the boy who cried wolf then."

To avoid disclosing my concerns about his mental state, I trotted out an excuse even I recognized as lame. "What you're asking me to do today would be against the law."

When he sneered, his mustache revealed the curl of his upper lip. "Because you never broke the law before."

He had me there. "This is different."

"How?"

The pain I felt at refusing him came out as petulance. "Because you won't tell me why, for one thing. Who is this woman? Why do you need to know about her background? Is she into something illegal? Is she in mortal danger? What?"

Billy shot to his feet so fast he overturned his chair. Pegg, who had been watching us from a distance, snapped to attention and reached for his radio. He was unarmed, as was standard for correctional officers when in places where they could easily be ambushed by prisoners.

"Is there a problem, Cronk?"

The prisoner burned me with his glare. "Forget I asked."

"Billy?"

"You don't have to visit again—not for a while." Then he drove the shiv through my heart. "Tell Aimee I love her."

2

I left the prison in a daze.

What was I going to tell Aimee Cronk?

"I'm sorry, but I can't help your husband because his acute paranoia has become chronic?"

I knew that the correctional system dealt with "problem" prisoners by handing out mood-altering medications like biscuits to begging dogs. But to the best of my knowledge, Billy had never taken any prescriptions, not even the antidepressants we had encouraged him to try during the first dark days of his incarceration. If anything, he looked healthier just now than he had in ages.

I could still recall Billy Cronk's first months in prison, when, out of despair and disgust, he had stopped exercising and told the barber to shave off his hair: a voluntary Samson. His regimen of self-punishment didn't stop with letting his muscles go soft. He'd also allowed himself to be battered and bloodied by inmates he could have knocked cold with a single punch. Every time I visited him, he seemed to have a fresh bandage, a new set of stitches. He lied to me about how he'd received them, just as he lied about the incident that sent him to the Supermax the first time. He'd claimed he defended himself from a new prisoner looking to show his hardness by coldcocking the largest guy in the pod. The real story was far more disturbing.

Because Billy had taken beatings without fighting back, he acquired a reputation as a punk. Inevitably some of the wolves had gotten it into their heads to gangbang the cowardly new fish. Submitting to rape by a trio of likely HIV-positive thugs was one punishment

Billy refused to accept. All three of his attackers ended up in the intensive care unit. One never recovered his sight.

And Billy had landed in the Supermax. He did months in solitary confinement.

I had never been allowed inside the Special Management Unit, or SMU, as it was euphemistically known, and Billy refused to tell me about the experience, but I'd heard plenty of horror stories. Inmates sent to the prison's Supermax building spent twenty-three hours a day in cells smaller than my mom's walk-in closet. Their rooms were lit constantly and blindingly, with no clocks to mark time. Prisoners in the SMU were denied books, televisions, and radios. Even toothbrushes were forbidden. Sometimes, if they created trouble for the COs, they were also deprived of blankets and even clothing. Their cold meals were shoved through a slit in the door. Insane prisoners not uncommonly sought revenge on their captors by splashing them with cocktails of feces, blood, and semen.

Whenever I thought of the Supermax, I heard the voice of the Reverend Deborah Davies in my head. She was one of the Warden Service's two female chaplains. Before that, she had volunteered her pastoral services in correctional facilities across Maine.

"History is going to judge us for the six million Americans we have consigned to our gulags," she'd told me. "And our descendants are going to hate us the same way we despise our slaveholding ancestors."

I had sent too many evil men to jail to hold with all of her progressive notions.

"You've got to acknowledge it's a form of torture, Mike," she'd said.

"That's for someone else to decide."

"None of us gets off that easily, my friend."

I hadn't known what to expect when Billy emerged from solitary, and I'd approached my first visit with trepidation. I was shocked to find that he had begun exercising again and had grown out his hair and beard. He had seemingly climbed out of the pit stronger than when he had been tossed into it. Except for the paleness of his complexion, he again resembled the Billy Cronk I had first met: a Norse god fallen to earth.

After his surprising physical rebirth, had I been wrong to believe that he would emerge from prison with his mind intact, too?

I rolled down the window to feel the slap of air against my face. Then, because I am nostalgic by nature—perversely so, according to my friends—I turned down a back road I had patrolled years earlier as a newly minted warden. Here, on the Maine Midcoast, I had made my first arrests, saved my first lives, lost my first love.

Almost at once I noticed the difference in latitude from where I had begun the day. While the benighted forests around Grand Lake Stream were still encased in ice, the snow here had largely melted, even in the ragged shadows of the evergreens. Pussy willows clustered along the roadsides, begging to be cut for vases. Elsewhere, the reddening buds of maples added an erotic blush to what would otherwise have been a landscape of unbroken grayness.

One other seasonal change announced itself. During my brief sojourn in the North Woods, election signs had sprouted from the rotting snowbanks and flooded lawns.

The primary would not be held until June, but our current governor—a man nicknamed the Penguin because of his physical and ethical resemblance to Batman's comic-book foe—was in trouble. His approval rating was underwater, and he was facing a formidable opponent, the state's leonine attorney general. Campaign consultants had advised Henry "Hal" Hildreth III to downplay his wealth by choosing a slogan (*HAL!*) meant to imply he was a relatable man of the people.

The Penguin's roadside signs, by contrast, bore the message the governor himself had chosen for his reelection bid:

BECAUSE FREEDOM ISN'T FREE

I couldn't read those words without thinking of the cage in which I had abandoned my friend.

Again.

My drive through these nostalgic woods had for once failed to revive my spirits. With a weight pressing on my shoulders and nowhere else to go, I headed home.

* * *

When it had become certain that I would be working out of the Bangor office, I had purchased a four-room cottage set amid ten acres of mixed woods in the seaside village of Ducktrap. It was one of those New England hamlets with a full graveyard and an empty schoolhouse. Half a mile from my place, a crumbling old farm had an actual family plot in its front yard. No wonder the dump had scared off potential buyers for the past decade.

My home wasn't in such dire shape, but it definitely needed some love. Its pine floors were warped and its joists leaned every which way but upright. On the plus side of the ledger: the fieldstone foundation was solid, the roof didn't leak, and a nearby nest of Cooper's hawks kept the red squirrels from invading my attic.

Best of all, a river flowed along the bottom of the property. Every fall, a dwindling population of Atlantic salmon returned to the Ducktrap to spawn—one of the last places this still happened in the United States—but the brackish waters also held sea-run brook trout, striped bass, even a few shad. In the woods I found the tracks of occasional bears and wayward moose. At night, sitting on the porch, gazing up at the sky, with the stars as sharp as diamonds, I could persuade myself I lived someplace wild and remote.

I parked my Scout in the dooryard beside my government-assigned vehicle, an unmarked Jeep Compass. I missed the truck I used to drive when I was a patrol warden. My promotion had come with costs as well as benefits.

When I stepped through the mudroom door and continued into the kitchen, I realized that something was amiss. Someone had been inside my house during my vacation.

I found the explanation on the table in the form of a note:

I was in the neighborhood.
Check your refrigerator.
You're welcome.

The message was unsigned, but the identity of its author was no mystery.

Danielle "Dani" Tate and I had been dating for two months. She was a state trooper assigned to southwestern Maine, close to the New Hampshire border, so our relationship was by circumstance long-distance. Having a two-hour drive between us was also my preference.

Not long before, I had been living with the daughter of my friends Charley and Ora Stevens. Stacey and I had been together for years, and the expectation was that we would get engaged and married. But she was fighting inner demons more powerful than she was.

I knew how that felt. I also knew that I couldn't help her.

I still loved Stacey. I doubted I would ever stop loving her. She would always have a claim to some piece of my heart.

For that reason, I had been trying to take things slow with Dani. Only now did I understand that my giving her a set of house keys had, perhaps, sent a different message.

She had stocked the refrigerator with greenhouse greens, locally pressed apple cider, and cream in a glass bottle from the dairy down the road; the freezer contained two organic chickens. My year's supply of microwave burritos had been forcibly evicted. Dani wasn't the only woman in my life horrified by the junk I ate. But she was the first to take aggressive action against my bad habits.

I was simultaneously shocked and tickled. I checked my watch and realized that she would still be asleep. When she worked the eight-to-eight overnight, she normally rose at five P.M. I sat down with my phone and brought up her contact.

The screen showed the picture of a woman with a square face, blond hair, and stone-gray eyes. Few people would have called her beautiful. But in this rare photograph she was beaming. She had the most amazing dimples that only appeared when she was happy.

I smiled, clicked on the image, and began typing:

> I didn't realize that when you said, "You need to start eating better," you meant immediately.

After I pressed send, I immediately second-guessed myself.

Dani and I hadn't communicated since I'd gotten the panicked call from Aimee. In prison, Billy had all but begged me not to share what he'd said with my new girlfriend, the state trooper. He and I both knew that Danielle Tate wouldn't look the other way where the laws of Maine were involved.

Yet I had to explain why I was home when I'd planned on spending the next three days fishing in Washington County.

> Seriously, though, thank you for the food. I've had an
> interesting day. I need to tell you about it.

Interesting?

I deleted the adjective and typed in *weird*. Then *crazy*. Then *insane*.

Upon further consideration, I erased everything and sent Dani a two-word message:

> Call me.

I took a quick shower, then wiped a window in the foggy mirror so I could see myself to shave.

I missed having a buzz cut. When I'd been promoted the year before, my captain had asked me to grow out my hair in the event I was called upon to do undercover work. The truth was, my frequent appearances in the news had made it all but impossible for me to conduct covert operations within the state of Maine.

But at least my longer hair concealed the scar on my upper forehead. It was a reminder of a bar fight I'd been in when I was twenty-one, at a backwoods roadhouse called the Dead River Inn. At the time I had no clue how many scars I would acquire in the rough-and-tumble years ahead:

A star-shaped burst of permanently bruised capillaries from the impact of a bullet against my ballistic vest.

A white line on my forearm where a meth head had cut me to the bone.

A permanent lump at the base of my skull from a baton that had slammed me into unconsciousness.

A cluster of dead nerves in my hand where I'd torn ligaments in an ATV crash.

So many scars. Not all of them external.

I put on a pair of Levi's and a faded COLBY MULES T-shirt, started a fire in the woodstove to banish the spring chill from the house, and popped the lid off a bottle of Molson Export ale. Craft brewing had become a big thing in Maine, but I'd found I had no palate for spice notes and fruity undertones.

For dinner, I grilled a couple of deer-meat burgers in a cast-iron pan that smoked so intensely I had to open a window. Afterward, I poured myself three fingers of bourbon and settled down in the living room to decide what to do with my remaining vacation days. I could drive back in the morning to Grand Lake Stream. But what's the old quote about how you can't step into the same river twice?

There would be no way, after my visit to the prison, that I could enjoy myself catching salmon. What I needed, I realized, was a project. But spending my vacation unpacking boxes and repairing holes in the drywall seemed a poor use of my precious time off.

I slugged down the liquor, pushed around the embers in the stove with a poker, then threw on an oak log that would take the whole night to burn.

As I was dusting my hands, my phone vibrated on the side table. I expected it to be Dani.

Instead it was a text from the mentalist Aimee Cronk:

Shame on you, Mike Bowditch.

3

I tried to message her back, but she wouldn't respond. Nor did she pick up the phone when I called. She'd said everything in that simple scalding text. I had failed her husband when he needed me—and not for the first time.

I slouched in my leather armchair, listening to the fire hiss and crackle inside the stove like a caged imp. Instead of refilling my glass with bourbon, I went into my mostly unpacked office and removed a cardboard box from a desk drawer.

After Billy's sentencing, I had obtained a copy of the trial transcript. My intention had been to search for a legal loophole he might be able to exploit in his appeal—or so I had told myself. The reality was that I had acquired this document as an instrument of self-torture. I was as much of a masochist as my friend.

The relevant pages were dog-eared and grease-stained from my fingertips. The dramatis personae of the courtroom were identified by our roles: the Prosecutor (Attorney General Henry "Hal" Hildreth), the Court (the Honorable Martha Meade), the Defense (Mark Clark, Esq.), and the Witness (me).

PROSECUTOR: Warden Bowditch, where were you when the defendant shot and killed Todd Pelkey?

WITNESS: I was on the top of the gravel pit.

PROSECUTOR: And you had an unobstructed view of the bottom?

WITNESS: Yes.

PROSECUTOR: And you knew he was dead?

WITNESS: I suspected he was dead.

PROSECUTOR: Where was Lewis Beam relative to the defendant at that time?

WITNESS: On the ground. Ten to fifteen feet away from Billy.

PROSECUTOR: And what was he doing?

WITNESS: Crawling away.

PROSECUTOR: It was the defendant who had broken his arms, correct?

WITNESS: It was a life-and-death struggle. Billy was just defending himself.

THE COURT: Witness is instructed to answer the question.

PROSECUTOR: It's all right, Your Honor. The witness has affirmed that the defendant was the one who shattered Mr. Beam's arms, rendering him helpless to defend himself.

DEFENSE: Objection. The prosecution is assuming facts not in evidence. We can't know whether Lewis Beam was helpless or not. Neither could my client at the time.

THE COURT: Sustained.

PROSECUTOR: Warden Bowditch, did you see any weapons on Mr. Beam?

WITNESS: At that point, no.

PROSECUTOR: Did you see any weapons on the defendant?

WITNESS: Yes, an AR-15 rifle. He'd used it to save my life by killing Todd Pelkey before Pelkey could shoot me.

PROSECUTOR: We're not talking about Mr. Pelkey now, Warden Bowditch. We're talking about Lewis Beam, who was *trying to crawl* to safety while the defendant pointed a loaded rifle at the back of his head.

DEFENSE: Your Honor!

THE COURT: Is that an objection?

DEFENSE: The prosecutor is testifying again.

THE COURT: Sustained. The prosecution will refrain from making speeches until closing arguments.

PROSECUTOR: I apologize, Your Honor. Warden Bowditch, in your statement you said that you called to the defendant, "Billy, don't do it." What was it that you thought he was going to do?

WITNESS: I didn't know what he was going to do.

PROSECUTOR: Your Honor, permission to treat the witness as hostile.

THE COURT: I was under the impression he was your witness, Mr. Attorney General.

PROSECUTOR: So were we, Judge. So were we.

THE COURT: You have my permission.

PROSECUTOR: Warden Bowditch, isn't it true that having just watched the defendant shoot and kill Todd Pelkey, you believed he was about to do the same to Lewis Beam?

WITNESS: What I was trying to tell Billy—Mr. Cronk—was that in my opinion Beam no longer posed a threat.

PROSECUTOR: Did the defendant give any indication he had heard you?

WITNESS: He seemed to be having a flashback to his time in combat.

PROSECUTOR: Are you an expert in post-traumatic stress syndrome?

WITNESS: I have personal experience with it.

PROSECUTOR: And yet the defense hasn't included you on its

list of expert witnesses to testify on the subject of flash-backs in combat veterans.

DEFENSE: Your Honor, the prosecutor is badgering now.

PROSECUTOR: The Court has already ruled that the warden is a hostile witness. It's understandable and admirable that he wants to defend his friend, the man whom he believed had just saved his life.

THE COURT: Let's hear a question, Mr. Attorney General.

PROSECUTOR: Of course, Your Honor. Warden Bowditch, how did the defendant respond to your concise communication to him that you were no longer facing a material threat to your lives?

WITNESS: He shot Lewis Beam in the head.

PROSECUTOR: He blew apart the skull of a man with two broken arms. Is that right?

WITNESS: Yes.

THE COURT: Louder, please, Warden.

WITNESS: Yes.

As always happened after I reread the transcript, I felt as hollow as the abandoned house down the road.

"Damn you, Billy," I said to the empty room.

Against my better judgment, I opened my laptop and belatedly began my search for Dawn Richie.

I found next to nothing except for an item on the website of the *Machias Valley Observer* announcing Correctional Officer Richie's promotion to the rank of sergeant several years earlier. This press release was the only evidence I could find (without accessing government databases) that the woman existed.

There was nothing unusual in this. In Richie's line of work, and mine, it paid to protect your privacy. Minimizing one's cyber-footprint was simple prudence when you made enemies of danger-ous and vengeful human beings.

But I was impressed with Dawn Richie's success at persuading others from blowing her cover. I discovered no posted real estate transactions, no social media mentions, no photographs snapped at weddings. The woman might as well have been a phantom.

Once again, I woke up to the sound of my cell phone.

"Hello?"

"I had to work a fatal over on 302," Dani said, explaining why she hadn't returned my call sooner.

"What happened?" My mouth felt cotton-stuffed from the liquor.

"A box truck veered across the median, sideswiped an SUV, which crashed into a tree and burst into flames. Then the truck flattened a Honda being driven by this little old couple. The husband and wife both died at the scene, which I guess might be a blessing. The driver of the SUV was charred from head to foot but was still alive when a couple of passersby pulled him out. And the guy who started it all, the one driving the truck, walked away without a scratch."

"Jesus."

"We think he's amped up on something. Adderall or Ritalin. Maybe some designer stimulant."

I propped myself up against a couple of pillows. "Sounds like a wonderful way to start your shift."

"The commander's put me on traffic duty, detouring westbound vehicles out through Casco. The main road's still closed until the wrecks can be hauled off and our guys can finish mapping the site. What's going on with you? Why are you home so soon? I thought you were going to fish with Charley for a few more days?"

"Aimee Cronk asked me to go see Billy. She said it was an emer-gency."

"Did something happen to him?"

"He's having one of his semiannual freak-outs." As soon as I spoke the words, I regretted them. "This time, he might have some legitimate concerns though."

"Are the wolves after him again?"

"No, it's not that. Not this time. It's hard to explain. Billy has always been his own worst enemy."

"I don't know what to tell you." She sounded distracted. "I know you consider Billy Cronk a friend and all, but you always seem to end up in a dark place after you visit him. I'm sorry your vacation got cut short for no good reason."

"Thanks for all the food, by the way."

"You'll be paying me back for it. Don't worry. And you really do need to clean your house. I am happy to be your dietitian, but I draw the line at being your maid."

I let out a laugh. "What were you doing in Ducktrap, though?"

She hesitated, and I realized she'd been lying about being in the neighborhood. She'd traveled two hours from her apartment for the sole purpose of restocking my refrigerator. It seemed an extravagant gesture, given the casualness of our relationship.

Suddenly, I heard a loud crunching noise on her end of the phone. Definitely metal on metal.

"God damn it! Can you hang on a second, Mike?"

She muted the call.

While I waited for her to return, I realized how desperately I needed to talk with someone—anyone—about Billy's paranoid request. But sharing his secret, especially after he'd told me not to, would be an unforgivable violation of his trust. However bad I was feeling, I needed to keep the incident to myself.

When Dani returned to the phone, her voice had acquired a blunt edge. "I need to call you back. A car just tried to pull a U-turn to avoid the detour and smashed into a Jeep. That's my life these days: one car crash after another."

I knew the feeling.

4

Early the next morning, I saw two gray foxes cross my yard and disappear, single-file, into the cedars along the river. A late-breeding pair, I had to assume.

When I was young, before my mom had grown tired of my dad's drinking and womanizing and had decided to escape the North Woods for a new life in suburbia, I had once awoken to strange noises coming from outside our cabin. My child's brain conjured up two little dogs lost in the wilderness.

Deeply worried, I asked my father what poor animals were making those high-pitched cries, and he told me with a lewd grin that they were mating foxes. He said that the male and the female were inseparable during the spring.

"Once I caught a vixen in a leghold trap." His voice had been rough from beer and Marlboros. "But instead of running off, the dog—that's the male—stayed close to hand. Even when I came right up on them, he wouldn't abandon his bitch. You should have heard the little bastard growl at me."

Bastid was how he pronounced the word.

"What did you do?" I'd made the mistake of asking.

"I shot them both, of course." Then he added, "Although it saddened me to do so."

There was Jack Bowditch for you: a death dealer with a heart of gold.

My dad would have loved running a trapline on this wet, wooded property of mine, so rich with furbearers.

Like Billy Cronk, he had been a combat veteran—a Ranger in Vietnam—who had come home decorated with scars and medals.

But my father's crimes had never landed him in jail for more than a few weeks. The past was his personal prison.

At times I wonder if it is mine, as well. Sometimes it seems as if I have escaped. Then I will hear the baying of bloodhounds on my trail.

Standing there, thinking of those two war veterans, I decided to return to the fenced hilltop in Warren. I wasn't sure Billy would consent to see me after our argument. But I owed it to him, and my conscience, to learn what had prompted his odd request that I investigate Sergeant Dawn Richie.

The sun had barely cleared the crowns of the trees. In my neighbor's field Highland cattle had trod a muddy, manure-strewn path from the barn down to the creek. Steam rose from their nostrils as they stood stupidly in their pasture, their shaggy sides matted with ice.

Instead of the coastal route to the prison, I chose to take the country road that skirted the western slopes of the Camden Hills. The unlit shoulders of the mountains were cloaked in velvet shadows. Then, below Maiden's Cliff, sunlight sparkled off the thinning ice on Megunticook Lake. The sudden, unexpected brightness made me grope for my sunglasses.

My phone vibrated in my pocket.

"Where are you?" asked Aimee Cronk.

"On my way back to the prison. I'm not happy with where I left things with Billy yesterday. I'm hoping he'll tell me what's really going on with him."

"The prison? You need to get to the hospital!"

My studded tires skidded on the pavement. "The hospital?"

"Billy was stabbed! I don't know the details. He's being taken by ambulance to Pen Bay Medical Center. It sounds bad, Mike. I'm scared. Really, really scared."

"I can be there in ten minutes."

"I need to pick up the kids from school, and then it's a three-hour-plus drive if the damned Tahoe doesn't blow a head gasket. What if he dies before we get there?"

"He won't."

"How can you say that?"

"Because Billy is as tough as they come."

"Oh, Mike." Her voice broke. "You're so naïve."

I had installed a two-way radio in my personal vehicle in case I found myself nearby during an emergency and could provide assistance to first responders on the scene.

When I switched on the radio, a cacophony exploded from the speaker. The chatter was so fractured—so many units were responding at the same time—that I had to piece together the narrative. I gathered that five ambulances had either arrived at or were en route to the hospital from the prison. Whatever mayhem had occurred had involved more people than just Billy.

I hit the gas along the potholed roads, at one point scattering a parade of turkeys head-bobbing across the asphalt. A car, coming in the opposite direction, flashed its high beams at me. But I sped along, undaunted, until I came to the medical center in Rockport.

Two ambulances were lined up outside the emergency room as paramedics, assisted by hospital personnel, worked quickly to unload stretchers. The parking spaces outside the ER were jammed with government vehicles: prison transports, squad cars from the neighboring towns, state police cruisers, black SUVs with the Knox County sheriff's star on their sides.

Rather than trying to enter the building through that logjam, I continued to the main drop-off circle. I had visited the hospital enough times while I'd been stationed in the Midcoast—both as a first responder and as a patient—that I knew all the shortcuts.

I clipped my badge, my holstered sidearm, and my cuffs to my belt. Then I dashed through the automatic doors.

The Knox County sheriff had had the presence of mind to station a deputy in the lobby to prevent curiosity seekers from sneaking down the hall to the ER and surgical wing. Seeing me rushing forward, the lanky officer held out his arms as if we were in a game of red rover. Then his freckled face cracked into a grin.

"Bowditch?"

"Skip?"

I hadn't seen Skip Morrison in ages, but when I'd been stationed in the area as the district warden, I had considered him something of a friend. We'd gone out for beers and conversation more than once, the conversation consisting of me nodding along to his cracker-barrel monologues. The guy was congenitally incapable of shutting his mouth, but at least he was interesting.

We'd both risen in the world since those days. Skip was now the chief deputy for Knox County.

"What are you doing here?"

"One of the prisoners who was stabbed is a friend of mine. I need to see him."

"The sheriff says I'm not supposed to let anyone by except essential personnel. It's a frigging MASH unit in there, from what I hear."

"Do you know what happened at the prison?"

"Two inmates attacked a couple of COs with homemade knives in the laundry room, and it turned into a bloodbath. One of the guards is dead, another is injured. And a third prisoner managed to get himself stabbed, too."

"Do you know the name of the CO who was killed?"

"I haven't heard yet. But the one who was wounded was a female sergeant."

"Dawn Richie?"

"That sounds right. Who's your friend who was stabbed?"

"Billy Cronk."

"I know Billy! That guy could pull your arm from your socket, then beat you to death with it. Everybody in the joint is afraid of him." Skip's face darkened. "Do you think he was one of the two attackers?"

"He wouldn't assault a guard except in self-defense."

"How sure are you of that?"

"Can you please just let me past?"

He frowned as if preparing to say no, then surprised me with a smile. "Promise to circle back and tell me what the heck's going on. You know how it kills me being out of the loop."

I started down the carpeted hallway. On the left side of the passage was the ER; on the right was surgery. Seriously injured patients would be wheeled across from one side to the other.

I hadn't made it fifty feet before an urgent voice came over the loudspeaker: "Code Silver, Surgical Care. Repeat: Code Silver."

The codes that hospitals use are different from the "ten codes" used by police, fire fighters, and other first responders.

Anyone who has ever seen a TV show set in a hospital knows that a Code Blue is a medical emergency: a patient flatlining.

Code Red indicates a fire.

A Code Silver is less intuitive but makes sense when you think of the traditional color of gun barrels.

Despite the massive law-enforcement presence, someone in the surgical unit had grabbed a weapon and was, presumably, threatening the life of another person. An active shooter was loose in the suite of operating rooms.

I drew my SIG P239 from its holster, performed a press check to ensure a round was loaded in the chamber, and brought the gun in a two-handed grip up near my chest, ready for whatever might come bursting through the sliding doors between me and the incident scene.

As I neared the first entrance, I heard shouting. Men's bellicose voices, layered one on top of the other. A Babel of repeated commands for someone to drop a weapon.

Nothing happened as I crossed the sensor plane of the automatic doors. The hospital must have gone into lockdown mode. I couldn't see a thing through the translucent panels. The good news was that security had closed off the obvious exits from the surgical wing. The bad news was that I was now cut off from the action.

My only option was to rush back the way I'd come and circle around the outside of the building to an entrance where a platoon of cops would already be drawn up.

Or is it my only option?

The hospital was an older building that had been partly retrofitted with modern technology. The result, I'd noticed on one of my prior visits, was a mishmash of security measures. Mirrored hemispheres on the ceilings contained all-seeing cameras. Certain doors only opened with a swipe of a card, others with a series of numbers punched into a keypad.

But plenty of old-fashioned doors with old-fashioned locks secured with old-fashioned bolts remained. What I needed to do was locate one of them.

I ducked into the now-vacated postoperative unit. Before me was an empty desk. Beyond were a series of spaces, some actual rooms, others just curtained enclosures where anesthetized patients normally lay in wheeled beds, waiting to return to consciousness or having just done so. In the lobby the *Today* show continued to play on a television set to an audience of empty chairs. The hosts were discussing healthy treats to put into kids' Easter baskets.

As I rounded the desk, I was startled to find a young woman in scrubs on her knees. She was pressed against the desk the way a frightened dog presses itself against its owner's leg.

I'd been wrong to assume the unit had been cleared, I now realized. Nurses and visitors were hiding behind every curtain and closed door. The administration had walled off the ER when they'd initially brought in the prisoners, but the Code Silver had caught them off guard. There simply hadn't been time for security to evacuate the expansive critical-care wing when the prisoner escaped. It was all they could do to initiate their shelter-in-place procedures.

"What's happening?" the woman in scrubs whispered. She had horrible acne and looked too young for whatever job she might have had in a hospital.

"An armed prisoner is loose. I need to get into the surgical wing."

"You keep going down the hall."

"The automatic doors are locked. Is there another way in from this side?"

"No."

"Are you certain? Maybe there's a way you never use yourself."

She shook her head no. But I knew she had to be overlooking something. This part of the hospital was a warren.

Across the room, seemingly in the right direction, I saw a door labeled JANITORIAL.

As I hoped, it seemed to be a pass-through, accessible to custodians moving between surgery and post-op. The room stank of headache-inducing chemicals and was jammed with custodial carts.

The shelves contained neatly folded bedclothes and cardboard boxes containing who knew what.

I crossed to the opposite door and pressed my ear against it.

More shouting. The words shapeless. Just noises.

Then the doorknob rattled. Someone was trying to open it. But the bolt was still shot.

I reholstered my service weapon. With my left hand, I reached for the lock. It made the softest of clicks. I closed my hand around the knob.

What happened next took only seconds, yet it unfolded in super–slow motion.

As I pulled the door inward, I felt movement. A gore-soaked man had pressed himself against the lintel. He had coffee-colored skin and a neck as thick as my thigh, and he was holding a pair of surgical shears to the throat of a woman in scrubs. The cutting edge had already given her a ruby necklace of blood. He must have had his other arm wrapped like a python around her waist.

Facing both the man and his hostage—and now me—was a semicircle of firearms. The faces of the officers holding them were blurred. The barrels of their weapons were the only things in focus.

The inmate stutter-stepped as he felt his structural support disappear behind him. Whatever he'd expected, it hadn't been the previously locked door opening of its own accord.

He rolled his eyes sideways, trying to catch me in his peripheral vision. I grabbed the wrist holding the shears and gave it a yank, throwing my weight backward. Both the hostage taker and the hostage fell with me through the doorway.

Time seemed to stop. I became aware of the smell of shampoo in the woman's hair. I saw the shears still clenched in the prisoner's hand as the sharp edge slashed within an inch of my eyeball.

A gunshot exploded, shattering the moment like a hammer breaking a mirror.

Then gravity kicked in again and we continued our fall.

The woman knocked the wind from my lungs when she landed on top of me. A split second later, I felt the considerable weight of the inmate slam my shoulder to the floor. I smelled gun smoke. I even thought I heard the spent shell casing bounce off a hard surface. I turned my head and stared into the ragged red hole in the center of the dead man's forehead: a third eye already focused on the world beyond this one.

5

The prisoner's name was Darius Chapman. Despite his clothes being blood soaked and half-shredded, his identification tag was still clipped to his shirt pocket. I had never heard of him before.

But I recognized the correctional officer who'd shot and killed him: Rancic, the dark-eyed man behind the prison body scanner. I watched the guard as he holstered his still-hot weapon. From his self-possession and the hardness with which he returned my gaze, I suspected that Chapman wasn't the first man Rancic had killed in his life.

The nurse was lifted off me, then rushed away to be treated for the laceration to her neck.

Brother officers helped me to my feet.

A man in physician's scrubs examined Chapman's corpse on the floor for a pulse.

I was escorted to the ER, where another doctor sat me down on a gurney. He instructed me to remove my jacket, which had been contaminated by blood, and toss it into a hazardous-waste bin. Next, my shirt, also stained. I was relieved I got to keep my pants.

With the help of a nurse who appeared at his unspoken command, the doctor swabbed the gore from my face and applied some sort of neutralizing agent to the potentially disease-carrying brain matter in my hair. He checked me for open wounds. Finding none, he walked off without a word, the silent nurse trailing behind.

A state trooper told me to sit tight until I could give a statement on what had happened with Chapman, but I got up anyway. I had no intention of waiting there, bare chested and shivering, until the scene commander could delegate an officer to interview me.

Hospital staff rushed back and forth along the hallway, and assorted cops and prison guards milled in and out of the now-open ambulance-bay doors.

"Where's Billy Cronk?" I demanded of one of the interchangeable guards.

"Surgery."

Once more, I crossed the hall to the surgical wing. The operating rooms were all blockaded by thick-bodied men in uniforms. They didn't want a repeat of what had happened with Chapman.

I must have checked three different rooms and asked three different officers the same question.

Finally one of them answered, "Yeah, Cronk's in there. Why?"

"Is he going to live?"

"How should I know? I'm just guarding the door."

Someone tapped my shoulder. "Mike?"

Skip Morrison had finally relocated me. The chief deputy gave me one of his Howdy Doody grins. "Nice abs!"

I had almost grown accustomed to walking around bare chested. "There was blood and brains on my shirt. I had to throw it away."

"Likely story! I hope you're telling everyone that it was me who told you to sneak in the back way. I want credit for taking down Chapman, too."

The idea of being credited with anything baffled me.

"How the hell did he get loose?" I asked, knowing that Skip was such a busybody, he would already have the story.

Chapman, it seemed, was one of the lucky survivors of the knife fight back at the prison. But he had been stabbed in the torso so many times he was springing leaks everywhere. The COs put him in restraints and kept him locked up for the ambulance ride. That's standard operating procedure at the prison. Rancic rode along with the emergency medical technicians to provide security.

The EMTs did everything to stop Chapman's abdominal bleeding. Pressure, bandages, hemostatic gel—but an artery was giving them headaches. Five minutes out, the prisoner fell quiet. When the ambulance arrived, the emergency personnel rushed his stretcher into the ER, where a doctor waved them into surgery without a stop at triage.

The attending surgeon requested that Rancic remove the cuffs because they were going to be in the way. After Rancic unlocked the manacles and before another officer applied the bed restraints, Chapman stopped pretending to be unconscious. He grabbed the nurse who was cutting off his clothes with surgical shears and pressed the scissors blade to her throat. Hostage taker and hostage backed from the room. Chapman was trying to feel his way toward safety even as cops convened from other parts of the hospital. Rancic followed the scrum, and when he had a shot, he took it.

I had never transferred a prisoner from an ambulance stretcher to a hospital bed, but even I knew better than to remove restraints before new ones were in place.

"You don't think that's weird?" I asked Skip.

"The level of incompetence? No, I think that's par for the course at the prison."

"I'm talking about the fact that the same CO who unchained the guy was the one who killed him."

"If I had to guess, I'd say Novak was trying to make up for having screwed up and nearly gotten a woman beheaded."

"Novak? Is that Rancic's first name?"

"The guy's a Gypsy, from what I hear."

I crossed my arms against a sudden draft. *"Romany."*

"What?"

"*Gypsy* is considered an ethnic slur. They prefer to be called Romany. I don't know what the term is for an individual."

Skip pulled on his freckled earlobe. "I hope you haven't gotten all PC on me, Bowditch."

"What's Rancic's résumé? I don't remember meeting him when I was stationed here."

"He's a new hire, six months on the job. I'm not sure where he worked before."

"He struck me as a veteran CO."

"A veteran CO wouldn't have allowed a prisoner to get free."

It was a good point. "What can you tell me about the man he killed?"

"Chapman?" Skip said in a faux-wistful tone. "That's a different story. We held Darius in the county lockup briefly before his trial for armed robbery. You probably remember those banks that got held up around Rockland, a couple years ago. Anyway, Darius and I shared some quality personal time, and let's just say I won't be buying a bouquet of flowers for his grave. That man went from calm to crazy faster than a Porsche goes from zero to sixty."

"So there's no known connection between the two of them? Rancic and Chapman?"

Skip set a long hand on my shoulder with affection. "Have I ever told you what a beautiful thing your paranoia is?"

The irony wasn't lost on me. I had unfairly labeled Billy Cronk as paranoid when the threat to him had been real. Meanwhile, my deputy friend was accusing me of being a conspiracy theorist.

"Tell me what happened at the prison," I said. "How did it start? Who stabbed who?"

"Oh, there are rumors galore. But nothing I believe. At the moment it's safe to say that the people who know aren't talking. And the people who are talking don't know. Listen, it's been good catching up, but I'd better boogie."

Before he could go, I asked him if he might have a spare shirt or jacket in his cruiser I could borrow. Five minutes later he returned with a self-satisfied grin and a novelty tee he'd picked up at the Maine Lobster Festival.

This one was red, white, and blue. An eagle clutched two pistols in its talons. On the back, words were written in an appliqué script meant to resemble the handwriting of the Founding Fathers: I'M SORRY BUT I CAN'T HEAR YOU OVER THE SOUND OF MY FREEDOM.

Skip had professed ignorance, but it struck me that certain facts had been established. Billy Cronk, Darius Chapman (now deceased), and one unidentified prisoner (also deceased), had been in a knife fight. In this mêlée, a correctional officer had also been killed and Sergeant Dawn Richie had been wounded severely enough to require transport to the hospital.

I leaned over and put my face in my hands. Billy was only a few years from completing his sentence for manslaughter. I had professed to Skip that my friend would only have attacked a guard in self-defense. But given his recent behavior, his vague accusations against Dawn Richie, how certain could I be of that?

What am I going to tell Aimee?

I thought of her speeding south, her balky, rust-bitten Tahoe loaded with Cronklets. When she arrived, would the troopers even let her see her husband? Not if he was a suspect in the assassination of a correctional officer and the attempted assassination of another.

Although the hospital was still teeming with troopers, deputies, and municipal cops, I seemed to be the only game warden present. No surprise there. Unless a prisoner escapes and our tracking skills are needed, we are not generally brought in to deal with crises in the correctional system.

A smooth-faced trooper tapped my shoulder. "The hospital is asking nonessential personnel to clear the ER, Warden."

I caught sight of a black-haired man dressed in a fancy suit on the far side of the surgical suite.

"Just a second," I told the trooper. "Hey, Steve! Steve Klesko!"

The state police detective paused midstep and searched for the person who'd shouted his name. When he finally saw me, he made an exaggerated face signaling dismay.

Detective Steven Klesko and I had cooperated on an investigation the previous November on an island twenty miles off the coast. A negligent hunter had mistaken a woman for a deer, we'd been told. What had actually happened was far more twisted than that simple scenario.

I hadn't covered myself in glory during the Ariel Evans case. After it was over, I'd received reprimands from my superiors for failing to communicate my findings, for refusing to coordinate my actions with them, and for exceeding the scope of my authority in arresting a suspect in the killing.

But at least one good thing had come out of my first homicide investigation. Klesko and I had become friends. Along with some of his college buddies, I had joined him on a marathon snowmobile trip over the winter—five hundred miles across northern New England. To my surprise, he'd even asked me to be a groomsman in his upcoming wedding.

"Mike, what are you doing here?"

"I was nearby, heard what happened at the prison, and thought I might be of help."

"That's bullshit. You couldn't control your curiosity."

"Are you in charge of this thing?" I asked, meaning the Gordian knot of interlocking crimes that needed to be untangled.

"Lucky me, right?"

In Maine all felonies committed by incarcerated persons and all suspicious deaths of inmates are investigated by the state police. The policy was put in place by a former governor who realized it was an obvious conflict of interest for prison wardens to investigate their own officers for potential negligence or misconduct.

"If you have a minute, I'd like to buy you a cup of coffee," I said.

"I don't have a minute. But I never pass up free coffee."

Klesko wasn't handsome in the conventional sense. His hairline was too low, his eyebrows too close together, his eyes too sunken in their sockets. Decades of playing hockey, including a stint in the minor leagues, had left him with a dented nose he hadn't bothered to straighten. But he carried himself with an athlete's grace. Most important, he seemed utterly at ease inside his own skin. And isn't that the essence of charisma?

After we'd found the coffee machine and a quiet corner, I asked, "How is Dawn Richie doing?"

"She's got a facial laceration and some superficial defensive wounds on her extremities, but nothing life-threatening."

"Have you interviewed her yet?"

"I've been waiting for the docs to give me the go-ahead, but it should be any minute now. Sergeant Richie was the first one transported. Why are you asking me these questions, Mike?"

"I'd like to sit in on your interview."

"I'm sure you would!" It took him more than a few seconds to realize I was serious. "I hope you realize how out of the question that request is. On what basis should I allow you to be in the room?"

Once again I found myself at a decision point. I was the friend of one of the inmates who had, perhaps, attacked Dawn Richie. That same inmate had instructed me to pry into her private life. Sharing that information with the police would be yet another betrayal of a man I had already doomed once.

But Steve Klesko was a fellow law-enforcement officer, and my duty was to share whatever information I possessed that might assist his investigation. I couldn't save Billy from himself. If that reality hadn't been obvious before, it was now.

"One of the injured prisoners is a friend of mine. I actually visited him yesterday, and we had a disturbing conversation. His name is Billy Cronk. Can you tell me how he's doing?"

"The docs think he's going to pull through. I take it you believe your conversation is relevant to the stabbings."

"It might be."

His conjoined eyebrows rose. "Well?"

"Before I tell you, I'm hoping you can give me some assurances."

"Come on, Mike. You know I can't do that."

"I don't want to worsen his legal situation."

Klesko scratched a temple where a few gray hairs had recently appeared among their darker fellows. "What exactly do you think happened this morning?"

"I don't honestly know."

"Your friend Billy Cronk was the one who saved Sergeant Richie's life. If not for him, those two other inmates would have cut her throat. Your friend's the hero of the day, dude."

6

It took a moment for Klesko to register my stunned reaction to his words. "What were you under the impression happened at the prison this morning?"

"My first thought, when I heard Billy was involved, was that something had triggered him to go berserk. He has a history of flashbacks to the war. They sometimes end in violence. It was how he landed in prison."

A note of caution crept into his voice. "When you talked to him yesterday, did he seem like he was on the verge of a psychotic break?"

"Maybe."

"Did you warn anyone?"

"The COs would have locked Billy up in the Supermax as a precautionary measure. If he wasn't crazy yesterday, he would have been after a couple of weeks in solitary. I couldn't do that to him based on nothing but gut feelings."

Klesko stared straight into my pupils. The unsettling sensation was of being appraised by two different people with two different agendas. There was Steven Klesko, the detective with the Maine State Police, coldly assessing my actions. And there was my friend Steve, who heard the pain in my voice despite my attempts at hiding it.

After a moment he said, "You were the one who arrested Cronk, right? After he blew that guy's head off?"

"I didn't want to, but he told me it was the right thing to do. He said if I broke my oath, it would eat me alive."

"You also testified against him at trial?"

"Hildreth subpoenaed me. I wasn't in any position to deny the state attorney general."

"Tell me if it's none of my business. But have you talked to anyone about this? A professional?"

"There's a priest in Bangor I sometimes go to for confession."

Since my childhood, the church had rebranded it the Sacrament of Penance and Reconciliation. The penance part I got; I understood suffering. But reconciliation with my Creator had so far eluded me.

"What did the padre say?" Klesko had also been raised a Catholic and still attended mass.

"That God forgave me for sending my friend to prison."

"What more do you need than that?" Klesko deposited the empty cup in a trash can. "To make sense of this, I'm going to need to talk with Cronk. You can't be part of that. As for Sergeant Richie—"

A rotund orderly in multicolored scrubs chose that opportune moment to lumber over.

"Detective Klesko?" he said in a high-pitched voice that didn't match his body mass index. "The docs say it's all right for you to talk with the sergeant now. If you want to follow me . . ."

Klesko didn't say anything, but he gave me a sidelong glance that I read as permission to follow him. I didn't hesitate.

Dawn Richie wasn't remotely what I had imagined. I had expected a thick-limbed woman of late middle age. Instead I found an athletic person in her mid-thirties. Half her face was concealed beneath layers of tape and gauze, but her undamaged features were delicate, and the color of her eyes—a hazel that changed from brown to green—was mesmerizing. Only her helmet of mouse-brown hair fit the prejudicial stereotype I had carried inside the room.

She was sitting upright on a bed that could be adjusted for that purpose. She wore a papery hospital gown. Both of her hands were wrapped and rewrapped with bandages so that they looked like soft, white clubs or giant Q-tips. She had an IV, pumping saline I assumed, in the crook of one of her buff arms.

"I'm Detective Klesko with the Maine State Police."

She raised her bandaged limbs. "Excuse me if I don't shake hands."

"We're wondering if you feel up to giving a statement."

"Frankly, I'd like to get it over with." Richie turned her chameleon eyes on me. "Who's tall, dark, and silent over there?"

"I'm Mike Bowditch. I'm an investigator with the Maine Warden Service."

"A game warden! I don't hunt or fish so it can't be that I have an outstanding warrant against me." The bandages on her face made her smile seem lopsided. "I know why you're here, Warden Bowditch. You're a friend of Billy Cronk. I've seen your name on the sign-in sheets."

"I can leave the room if you'd like, Sergeant."

"Stay if you want. It won't change what I have to say."

From her specific Maine accent—Down East, coastal—I gathered she'd grown up close to the prison in Machiasport, where she'd started her career. People from away often assume there is a single Maine accent, but there are at least a dozen subtle regional varieties.

Klesko removed his smartphone from his pocket. "Have the doctors given you any medication that might impair your memory or otherwise affect what you have to tell us?"

"No, but if you want to bring me some, I'd appreciate it." She was a bit of a smart-ass, this Dawn Richie. "Just kidding! I've never been one for drugs or booze. I don't like the feeling of being out of control."

"I'm going to record this if you don't mind," said Klesko.

"Knock yourself out. Before we get started, I need to ask you about that gunshot. So I hear it was Rancic who took down Chapman?"

"That's correct," Klesko said.

This confirmation of the latest gossip seemed to please her. "How did he allow Chapman to get free of his cuffs? Darius wasn't exactly the Great Houdini. I know, I know. That's a question for later. You want to hear from me what happened in the laundry room."

"We'll also be reviewing the security footage," said Klesko.

"A lot of good that'll do you! Chapman and Dow were smart where they chose to ambush us. The washers and dryers block the cameras in that section of the room. It's a blind spot."

"Dow?" I said, already breaking my self-sworn oath of silence. "Which Dow?"

She let her gaze wander over me again with renewed interest. "We have a few Dows in the prison, but Trevor was the one who sliced up my face."

Klesko voiced his displeasure with me by clearing his throat.

"Sorry," I said.

Trevor Dow had been one of a handful of men I hated. He was a murderer and a drug dealer who had terrorized an entire town for years before I'd helped send him to prison.

And it was Billy who had stabbed the son of a bitch to death.

Jesus.

With the video recorder going, Klesko began his interview with the usual preliminaries; he stated his own name, the location, the date, the time, and identified everyone present in the room. Then he asked Dawn Richie to give her complete name and also spell it, which she did with amusement, then added, "*Richie* as in *Richie Rich*. Except I don't have two nickels to rub together."

Klesko smiled indulgently. "Let's begin."

"Do you want me to answer questions or just talk?"

"Give me an account of what happened in your own words. I might interrupt from time to time. I'll almost certainly need you to clarify some points at the end."

"Too bad you didn't bring popcorn," she said.

At approximately 7:45 that morning, Sergeant Richie had been called to the laundry room in B-Block by the guard on duty. The trustees assigned to the detail were reporting that several of the new industrial washers refused to start.

A quick inspection revealed that the units had been sabotaged—the control panels had been jimmied—and since the machines had been working the day before, and the door to the room had been locked overnight, the vandal or vandals must have worked the last shift.

Richie sent the morning crew back to their pods, since there was no way they could have vandalized the machines. The lone exception was Billy Cronk, who had put in extra hours the prior evening and was therefore a suspect. She then summoned the two trustees who had worked the night shift with him. Both Darius Chapman and Trevor Dow were considered dangerous men. Dow especially had a reputation for brutally sodomizing his unlucky cellmates, although no one had dared go on the record against him.

How they'd become trustees, Richie had no idea, but she claimed to have been unafraid of them. Plus, she had the most fearsome officer in the prison as her wingman. This was the previously unidentified guard killed in the encounter. His name was Kent Mears, and he had weighed three hundred pounds.

Billy had mentioned the brute to me during one of our recent visits. CO Mears sounded like one of those sadists who sometimes bluff their way through written tests, oral interviews, and personality assessments and secure their dream jobs as professional punishers. He had risen through the ranks to command the Supermax's "extraction team": the armored squad that invaded the cells of disorderly inmates to beat them to a pulp and haul them off to bleed, naked, in a restraint chair.

With Mears for a bodyguard, it was no wonder Richie had considered herself safe. Despite knowing about the spotty surveillance in the laundry room—that she might be invisible to the guard in central control—the possibility of being ambushed never crossed her mind.

She'd been grilling Trevor Dow when she heard Billy Cronk cry out, "Hey! What are you doing?"

The shouted question caused Mears to turn his back on Darius Chapman, who used the distraction to jab a concealed shiv into the guard's carotid artery. Richie never even saw the improvised weapon. All she saw was cartoonishly red blood jetting through the fingers of her bodyguard. Mears banged off a steel dryer as he toppled to the floor. Dying, he kicked the machine so hard with his duty boots they made black dents.

The next thing Richie knew, Trevor Dow was whipping his hand toward her throat. This time she saw a flash of metal. She raised a hand but felt the razor edge slice through skin and tendons all the way to the metacarpals. But her reflexes at least deflected the shank. The blade missed the arteries and veins in her neck but slashed deeply down the length of her face.

Dow came at her again, this time grabbing her bleeding hand, but she got her uninjured arm between them, taking cuts to her wrist and hand.

Her next memory was of Dow raising the shank for a backslash across her windpipe, when his eyes seemed to pop from their sockets. He began to jerk as if an electrical charge were flowing through him, short-circuiting his nervous system. Then suddenly he was toppling over: a dead tree in a gale.

Behind him stood Billy Cronk, panting, blood-spattered, the shiv clenched in his huge hand. He must have wrestled it away from Chapman, she concluded. On the floor behind Billy, Darius hissed obscenities as he clutched his stomach.

Richie braced herself against the laundry table, but she felt her legs give way as the shock wore off.

Billy Cronk caught her in his arms. Gently he laid her down on an unbloodied section of concrete.

"You're OK, Sarge," she remembered him saying, his glacier-blue eyes close to hers.

No one *ever* called her Sarge.

Then armored men were dragging Billy away. They hammered him with plexiglass shields, beat his arms and legs with batons. One of the guards sprayed an entire can of mace into those same icy eyes she had stared into, spellbound.

The correctional nurse from the infirmary appeared and began pressing what looked like a maxi pad to Richie's face. She felt hands all over her while the RN shouted for the clueless officers to maintain pressure.

Meanwhile, out of the corner of her eye, she watched as Cronk refused to submit. She saw him on his hands and knees while the blows fell hard upon his back and shoulders.

7

Klesko produced two plastic bags from a leather duffel at his feet. The first contained a strange rust-red object that seemed mostly made of plastic with a point at one end. I'd heard stories about the inventiveness of inmates, but fashioning a lethal weapon from picnic cutlery and a sharpened wood screw took a special kind of ingenuity.

"Does this look familiar, Sergeant Richie?" Klesko asked.

"That's the shiv Chapman used to kill Officer Mears, I'm guessing."

"The same weapon Billy Cronk used to stab Darius Chapman and kill Trevor Dow?"

"It's got to be, right?"

"What about this item?"

The second plastic bag contained a T-shaped hunk of stainless steel. The crossbar had been honed to a cutting edge while the short descender was wrapped in box tape to provide a crude grip.

"Did that come from a clipboard?" I asked.

Indeed it had, said Klesko. It was the metal section that normally springs shut against the backing.

"These are nothing special," he said, leaning over to me, the smell of peppermint on his breath. "Sometime at the crime lab I'll show you some of the shivs and shanks confiscated over the years."

"Are we finished?" Richie said from her bed.

Klesko glanced at his notebook. "I'd like to go back to something you mentioned earlier. You said that Officer Mears lost focus when Billy Cronk said, 'Hey! What are you doing?'"

"Yeah, so?"

I felt my heartbeat begin to accelerate. *Steve is wondering whether it was Billy's role to provide a distraction.*

"How would you describe Cronk's tone?" he asked.

"His tone?"

"Did he sound confused, surprised, rehearsed?"

Finally Richie got the gist. "You're wondering if he was in on it? Have you met Cronk, Detective?"

"Not yet."

Smiling seemed to cause her pain. "The man isn't smart enough to be part of a conspiracy. What's that line from *Winnie-the-Pooh*? Billy Cronk is a bear of very little brain."

All his life people had misjudged my friend's intelligence, me included upon our first meeting. While Billy was far from brilliant, he was no moron. Like his wife, he had suffered the stigma of having been born poor to undereducated parents and had been dismissed ever since based on his accent and limited vocabulary.

"How is Killer Cronk doing, anyway?" Richie asked. "I heard Chapman stabbed him before Billy wrestled the shiv away."

"He's still in surgery to repair the tears to his intestines. One of the knife thrusts passed between the bowels but nicked the outer wall of his colon. The doctors are concerned about sepsis if there was leakage into the body cavity."

"Leakage!" She made a sour face. "I mean, that sounds like a horrible way to die. Can one of you get me a drink from that sippy cup?"

Klesko held the straw to her lips. When she was done slurping, she shimmied herself upright.

"Are we done?"

"Almost. Do you have any idea why Chapman and Dow tried to kill you?"

She laughed until she began to grimace from the pain it must have caused her damaged body. "Do I have an idea? Yeah, I have plenty of ideas, starting with the fact that they hated my guts."

"What was the nature of their grievance?"

She smirked at Klesko's turn of phrase. "Those two had grievances coming out their sphincters."

"Can you be specific, Sergeant?"

"When I first started at the prison, I got catcalls. You expect that as a female CO. But if you rap a few knuckles, mace a few tear ducts, it mostly stops. But Chapman and Trevor never bent the knee. I gave them some time to rethink their attitudes in the Supermax."

Klesko loosened the knot of his tie. "Can you point to any specific occurrence—say in the past few weeks—that might explain the timing of the attack?"

"Why does it have to be something recent?" she said sharply. "For all you know they've been working on their master plan for months. What's that Klingon proverb? 'Revenge is a dish best served cold.'"

"Isn't that a line from *The Godfather*?" asked Klesko.

"The wops stole it from the Klingons. Excuse me if anyone here is Italian."

There seemed nothing left to say after that.

Outside, in the hallway, I found myself studying the ceiling tiles as if I were a certified ceiling-tile inspector.

"What's on your mind, Mike?" asked Klesko.

"Did you notice she never commented on being slashed across the face?"

"No."

"I know plastic surgery can fix scars. But what kind of woman—what kind of person—doesn't give a shit about being disfigured? Either she's good at hiding her feelings, or she's one of the most cold-blooded people I've ever met."

The hospital staff were trying to return to normal operations, but the media had caught wind of the story, and journalists were now attempting to talk their way inside the building. Through the nearest window, I saw three news vans with satellite antennas lined up in a pretty little row.

With Klesko's help, I secured permission from the officer in charge to hang out in the waiting room until Aimee and the kids arrived. The deputies blocking the entrance were instructed to let the hero's family inside.

"I'd like to be in the room when he wakes up," I told Klesko.

"That, I am afraid, is a bridge too far."

"Why?"

"I need to get his statement before he talks with anyone else, which means we have to wait for the anesthesia to wear off. Given your relationship, I can't have you in the room for that conversation."

"You're still worried that Billy might have played a part in the attack?"

"I can't dismiss the possibility outright."

"Even though Dawn Richie said he was too dumb to conspire in anything?"

"I think it's safe to assume that the dead prisoners hated your friend. There's also the matter of potential lawsuits. If Mears's family—or, hell, Dow's or Chapman's—decides to sue the state, how is it going to look if you were in the room for the interview, potentially coaching him."

"Understood."

After Klesko had moved off to confer with his colleagues, I noticed a familiar pale person in a midnight-blue uniform at the soda machine. Aside from the COs assigned to Billy, most of the other guards had returned to the prison. Those who remained I took to be friends of Dawn Richie's. Maybe, like me, they were waiting for a chance to visit with their injured comrade.

But something about the way Pegg was standing was odd; slightly hunched, muscular arms hanging at his sides, he gazed with fascination at the shelves of Coke and Sprite. It wasn't the posture of a man struggling to make a decision. It was the posture of a man frozen in place by a magic spell.

"Pegg."

He didn't react until I tried again, my voice louder.

"Oh, hey, Warden Bowditch."

His eyes, I had noticed, tended to be on the pink side. But his sclera were fully bloodshot now.

"Are you OK?"

"Me? Yeah, I'm chill. You can call me Tyler by the way."

"Hell of a thing this morning. Were you there when it happened?"

"No, but I saw the laundry room after. That was some bad shit that went down. Mears getting stuck in the throat. Dude fell hard, too. We all thought he was bulletproof, you know? Like, no way could any con take down Mountain Man Mears."

Despite Pegg's jive-talking, there was no missing how shaken up he was.

"How long have you been working at the prison?"

"Four months." He offered a shaky smile. "The cons call me a newjack."

"So this was probably the worst thing you've seen?"

"The worst? More like the latest."

"We don't know each other, but if I were in your shoes, I'm sure I'd be reconsidering my career choice after something like this morning."

He turned his gaze to his boots. "Nah, I'm chill."

"Let me ask you something then. Had you heard anything about prisoners conspiring against Sergeant Richie?"

He shook his head vigorously from side to side: a no. But he didn't say the word, I noticed.

"Are you sure about that?"

"One hundred percent."

"It sounds to me like she's made a lot of enemies since coming over from Machiasport."

His cheeks darkened, the color close to wine. "I already said I didn't hear nothing."

"So you have no idea why Chapman and Dow ambushed her in the laundry room?"

"Fuck no."

"Really?"

"Those guys were fucking animals. They didn't have to have a reason."

"I'm not sure I believe you, Tyler."

In a split second the anger was gone, replaced by manifest fear. "Is Richie saying something? What is she saying?"

I held up a hand. "The sergeant didn't even mention your name. But I'm getting the feeling that you know something—or maybe suspect something—and it's causing you stress."

Now the anger flared back up, but it was a poor cover for the terror inside him. "A CO was killed and I had to mop up his blood. So, yeah, I am feeling a little stressed out."

"I know what it's like to lose colleagues in the line of duty. Some of them were friends. I found it helpful to talk it out afterward."

"You don't know me, man. You don't know the first damned thing."

8

While I was waiting for Billy to emerge from his cocoon of anesthesia, yet another detective pulled me aside. He needed a statement on the role I'd played in disarming Darius Chapman. My interviewer didn't approve of the word *execution* to describe what Novak Rancic had done, but it scarcely mattered: a dozen other eyewitnesses, including the nurse who had been taken hostage, would claim it had been a righteous kill.

The hospital having returned to normal, I drifted down to the cafeteria at the opposite end of the building. I ordered a couple of eggs and two grilled English muffins and was shoveling in my second breakfast while I checked the messages on my phone.

Word had gotten out among the Maine law-enforcement community, and the majority of my texts and emails were of the "What the hell happened?" variety. I answered my friends with candor, my supervisors with circumspection, and ignored the rest. The busybodies could get their gossip elsewhere.

Dani Tate had left a four-word voice message: "I'm on my way."

It occurred to me that I didn't know how to feel about that statement. She would have finished her shift and would be driving without sleep under the assumption that I needed moral support—or perhaps she was merely eager for an excuse to come visit.

Through the cafeteria window I watched a mixed flock of cedar and Bohemian waxwings alight in a crab apple. It took the birds mere minutes to pick the tree clean, and just like that, they disappeared into the air. I felt a wave of calmness pass through me: the first in days, it seemed.

"Warden Bowditch?"

I turned to see a man in a pin-striped suit tailored for a power lifter. He had dark curls, but his goatee was touched with frost. The graying beard gave me trouble because I knew I recognized him—by his physique, by his dapper dress, by his unusually long eyelashes—but couldn't remember where we'd met. Then came the spark. He was Angelo Donato, yet another official from the Maine State Prison. He looked to have aged a decade in the four years since I'd last seen him.

The two of us had locked horns when I'd visited the prison to ask about a mutual friend, Jimmy Gammon—who'd served alongside Donato as an MP in Afghanistan—and who had later committed suicide.

I gripped his outstretched hand and felt the calluses on his palm where he gripped the barbell. "Sergeant Donato."

"I wasn't sure you'd remember me. But I'm a deputy warden now."

"Congratulations."

Not until then did I notice a uniformed CO standing a short distance from us. He was whip thin with a trimmed mustache that made him look like a British subaltern and stood as if called to attention by a commanding officer. There could be no question that the military-looking man was Donato's minion.

"I wondered if you had time to answer a few questions." Donato sat down across the table without waiting for my permission. He moved aside a vase of dried flowers to have an unobstructed view of me.

"Do you want a Gatorade or a vitamin water, sir?" asked the mustached guard, whose uniform sleeve bore sergeant stripes.

"I'm fine, Hoyt. But maybe you could give the warden investigator and me a few minutes?"

"Ten-four."

After the guard had marched off, I said, "You've done a better job of keeping up with my career than I have with yours. So I take it these questions are sensitive as well as important or you wouldn't have wanted to ask them in private."

He had a disarming smile. "You always were a smart guy, Bowditch."

"Thanks."

"Too smart for your own good." He folded his big hands on the tabletop. No wedding ring. Just a circle of lighter skin where a band would have been. But most people who worked at the prison removed their valuables before going to work. "I want to know what Billy Cronk talked to you about yesterday."

"The dismal state of the Patriots' secondary."

"Be serious."

"I don't see how it's any of your business."

"It's my business if your friend had foreknowledge of the attack on Mears and Richie."

I crossed my knife and fork on my yolk-stained plate. "If he had foreknowledge of anything, I doubt he would have come near that laundry room. I don't know if you have had a chance to speak with your sergeant yet, but she's claiming it was Billy Cronk who saved her life."

"I've heard what Dawn is saying," Donato said in a skeptical tone that hinted at some secret knowledge.

With his hands resting on the table, I reconsidered the sallow circle of skin on his ring finger. There was no indentation in the flesh. Donato hadn't worn a wedding band for a long time. I remembered a photograph on his desk at the prison of a wife and young children taken the day of his return from the war.

I pushed my chair away from the table so I could cross my legs. "I was under the impression the investigation into this morning's attacks was being handled by Detective Klesko of the Maine State Police."

"That's correct, but we're conducting our own inquiry. It includes an audit of security protocols. When prisoners have found a way to exploit a hole in our systems, we need to identify the breach and patch it immediately. We have the safety of our staff—and other inmates—to consider."

I saw no need to respond. The smell of a frying hamburger wafted from the hospital kitchen.

Donato picked up the salt shaker as a plaything. "Cronk wanted to talk with you about Sergeant Richie, right? What did you talk about?"

"We agreed that the Patriots need to draft a cornerback, which means they'll probably take a long snapper instead."

He spoke without looking at me. "It would be a mistake to test my resolve."

I found the expression odd, almost old-fashioned. "It wouldn't be my first mistake of the day."

My phone vibrated on the table. I turned the screen faceup. A luminous photograph shone up at me, identifying the caller as Aimee Cronk.

"I need to take this."

Donato rose to his feet. He adjusted his cuffs and straightened his tie. He smoothed his goatee with his fingers. The purple shadows under his eyes seemed pronounced from this angle. The man wasn't much older than I was, but he looked as if he'd barely survived a head-on collision with middle age.

"Billy Cronk is no hero," he said, looming above the table. "The man's a wild animal who should spend the rest of his life in a cage."

As he stalked away, pursued by his right-hand man, Sergeant Hoyt, I answered the phone.

"Aimee?"

"Mike, where are you?"

"In the cafeteria."

"We're here at the hospital, but they won't let us see him!"

"Billy was still anesthetized when I was last there. He had just gotten out of surgery."

"But the guard says he's awake. A detective's in his room interviewing him. He should have a lawyer in there. He has a right to an attorney!"

I rose from the table. "I'll be right down."

I heard Aimee Cronk even before I rounded the corner to the waiting room.

"You had no business interrogating Billy without him having legal counsel present."

Steve Klesko said with strained patience, "Your husband isn't being investigated for a crime, Mrs. Cronk."

"It don't matter. It's the prosecutor who'll decide if it was self-defense, and if he says otherwise, you'll wish you'd Mirandized the shit out of him. Not to mention that our lawyer will claim Billy was drugged up when he spoke with you. So there's a consent problem for you there, too, *Dee*-tective."

Aimee was standing toe-to-toe with Klesko, although she was close to a foot shorter than he was. She wore a man's chamois shirt that hung on her curvy body like a tunic, jeans she'd patched herself, and a stunningly white pair of sneakers. Her red-blond hair was cinched in a topknot, and she was wearing what Billy called her "sexy librarian" glasses.

Klesko seemed to be bending backward from the short woman's frontal assault. "Please, Aimee—"

"It's Mrs. Cronk to you. And how come his own family can't see him if he's alert enough for the third degree?"

"He's still an inmate in the custody of the Maine State Prison. It's up to them if he can have visitors. You need to take it up with an official—"

"Really? You're gonna play that card?"

Klesko needed rescuing fast.

"Aimee?"

I'd been nervous about my reception, but she threw her arms around me with such force I was glad her hyper-jealous husband wasn't there to see it.

Across the room, I could see her children, the five blond Cronklets, occupying couches and chairs beneath the lone television set. They had already spilled sunflower seeds all over the carpet. Someone had tuned the TV station to a financial news network, and the backwoods ragamuffins were watching it with the intensity of day traders waiting for the next earnings report to drop.

"They won't let us in, Mike," Aimee said.

"So I heard."

"What are you going to do about it, I want to know."

I might have repeated Klesko's line that the decision remained in the hands of the prison officials, but I knew Aimee Cronk well enough to know how poorly that excuse would fare with her.

Fortunately, the deputy warden, Angelo Donato, had also made his way to the surgical wing. He stood in the doorway, conferring with three guards: the mustached sergeant he'd called Hoyt; the white shadow, Tyler Pegg; and a big guy with a shaved head who kept his back to me.

"Deputy Warden Donato!"

"Warden Investigator Bowditch."

"Your guard won't let Mrs. Cronk in to see her injured husband."

The twinkle in his eye announced his pleasure in having something to hold over me. "The rules are to protect the safety of everyone involved, including the medical personnel."

I glanced back at Klesko, figuring a good word from the detective might help, but he was already beating a retreat.

I tried an appeal to whatever heart powered Donato's massive chest. "You were an MP at Bagram Air Base, correct?"

"I know where you're going with this. I am aware that Cronk did a tour in the Sandbox."

"And Afghanistan."

"The Maine State Prison isn't a branch of the VA. His military record isn't our concern. His criminal record is."

Most bureaucrats, in my experience, have a fear of unknown outcomes.

"What do you think the TV reporters out there are going to report," I said, "when they learn you wouldn't permit an injured hero to see his wife and children?"

"What makes you think I give a shit what those bubbleheads have to say?"

I should have known that particular threat wouldn't work. Donato and his boss, the head warden, were protected by the governor, whose contempt for journalists was the stuff of legend.

"How about a trade then?" I played the last card in my hand. "I tell you what Billy and I talked about in exchange for letting Mrs. Cronk and her kids see him."

He rubbed his goatee in a way that suggested he'd only recently grown it. Facial hair was still a novelty. "The wife only, and she will be supervised by one of my men."

Aimee was watching me with a bottled fury. She flared her small nostrils and raised her red-gold eyebrows. *Be a man and make the call,* that expression was telling me.

"All right." Then I added, to everyone's surprise including my own, "But I want Pegg to be the guard in there with her."

"Me?" the pale young man said.

"Billy trusts him," I explained. "I assume you do as well, Donato."

He eyed his own man with open suspicion. "Of course I do."

I was tempted to ask Aimee if her kids needed supervision, but they were clearly waiting with keen anticipation for Microsoft's earnings report. While Pegg escorted her in to see Billy, Donato and I stepped into the corridor that separated the ER from the surgical care unit. The hospital had decorated the long hallway with black-and-white photographs of Maine's maritime past: ships under sail, wharves all afire, sea captains laughing in the face of storms.

"Billy Cronk wanted to see me because he had concerns about Sergeant Richie's safety."

"That, I'm afraid, is a lie."

"What reason do you have to say that?"

"I am under no obligation to share my reasons with you, Bowditch."

We had arrived at a stalemate. Instead of returning his intense gaze, I stared at the center of his forehead, knowing it would make him uncomfortable. After nearly a minute of silence, he raised his fingers to caress his goatee again.

"Have it your way. I'm pulling Cronk's wife out of there. She can see him again when our nurse practitioner says he's ready to leave the infirmary. That might be a while."

The desperation in this threat made me understand what was really eating at him. "You don't trust Dawn Richie."

"Excuse me?"

"You and I haven't agreed on much, Angelo, but you've always struck me as a natural leader. And a good leader protects his people. Somehow, though, I'm not getting the vibe that you feel overly protective of Sergeant Richie."

A janitor pushed a clattering cart past us. The distraction gave Donato the time to collect himself.

"You should write novels," he said in the affectless tone which was his default.

"Maybe in my retirement."

Suddenly, seemingly out of nowhere, a song began to play. I recognized the heavy-metal riff: "Enter Sandman" by Metallica. It had been a favorite of our mutual friend, the late Jimmy Gammon.

Donato produced a cell phone from his pocket. He cupped a hand to his free ear and began to turn away from me for privacy. "Yes, sir?"

But the person on the other end—and I was fairly certain I knew who it was—had news that shattered his composure.

"You're fucking kidding." He paused to absorb a reprimand from his superior. "I apologize, sir. That language was out of line. How long before he gets here?"

The answer was as unwelcome as the rest of the information he'd received.

"Yes, sir. I'll do my best to stall. But you know how he hates waiting."

Donato shoved the phone back into his jacket so hard it was a wonder he didn't punch a hole in the lining. "The governor is coming."

"Tough break."

He seemed to withdraw into himself as he processed my remark. Donato was clearly having trouble sizing me up. He had a natural facility for placing people into categories, and it bothered him that I resisted his best efforts.

He signaled down the hall for Sergeant Hoyt.

In Donato's haste to intercept the chief executive, he forgot about Pegg.

I wasn't sure I should be happy about the news he'd received.

The Penguin was coming, and no one could predict the chaos he was about to cause.

9

I took a seat in the waiting room among the Cronklets. Aimee and Billy had four boys—Logan, Ethan, Aiden, and Brady—and one girl, Emma, who ran the entire house. Fortunately for me, the kids remained fully under the spell of the television. One of the few things in life that chilled me to the marrow was having to make small talk with children.

Reporters kept trying to argue their way past the local cop the hospital had called in as backup to their security.

The journalists would get their pictures soon enough, the minute the governor arrived. The Penguin both hated the media and yet loved nothing better than having a television camera focused on his face and a microphone pointed at his mouth. He would be sure to drag a whole cavalcade of reporters in with him to record his expression of sympathy to Dawn Richie.

Why else would he be coming to the hospital if not to be photographed with the courageous CO who had survived a brutal attack by two convicts?

Billy Cronk, I suspected, would conveniently be omitted from the narrative. His role in the fracas was too complicated for propagandists, who painted only in primary colors.

For my part, I was chafing to escape the germy confines of the hospital. Dani had said she was headed to the Midcoast. I kept glancing up every time someone entered the room, hoping it was my girlfriend.

Instead, it was Aimee who saved me. She looked relaxed, even a little flushed and rumpled, as if an act had transpired between husband and wife that couldn't have been possible under such tight supervision.

"Billy wants to see you."

"How did you arrange that?"

"I told the guard it was part of the agreement with Donato to let you visit. He's a good kid but not the sharpest crayon under the bed."

I stopped in the doorway when I saw Aimee kneel beside her little girl. "Aren't you coming?" I asked.

"I thought you understood. Billy wants to see you in private."

For a man who had come within millimeters of being disembow-eled and had just awoken from anesthesia, Billy Cronk looked damned amazing. He was pale from blood loss, but his pupils were tightly focused. Both wrists remained chained to the bed—the guards having learned their lesson with Chapman.

"Are you sure this was all approved?" Pegg asked as he let me inside.

"Cross my heart."

"You ain't gonna uncuff him or nothing?"

I sat down beside the bed. "I swear I won't let him loose."

"Because I need this job, you know."

"If you could give us a few minutes."

Being so pasty, Pegg was incapable of hiding his agitation. The slightest anxiety caused his facial capillaries to flush.

"This better be on the level."

As soon as he was gone, Billy said, without a hint of irony, "I like your shirt."

I'd forgotten I was still wearing Skip's novelty tee. "Forget my outfit. Jesus Christ, Billy. What the hell happened this morning?"

"I saw the shiv in Chapman's hand and acted on instinct."

"Before that, I mean."

"It was an ambush. Chapman and Dow wanted to ice the sarge. But they had to take out Mears first."

"You need to back up even farther. Yesterday, you hinted that Dawn Richie was dirty and dangerous. You asked me to look into her private life—which I did by the way. Then the next thing I hear is you've nearly gotten yourself killed saving her."

"I was wrong about Sergeant Richie. She's a stand-up woman."

This description didn't exactly jibe with my own impression of her. "What changed your mind?"

He darted his eyes at the door. "Something Dow said. When he slashed her, he said, 'This is what happens to rats.'"

So Dawn Richie was an informer? For whom? Against whom?

Before I could ask those questions, the door opened wide, and Donato stood there with his uniformed henchman, Hoyt, behind him. Poor Pegg was nowhere to be seen.

"Get the fuck out of here, Bowditch!"

"Please don't blame Pegg for my being here."

"Don't tell me what to do, asshole."

The radio crackled on Hoyt's shoulder. The governor had pulled up to the hospital entrance in his two-car motorcade.

Donato came close to grabbing me by the collar. "Out! Now!"

It was lucky for him that he didn't put his hands on me. Probably lucky for both of us, given his considerable strength.

I glanced past him at my friend chained to the bed. "I'll find a place for Aimee and the kids to stay. I'll take care of everything. Whatever you do, don't talk to these guys."

The door shut in my face.

I wanted to be nowhere in the vicinity when the Penguin made his grand entrance.

During his single term as governor, he had hired lobbyists who represented polluters to oversee the state agencies (including my own) charged with protecting Maine's environment. Despite living in one of the most beautiful places in the world, his only regular encounters with the outdoors seemed to take place on manicured golf courses. Even then, from what I'd heard around Augusta watercoolers, he had spent most of his time at the nineteenth hole.

I slipped through a side door and wandered around the front of the building, toward my Scout, so I could change my shirt, at least. The wind had shifted, and I could smell Clam Cove, the tidal flat just over a knoll from the hospital. Three ring-billed gulls were fighting over a KFC bag until a larger herring gull swooped down and plucked the greasy prize from their midst.

After I'd pulled on a fleece quarter-zip, I remembered my promise to Billy.

It being April, arguably the worst month to visit the Maine coast, I had my choice of motels. I made a reservation at the nearest establishment for two adjoining rooms. I left my credit card number, telling the manager the Cronks' stay would be open-ended and that he should bill me for all of their expenses.

My mother had left me some money in her will, a generous trust fund. In the note she had written on her deathbed, she had included a quotation from Dorothy Parker. (My mom had loved sending me memes she'd found on the internet.) "If you want to know what God thinks of money, just look at the people he gave it to." The quote might have been a warning not to let my newfound wealth change me. More likely, she'd found it a funny zinger.

I texted Aimee with the reservation confirmation for the Happy Clam Motel, and she replied with only slightly less reserve than her husband:

> We appreciate your charity, Mike. Hard as it is to accept.
> Thank you.

Aimee Cronk was the last person who would let me use a financial gift as a balm for my conscience, especially when she knew I'd done nothing to earn my newfound riches.

I became aware of a car creeping up behind me, heard the burp of a police siren, turned, and saw a powder-blue Ford Interceptor Utility with its light bar flashing. The brand-new vehicle had been built on the same platform as the civilian Explorer model with one major difference: under the hood of this unassuming SUV was a monster 3.0-liter, turbocharged V-6 engine capable of accelerating to one hundred miles per hour in less than fourteen seconds. Dani had given me all the specs when she'd been handed the keys two weeks earlier.

She leaned out the window. "Please clear the lane, sir!"

I circled around to her side of the idling vehicle. "I was wondering when you were going to get here."

Smiling, she removed her shades, and the sun hit her unusual irises, which seemed to change from one shade of gray to another, depending upon the quality of the light. At the moment her eyes were the color of pebbles washed up in the surf.

"I had to wait for the governor's motorcade. I expected to see you in line to shake his hand."

"Very funny."

"I've been getting updates on the drive over," she said in a soft speaking voice that bore no resemblance to the gruff tone she employed as a trooper. "It sounds like a real mess for the prison. Hal Hildreth has already come out calling for hearings. I think the AG sees the incident as an opportunity to attack the governor's oversight of the Department of Corrections."

"Are politicians born without souls or do they lose them during puberty?" On cue, the wind blew the sulfur smell of the clam flat to my nose. "On the positive side, Billy's surgery went well. He looks like he's fit to cut a cord of wood."

"Wait a second. They actually let you in to see him?"

"Not exactly."

"You used subterfuge then?"

"I suppose you want to know all the gory details?"

"Actually"—she flashed her dimples—"I had something else in mind. You want to go somewhere and make out?"

10

Dani raced me back to my house and beat me by a mile.

I'd always been impressed by her reflexes behind the wheel. If she had chosen a different path, Danielle Tate could have been a champion NASCAR driver.

Or a mixed-martial-arts fighter.

Dani held a black belt in Brazilian jiujitsu that wasn't some phony honor handed out by a storefront sensei. She had recently tossed me onto the bed using something she called an *uchi mata* throw: a judo technique for which I had zero defense. Nor had I wanted one.

She might also have considered a career as an Olympic marksman.

During her last qualification, she had scored highest in her troop using the standard semiauto, the shotgun, and the AR-15.

Because of these achievements—or to diminish them—she had acquired the nickname of Bulldog, which she wore with sullen acquiescence. The name was meant as a friendly tribute to her tenaciousness, her male sergeant had told her. But Danielle Tate was a woman, and she understood what was really going on.

When I pulled into the driveway behind her, she was already standing beside her cruiser with a triumphant grin. She was still properly dressed in her trooper's blue uniform, but she had left her Dudley Do-Right hat on the passenger seat and pulled off the scrunchie she used to secure her hair. The sunlight brought out the honey-gold streaks amid the darker blond.

The men who thought this self-confident, vivacious woman was a dog were blind as well as chauvinists.

"Took you long enough."

"Keep in mind that my Scout doesn't have a rocket under the hood."

"As long as there's a rocket in your pants."

The last time I had blushed in the company of an attractive female was at a junior high school dance, but Dani's aggressive sense of humor turned me red as a beet.

We were all over each other before we'd made it inside the mudroom door. Laughing, we unlaced our boots and kicked them across the dirty floor. Then she was in my arms. At five-four, she was one of the shortest women I had been with. Standing embraces were difficult for us. After a few seconds of fumbling, she decided "To hell with it" and leaped up and wrapped her strong legs around my waist.

I laid her down on the kitchen table and unbuckled her leather gun belt and draped it creaking over the back of a chair. I had to remove my badge, cuffs, and holstered weapon before she could yank my pants down, lest the loaded gun drop to the floor.

Like all police these days, she wore a ballistic vest under her shirt, which had definitely not been designed for afternoon romps. I needed her help to get it off. The woven Kevlar had flattened her pear-shaped breasts. Because of her daily sessions at the punching bag and weight bench, she had acquired a muscular back and shoulders. She would have resembled a professional gymnast from behind if not for the broadness of her hips.

She sat up, pulled the fleece over my head, and laughed with delight at the sight of my bare chest and abdomen. Then her gaze fell lower and she laughed again.

"I shouldn't have worried about that rocket."

An hour later, we were lying in bed, naked, but with the bunched covers down over our bare feet. Dani rested her head against my chest and kept one hand flat on my stomach, which was still rising and falling from the exertion of our second bout. She wasn't even out of breath.

"How were you able to do that on no sleep?" I said in genuine amazement at her stamina.

"I'm younger than you."

"What? I'm only three years older than you are."

"Yeah, but you're thirty and that's officially middle-aged."

"I hope not."

She tickled my chest hair. "I'm starving."

"Do you want me to get up and make something?"

"Not yet."

"This is the third time we've been together in my bed and the third time you've passed on my cooking. Kathy told you I was a bad chef, didn't she?"

I was referring to our mutual friend Sergeant Kathy Frost. Dani had begun her career in law enforcement as a game warden. She had taken over my Midcoast district after I had been transferred to the windswept barrens of Down East Maine. Kathy had been the field-training officer to each of us in turn, and we remained close, even after she had been medically retired because of a gunshot wound.

Dani neither confirmed nor denied what she'd heard about my culinary capabilities. "That's not the reason I want you to stay in bed."

"I think I might need a break before I can go again."

She lowered her hand to my groin. "I'm not so sure about that."

The moment didn't last. She rolled off me and sat up, using a pillow to prop her back against the headboard. The expression on her face told me an intimate disclosure might be forthcoming.

"We're having fun together, aren't we, Mike?"

"God, yes."

"The thing is—I need to know—is that all this is?"

Her question tied a knot in my tongue. "You know I care for you, Dani."

"No offense, but that's a bullshit answer."

"I'm enjoying myself. I hope you are, too. Beyond that, I'm not trying to get ahead of things. I think you know why."

Her gray eyes became granite. "I remember Stacey. The problem is, I care for you, too."

"Can't this be enough for a while?"

"I thought so at first. But I want more."

"Oh."

She'd shaken her own self-confidence. "This is the time when you say maybe we should take a break."

"I don't want to hurt you, Dani."

"It may be too late for that. One of the reasons I drove all the way over here was to have this conversation in person. That and the sex." She smiled shyly as she lifted my hand off her arm. "I'm not asking you to lie to make me feel better. I know you're not an irresponsible man—at least when it comes to other people's emotions—and I know that it's natural for you to want to enjoy some freedom after being with Stacey. But I waited such a long time for this."

"You waited longer than I would ever have expected."

She seemed to perceive something in my remark that bothered her. "Just to be clear, I didn't save myself for you or anything."

"I get that."

"But I can't deny that I waited. Ask yourself why I did that."

I knew why.

"You don't need to say anything. But the way I see it, Mike, you've got all the information you need to make a decision. I should try to take a nap. I won't be any good tonight if I go on patrol after no sleep."

I tried to rise. "You should eat something. I'll make sandwiches."

She pushed me against the mattress. "Better let me."

"You don't even trust me to make a sandwich!"

Her response was to swing her legs off the bed and pad naked out to the kitchen. I lay there feeling my heart flop around my chest like a caught fish.

While Dani slept, I took a shower, put on some jeans, and closed the bedroom door.

She hadn't exactly given me an ultimatum, but she'd made it clear that the status quo could not and would not continue.

When we'd first met, just after she'd graduated from the academy, I had dismissed her as a girl with a chip on her shoulder.

Then, over the years, I'd noticed Danielle Tate becoming more self-assured, less impulsive, harder to read. I'd watched her grow into herself as a person. She was a woman who knew what she wanted, and she had wasted no time making her move after my relationship with Stacey had ended.

I made a pot of coffee and sat at the table with a steaming cup. A feeling of serenity passed through me, as it always did, looking at the world outside my window.

I wondered if I would see those foxes again. I needed to install game cameras around the property to capture all the nocturnal goings-on. They might also provide some small security if a villain from my past came sneaking out of the woods.

That thought brought to mind Dawn Richie again and the enormous effort she must have taken not to leave traces of herself online. Which in turn made me curious about the circus that had accompanied the governor's visit to Pen Bay Medical Center. I understood the Penguin well enough to know he would want pictures and video of himself congratulating the brave guard. Richie's carefully kept anonymity was finished as of today.

I opened my laptop and brought up the site of a news station out of Portland. As I'd expected, the prison attack was the big story. The video began with the reporter, a recent college grad with bleached hair and that staccato pronunciation they teach in broadcasting schools, setting the scene inside the hospital.

Then the video cut to the governor standing over a bed, deep in conversation with an injured person. Except the patient he was addressing wasn't Dawn Richie. It was Billy Cronk. Aimee and the Cronklets stood crowded together at the edge of the frame.

"Holy shit," I said aloud.

Next came a close-up of the Penguin speaking into the camera, his gin blossoms all aflower. "The people of Maine know I call things like I see them. Sometimes it gets me into trouble, being too honest."

The newbie reporter tried to ask a question and the Penguin snapped, "Don't interrupt me, please! Now everyone has heard what happened at the prison this morning. The investigation has already begun, I can assure you. When I arrived at the hospital, I asked for an update, and the first thing I learned was that a convict was nearly killed because he stepped in to save a prison guard. And I thought, 'How can that be? The man is a criminal!' So I asked to see this inmate's record. And here is what I discovered. Not only is the man a decorated combat veteran, but the reason he is in prison is because he used his constitutional rights to defend himself against two drug dealers."

Pelkey and Beam were actually dealers in illegal guns, but the Penguin wasn't far off.

"This cannot be happening," I said to my computer.

"What can't be happening?" Dani murmured from the doorway. She had pulled on one of my dress shirts. Her gymnast's legs looked good under the hem.

"The Penguin is going to pardon Billy Cronk."

"You're kidding!"

"He hasn't said the words yet, but just wait."

She wrapped her arms around my neck and leaned over my shoulder to watch the screen while the governor continued.

"But if he's in prison, people will say it's because he deserves it. Except here is what I have discovered, the secret no one wanted you to know. William Cronk didn't receive a fair trial. The prosecutor on his case didn't play fair. That's no surprise when you hear it was my opponent, Henry Hildreth the Third, who prosecuted the case."

"I think you may be right," Dani said, her breath humid on my ear.

"The attorney general is a well-known enemy of the Second Amendment. So of course he is going to seek the maximum punishment toward a man who defends himself with deadly force."

I hit the fast-forward button.

"You don't want to hear the rest?" Dani asked.

"Just the punch line."

The governor raised a finger in conclusion. "I will be instructing my office to draw up a pardon for William Cronk." He then placed a hand on Billy's shoulder. "Mr. Cronk, the people of Maine thank you for your service and your heroism, and we hope you and your family will forgive the actions of this rogue prosecutor, which resulted in a miscarriage of justice."

"You mean he's going free?" said Dani.

"I guess so. I don't know how pardons work."

Dani released me from her forceful embrace. "What a day!"

I let out a groan. "Shit."

"Why are you saying 'shit'?"

"Because now I might have to vote for the Penguin."

11

After Dani returned to sleep, I put on a sweatshirt and padded outside with my cell phone. I considered sending a congratulatory text to Aimee but understood the Cronks would need time to process the unexpected turn of events. As did I.

Nearby a robin laughed maniacally. I caught a flash of red as he flew off through the bare trees. The hints of color were subtle in the spring woods: green buds of birches, purplish catkins of alders, maroon spathes of skunk cabbage emerging from holes in the snow they had melted with their own thermogenesis.

Billy is going free!

Every so often I would let out a whoop, startling the chickadees that had begun swooping into the feeder. My mentor, Charley Stevens, had trained a flock of chickadees to eat out of his hand, but I lacked the patience for avian instruction.

Less than a minute passed from the time Charley's name popped into my head until the phone buzzed. I had read how the brain fools us into interpreting such synchronicities as evidence of telepathy. What happens is we forget the countless occasions when we're thinking about someone and the phone *doesn't* ring. So what was it with coincidences that they always made me shiver?

"I take it you've seen the news," said the retired warden pilot.

"Seen the news? I was part of it."

"I figured as much. You have an uncanny aptitude at finding yourself at the center of every hullabaloo. Besides, I knew it was a call from Aimee Cronk that took you away from the river yesterday."

"Did the fishing improve after I left Grand Lake Stream?"

"Doesn't it always?"

I knew the old geezer was waiting for me to give my full account of the past thirty-six hours. When it came to curiosity, Charley Stevens had every tomcat beat. So I indulged him. Given Billy's change of tune about Dawn Richie, I no longer felt oath-bound to omit any details.

"Did he explain what had gotten his hair up about Sergeant Richie in the first place?"

"We were interrupted before he could."

"I'd surely like to know. You said this woman was from Down East before she got the job in Warren. I thought I knew most of the turnkeys at the Machiasport pen."

"You're going to start snooping around, aren't you?"

"I'm retired. What else do I have to do?"

"I found it odd that the governor didn't even mention her name."

"My guess is her boss wants to keep Sergeant Richie out of the limelight as a protective measure. And it wouldn't do for them to pin a medal on her only to have her turn around and sue the state for gross negligence in failing to protect its COs."

"The way I figure it, this pardon is the Penguin's way of sticking it to Hildreth."

"Now I've gotten *you* calling him the Penguin, too. What a bad influence I've been."

"Stacey claimed we were bad influences on each other."

My mention of his runaway daughter seemed to suck the good humor out of him.

"You're right that Billy's deliverance is pure political theater," he said after an exhalation of breath. "I'm sure Hildreth is fuming."

"Do you think the pardon will actually happen?"

"I expect so. Tell me again about this guard you mentioned, the one who shot the prisoner he'd let escape."

"His name is Novak Rancic, and I heard he was an experienced corrections officer. I've seen the process guards use to transfer a prisoner from handcuffs to hospital-bed restraints. It's almost like Rancic went out of his way to give Chapman the opportunity to get loose."

"Be careful of coming to conclusions when you don't have all the evidence."

"You've told me that before, Charley."

"Have I?"

I heard the porch door open above me and saw Dani emerge buttoning up her uniform. She must have been unable to fall back to sleep. I used the handrail to pull myself to my feet.

"Meanwhile, now that Billy's safe, I can get back to enjoying my vacation."

"I was hoping you'd be headed back to Grand Lake Stream."

"I haven't made up my mind yet."

As I was hanging up, Charley said, "Give Trooper Tate my fondest wishes."

How had the old fart known that Dani was here with me? Maybe I had written off the existence of ESP too quickly.

"Charley Stevens sends you his fondest wishes."

"I bet he does."

Dani still considered Stacey to be an archrival, no matter that Dani was now the one sharing my bed. Her open jealousy both piqued and excited me, I had to admit.

"You must feel like you're getting a pardon, too," she said.

"How's that?"

"When Billy goes free, you won't have to carry around your guilt anymore. You can both move forward."

"It's not like I've been locked in there with him."

"No?" She shrugged her shoulders. "I should get going. I don't want to be late reporting for duty."

"And I don't want to be a bad influence."

"Then stop being one." Her tone was light, but the words landed hard.

"You were the one who came flying over here."

"You're right. That wasn't fair. All I'm asking is you think about what I said before. I'm not giving you an ultimatum, but . . ."

She kissed me with closed lips and was the first to pull loose of our embrace. We exchanged awkward goodbyes. Then, before I knew it, her Ford Interceptor was rumbling down the track of mud that was my driveway.

Slate-colored juncos returned to peck at the husks under the bird feeder.

April was too early for bare feet. I hurried inside to warm my refrigerated toes beside the woodstove. I wondered if it was too soon for a bourbon straight up.

Six hours later, I was no closer to deciding how to spend the remainder of my vacation.

All I knew was that, for the first time in years, I no longer needed to worry about the Cronks.

One of the decisions I'd made, in moving into my new house, had been to sell my television. I had only ever watched sports on it, and I preferred listening to baseball on the radio. There were plenty of bars and friends' dens I could visit when football season rolled around. And there was always the computer.

Now I retreated to my leather armchair and a copy of Edmund Morris's biography of Teddy Roosevelt. I'd been a history major at Colby but had found the demands of my profession—the long hours, the endless paperwork, the constant motion—had broken my habit of reading for pleasure.

Sitting there, I remembered Dani's gibe at me for being nearly middle-aged.

Thirty didn't feel old.

Except when it did.

Somehow I had forgotten that Roosevelt's first significant achievements came as the police commissioner of New York City. He'd rooted out corruption from among his own force, planted the seeds for what would become criminal-justice academies, and roamed the streets at midnight to observe his men in action. I wondered what TR would have done to reform the Maine prison system.

I fell asleep in my chair with the book open on my lap.

I had a dream that a fly had somehow found its way inside my house and had landed on my shoulder. It seemed to want to tell me something. But when I turned my head aside, it began to shriek.

I sat upright and the book fell to the floor. The lights were still on, but I had forgotten to add wood to the stove, and the room had grown cold. The buzzing was coming not from a fly, but from my phone.

It was nearly two A.M., and my friend Warden Gary Pulsifer was on the line. "I hope I didn't wake you."

"What's going on, Gary?" I expected the worst, as one always does at that hour.

"Listen, I knew you'd want to hear this as soon as possible. I think you might want to drive up to Pennacook as fast as you can."

It was an old mill town on the Androscoggin River in western Maine, most noteworthy in my mind for having been Dani Tate's birthplace. Pennacook sat at the foot of a chain of low mountains that were the trailing edge of the Appalachian Range. My sleep-fuzzed mind could think of zero reasons I might need to go there, especially at this miserable hour.

"Why?"

"Shadow's been hurt."

"Shadow?"

"That wolf of yours is bleeding to death in the back of my truck."

PART 2

All Stories Are About Wolves

12

Déjà vu.

"Will he live?" I asked the veterinarian.

"What do you want to hear?" Dr. Elizabeth Holman said.

"An honest answer to my question."

"Then no. He's not going to live. I doubt he'll make it through the next twenty-four hours."

The wolf lay motionless on the stainless steel table between us. He was even bigger than I remembered: seventy inches long from nose to tail, 140 pounds of muscle, bone, and sinew. His front claws were longer than jackknives. His canine teeth could have punched holes through the skull of a bull moose.

But his ordeal had left the powerful animal diminished. On his desperate flight through the forest, he had lost clumps of black fur and torn the pads of his feet to shreds. Those injuries were mild compared to what the surgery had done to him. He had an endotracheal tube jammed down his throat and a catheter taped to his foreleg where fluids were being pumped into his stagnant bloodstream. The vet tech had shaved his coat down to the skin in two other places: where the arrow had entered and where the point had exited. The rest of the carbon-fiber shaft had remained inside the wolf's body for God only knew how long. Days? Maybe even weeks?

Careful to avoid the pillowy bandage taped to his rib cage, I pressed my palm against the wolf's side and felt the faintest heat coming through my bare hand. I hadn't wanted to reveal my emotions to the vet or her assistant. Under the circumstances, it was important that I appear aloof, disinterested, professional. When in truth the attack upon the animal couldn't have felt any more personal to me.

What happened, Shadow? Who did this to you?

The small room was utterly unlike the surgical wing I had spent so many hours in the previous day. Yet I couldn't shake the eerie sensation that I was reliving that earlier experience. A priest had once described purgatory to me as a netherworld in which you were forced to suffer repeatedly with your sins until you could finally see them with moral objectivity.

"I'd like to have a look at the arrow."

"My assistant is bagging it up for you."

"None of you touched it, I hope."

Dr. Holman thrust out her bony chin. She was thin limbed and hollow cheeked in the way people are who run long distances every day, rain or shine. People who are so physically fit they appear terminally ill. I noticed a tiny gold crucifix held by a chain in the hollow of her throat. "We wear gloves when we operate, Warden Bowditch."

"I didn't mean—"

"The Pennacook Hospital for Animals isn't some fancy clinic like you have downstate, but we're fully accredited—"

"I didn't mean to offend you. I'm a bit sleep-deprived." With its fluorescent lights and white-painted walls, the operating room was too bright for my tired eyes.

"That makes two of us." Lips pursed, she looked me up and down. "Gary—Warden Pulsifer—tells me you're a warden investigator. Is that why you're not wearing a uniform?"

"Actually I am on my vacation. You can call me Mike by the way."

"My friends call me Lizzie."

I removed my phone from my pocket and found the recording function. "Can you repeat for the record what you told me before—about the exact nature of his injuries? And how you treated them?"

A divot appeared between her eyebrows. "I thought you were on vacation."

"I may need to open a criminal investigation, depending on what happened."

Her gaze drifted toward the door. "Wouldn't you rather we talk in my office?"

"Here is fine."

The answer displeased her because she was understandably exhausted and wanted to sit down. But I wasn't ready to leave Shadow's side. These were likely to be my last moments with him.

With her narrow hand, she drew an invisible line in the air above the anesthetized animal. "The arrow entered his body through his left upper trapezius, punctured and deflated the left anterior lung lobe, and pierced the skin through the right rib intercostal. The point had snapped off, but the shaft remained lodged inside his body until I was able to remove it. That was good luck. He would've bled to death if the projectile had worked its way loose before he came to us. As it was, he suffered a class three hemorrhage."

"Meaning?"

"He lost somewhere between thirty to forty percent of the blood in his body."

"What normally happens to a canine if he loses a third of his blood?"

"The same thing that would happen to you—massive irreversible organ failure leading to death. This animal shouldn't even be alive."

"I see." They had bathed the wolf before surgery, but an earthy, canine smell still rose like heat from his body.

"The danger now is pneumothorax and infection. His immune system has been badly compromised. But the longer he holds on, the more hope we have."

From behind me came a faint knock and Holman's assistant entered the room. Like the doctor, she wore blue scrubs, but everything about her shouted teenager. Her movements were clumsy, tentative. She refused eye contact. She had a complexion like pancake batter and a streak of pink in her hair.

"Is now a good time?" She carried a gallon-sized plastic bag. It contained a black stick with red-and-white fletching. A layperson would have called the synthetic material "feathers."

I extended a hand. "I'll take that."

"Shouldn't you be heading home?" Holman said in a motherly voice that seemed to suit her.

"Don't you need me to help remove his tube?"

"I'm going to leave it in a bit longer. And you need to get your kids ready for school."

"I'd rather stay, Dr. H."

"I'll be here."

"I'm worried that if I leave—"

"What happens next is all up to him now. It's out of our hands."

The young woman's eyes and nose began to run. "I never saw a real wolf except in a zoo. I didn't know there were wild ones around here."

"There aren't," I said.

She gazed at me with her lips parted. If there were no wolves in Maine, what was this thing before us? But I didn't explain my cryptic comment.

After she had closed the door, I raised the clear bag to the overhead light to examine the arrow. "This wasn't shot with a bow."

"You think somebody *stabbed* him with it?"

"That's not what I meant. How long would you say this is?"

"Fifteen inches, give or take."

"It's sixteen inches," I said. "The brand name has rubbed off, but it's a Spider-Bite. I'm guessing the X2 model. You said the point had broken off, but it didn't. If you look closely, you can see the shaft is intact. Only the broadhead is missing. It would have screwed into the end here. Imagine an arrowhead made up of three or four razor blades—"

The muscles in her thin neck grew tense again. "I know what a broadhead is. This isn't the first animal I've seen that was shot by an arrow, let alone impaled on a foreign body."

"That's just it. Technically speaking, this isn't an arrow at all. This is what used to be called a bolt or a quarrel. At sixteen inches, it's too short to have been fired by most recurve or compound bows."

Now it was her turn to rub her weary eyes. "I'm still not following you."

"Whoever fired it used a crossbow."

"Does that make a difference?"

"It doesn't make a difference to the wolf. But it might help me find the son of a bitch who tried to kill him."

We both fell silent. What Holman was thinking I couldn't imagine. Within me, a dark storm was raging.

The joy I had felt at the prospect of Billy's early release had been snuffed out. I couldn't even remember having experienced it. The previous day seemed a lifetime ago.

I stared down now at the dying animal, my heart a vessel for molten metal.

Here he lay, the big, bad wolf. Since the dawn of humanity, his kind had been the embodiment of our every nameless fear. Rather than confront our own psychic failings, we had used our terror to wage a campaign of extermination against these rival predators. We had shot them from planes and poisoned them with strychnine-laced baits and imprisoned them in zoos for our children to gawk at. Were we any less afraid as a result? I didn't think so. Humankind had created a sanitized, safety-cushioned world for ourselves—and we had never been more terrified.

I reached out a shaking hand toward the wolf. "Can you give me a minute alone with him, please?"

13

I had told myself I wanted something meaningful to do with my remaining time off. Now here it was.

Outside the clinic, the sky was as black as it had been when I'd arrived, but there was a hint of light now in the east. The air tasted crisp and metallic, and a scrim of frost lay across the lawn. April, in the Maine mountains, is a winter month. Not that I needed the reminder, having grown up not far from here.

In the darkness I could hear the thundering of the river across the highway. The Androscoggin has its beginnings in the White Mountains of New Hampshire, forty miles to the west. Snow had fallen heavily up in the Presidential Range that winter, and all the meltwater was rushing down to the distant sea. The flood carried great rafts of ice that made groaning sounds or even violent explosions when they slammed against each other in the surging stream.

The last time I had come through Pennacook, half a decade ago, it had also been nighttime, and the sky above the town had been sepia colored from the glow of the old Atlantic Pulp and Paper Mill. The smokestacks themselves had been illuminated all the way up from the ground, and the clouds of steam billowing from their mouths had reflected the light. I remembered the nonstop rumble of the huge machines that lived in the bowels of that enormous rectilinear complex. But mostly what I remembered was the sulfurous stench: as if hell itself were around the next bend of the river.

The paper mill had closed since my last visit. After announcing the community's apocalypse in a press release, its absentee owners had made noises about trying to find a new buyer even as they sold off everything of value, right down to the secretaries' desks. This I had heard from Dani, whose father had lost his job and, then, his will to live in the shutdown.

Now Pennacook had fresh air, a nocturnal view of the constellations, and a sky-high unemployment rate that perfectly correlated with the spike in drug overdoses and suicides.

"It's like the whole town just curled up into a fetal position," said Dani. "I never knew that a place could give up and waste away just like a person."

In the clinic parking lot, Warden Gary Pulsifer climbed out of his idling patrol truck to meet me.

His breath drifted sideways on the breeze. "How did it go in there?"

"Not good. The doc tried to hedge at first, but when I pressed her, she admitted he is going to die."

Pulsifer had a scrappy build and a pointed face. He was pushing fifty, which made him old for a warden, and his fox-colored hair had recently turned white around the temples, which made him appear even older.

"I'm sorry, Mike. I know that dog meant something to you."

"He's not a dog."

"Wolf dog then."

"Genetically speaking, he's a lot more wolf than he is dog."

"How do you know about his genes? Did you run his DNA through a doggy database?"

Pulsifer had one of the highest IQs in the Warden Service, and like most intelligent people, his brilliance was the wellspring of his problems. Because of his intellectual superiority, other wardens accused Pulsifer of mocking them even when he hadn't said a word—his default expression was a knowing smile that resembled a smirk.

"His first owner had him tattooed with identification information," I explained. "There are records of his lineage out West."

Shadow had come from Montana originally, and he carried the blood of Yellowstone wolves in his veins. He had been brought into the world by a man who specialized in crossbreeding wolf hybrids to eliminate as much of the domestic dog in them as possible. Later, the animal had passed into a cross-continental network that dealt in contraband until, improbably, he had found himself the property of two methamphetamine addicts in Maine. I had rescued him from their drug den three years earlier.

Pulsifer tucked his hands inside the heavy ballistic vest he wore over his shirt. The armor was covered with an olive-green fabric the same color as his uniform. From a distance, you couldn't tell he was bulletproof.

"When the woman who found him described the animal to me, I knew it wasn't a German shepherd or black morph coyote. It had to be your wolf dog. Sorry, I mean wolf."

"Shadow isn't *my* wolf."

"He escaped from your custody, correct?" Pulsifer's smile was thin and superior.

"You could say that."

"Then he's your responsibility. *N'est-ce pas?*"

I couldn't argue with him there.

Since Shadow had bolted for the wild, three years earlier, the semi-tame wolf had been glimpsed wandering through the high timber between the Rangeley Lakes and the surrounding mountains. Occasionally he had been spotted in the company of a she-wolf, whose place of origin and current whereabouts were both unknown. Having seen the violence done to her male companion, I found myself deeply concerned for her. Wild wolves had been expurgated from the state of Maine in the late nineteenth century, but a few wanderers from Canada appeared from time to time. I was grateful that Shadow had been neutered before he came to me, or I might have been personally liable for the reintroduction of *Canis lupus* to the Northeast.

"Do you want to get some breakfast at the Boom Chain?" Pulsifer said. "I'm paying."

My gaze rose to the hillside across the lot, behind which loomed the unseen mountains. "I'd prefer we go visit the woman who found Shadow."

"Because who doesn't love the cops knocking at their door at five-thirty A.M.?"

He had a point. "I guess I could use some breakfast. But since when do you ever pick up a tab?"

"Didn't you just turn thirty? Consider it a birthday present."

"My birthday was in February, Gary."

I had blundered into his carefully laid trap. "Well, mine's coming up at the end of the month. So I guess it's your turn to buy."

Fifteen minutes later, we were seated in the corner booth of the Boom Chain Restaurant under a pair of antique snowshoes and a stuffed coyote head mounted on the wall as decorations. We were the first, and so far only, customers of the morning.

A waitress appeared with a scorched-bottomed coffeepot. She had streaks of gray in her loose-flowing hair, an unzipped gray hoodie over her uniform dress, and a crooked smile of which she seemed utterly unashamed. I liked her immediately.

"Whatcha doing down here in Oxford County, Gary Pulsifer?"

"I heard the most beautiful waitress in Pennacook was working at the Boom and thought I'd come take a peek." He made a show of scanning the empty tables. "You haven't seen her around, have you?"

She rolled her eyes at me as she filled our cups. "Mister, don't you believe a word that comes out of this man's mouth. I ain't never seen his tongue—and I don't want to neither—but I'll bet you it's forked."

She took our orders: poached eggs and hash for Pulsifer, pancakes and a molasses doughnut for me.

I waited until she'd vanished through the swinging door. "You have a way with women."

Pulsifer extended a wanton arm along the top of the booth. He seemed to be unusually loose and relaxed: comfortable in a way I had never seen him before. "It's the burden I was born to bear."

"What about this woman who found Shadow?"

"Alcohol Mary."

"That's an unusual nickname."

"Mary's an unusual lady. She lives alone up on Number Six Mountain."

I wasn't aware that anyone lived up there; I assumed that the oversize hill fell within the boundaries of the state-owned land around Tumbledown Mountain. Number Six was a camel-backed knoll that watched over the rich farmland of the Sandy River Valley. What could possibly have lured the wolf pair this far south, into the human-populated bottomlands?

"On the phone you said she found Shadow on her doorstep?"

"Close enough. He was hiding under the roofed shelter where she stacks her firewood. It baffles me why any wild animal would choose to take refuge at the home of Alcohol Mary Gowdie. It's a wonder she didn't shoot him and use his pelt for a rug."

"I'm not clear on why she called you, though. Intervale isn't in your district. Doesn't Ronette Landry live over in Strong?"

Pulsifer raised his rust-red eyebrows, desperately in need of trimming. "Mary and I have some history."

"You're going to have to do better than that."

He seemed to rehearse several answers in his mind before he looked at me with guilty eyes.

"During my drinking days, I used to buy moonshine from her. I should have had one of those punch cards, I bought so much hooch. Buy ten gallons and get the next bottle free."

Pulsifer had been an alcoholic, then a recovering alcoholic, then an active alcoholic again. His longest period of sobriety had ended with a pint of Jim Beam we shared one night in his kitchen. I felt responsible for his slip even though I hadn't known about his addiction at the time. Now he was sober again. It had surprised and humbled me when he'd invited me to an AA meeting to present him with a medallion celebrating two years of continuous sobriety.

"Mary's got quite the distillery up on that mountain of hers," he said.

"I didn't realize a person could make any money doing that these days, booze being as cheap as it is."

"Her stuff is 190 proof and half the price of Everclear. Mary runs a few side businesses, too. Last year she made two hundred gallons of maple syrup." His sly smile returned. "You should see her sugar bush."

He knew perfectly well how that old Maine term—referring to a stand of sugar maples—would sound to my modern ears.

"She seems like quite the entrepreneur."

"Most gangsters are." He spread both arms, winglike, along the top of the booth. "So tell me about the shitshow at the prison. It sounds like someone really wanted that female sergeant dead."

"The men who tried to murder her are both dead themselves."

"Thanks to your buddy Cronk."

"Billy killed one of them—in self-defense."

"He seems to kill a lot of people in self-defense."

I tried not to bristle. "He nearly died of a pierced bowel, Gary."

"I'm sorry. That was out of line. I shouldn't have spoken that way about your friend."

The apology shocked me into silence. I couldn't recall the last time I'd heard Gary Pulsifer utter a contrite word.

His voice was softer when he spoke again. "You wouldn't know this, but there's a local connection to those homicides. The guard who got killed—Kent Mears—grew up in Pennacook. His dad still lives in town. What a miserable bastard the old man is."

"Miserable in what way?"

"I'm not allowed to say." Pulsifer clenched his eyelids shut. "I shouldn't even have mentioned him."

I realized at once that Old Man Mears must be a fellow member of Alcoholics Anonymous. Pulsifer had always been an incurable gossip. "Getting back to the matter at hand, what do you think your wolf was doing in the Sandy River Valley?"

"I told you before he's not my wolf."

His shrug indicated he was done parsing pronouns.

"Wild wolves have ranges of hundreds of square miles," I said.

"What about the lady wolf he's been spotted with? Where do you think she is?"

"Somewhere safe, I hope."

Even though we were alone in the restaurant, he lowered his voice. "Do you know how many people have called me the past two years swearing to have seen wolves out in the woods? And I've had to say, 'Must of been a couple of coyotes.'" He pronounced the word in the Western fashion: *ki-otes.*

"I appreciate your keeping the secret."

"It was in my own interest! Can you imagine what would've happened if the press got hold of a picture of those animals? The environmentalists would have rushed to the courthouse with a petition to outlaw all hunting and trapping up here because of the Endangered Species Act."

Pulsifer knew, as well as I did, that wolves were no longer listed as endangered for the ironic reason that they were presumed extinct in the eastern United States. How can something that doesn't exist be threatened with expurgation?

"That's a little alarmist, don't you think?"

"If you ask me, the worst thing that ever happened to deer in Maine was when coyotes moved in."

Like almost all the wardens, guides, and deer hunters I knew, Gary Pulsifer had a hatred for coyotes that bordered on the pathological. It wasn't so long ago that the state offered self-defeating bounties on their pelts. Wildlife biologists had discovered that coyotes react to attempts at eradicating them by reproducing more prolifically.

The waitress returned with our breakfasts.

"Do you know anyone in the valley who hunts coyotes with a bow or a crossbow?" I asked after she'd left us alone.

Gary doused his breakfast with hot sauce until his plate was a bloody mess. "I know plenty of guys who have tried and failed. Bowhunting coyotes isn't easy, even over bait."

I ate the doughnut in two bites. The phrase *wolfed it down* came into my head.

"I'll talk to Ronette and see if she can point me to the local bowmen," I said. "Maybe canvass the sporting good stores between Rangeley and Farmington and see who sells that brand of arrow. If I'm lucky, the bolt was bought locally and not ordered online."

Pulsifer dabbed with his napkin at the red corners of his mouth. "Does that mean you're finally going to pay a visit to Fairbanks Firearms?"

The name made my heart sink. "I suppose I will."

"If you do, tell Denis Cormier hello."

"My uncle and I aren't on the greatest of terms."

"But he's potentially one of your best sources." Pulsifer made another pass with the napkin. "You know, Mike, the odds of finding the guy who shot your wolf—"

"They're long odds, I admit."

"And even if you do find him, he's going to claim he mistook Shadow for a coyote. And the state says you can kill as many of them as you please, provided you do it by the book."

"You don't seem to understand my interest here. If Shadow dies, I need to know what happened to the female he's been seen with. Was she shot and killed, too? Maybe the hunter has her pelt hanging in his man cave. This is the only known wild wolf in the state of Maine we're talking about."

"And the chances of finding her in thousands of square miles of timber . . ."

"Improve considerably if I find the son of a bitch who wounded Shadow and learn where it happened."

Pulsifer lifted his gaze to the tin ceiling as if he could see heaven through it. "This is the part of the conversation where I remind you, as your union representative, that you can't break rules because you find them inconvenient. Now, if you'll excuse me, I need to use the *pissoir*."

While I waited for him to return, I stared at the mounted head of the coyote on the wall. The taxidermist had given the animal a postmortem snarl. The suggestion was that the vicious canine had been preparing to rip out the hunter's jugular when a well-placed bullet had ended its short, savage life.

What was it about human beings, I wondered, that we needed to categorize other creatures as "good" or "bad"? Nature cared not a whit for humankind's morality. And a good thing for us, too, or it would have wiped our small, selfish species from the earth eons ago.

14

In the gray light of morning the paper mill loomed over the town like an industrial fortress, abandoned and falling into ruin. I watched its snuffed-out smokestacks disappear in my rearview mirror as we drove up the hill until there was nothing behind and nothing ahead except trees and more trees. We were following the road that cut through the pass between the mountains.

Ahead of me, Pulsifer roared along in his black GMC Sierra. The patrol truck had a big 285-horsepower V-6 engine that found no challenge in the steepness of the grade even as my four-cylinder Compass labored to keep pace. I had taken my Warden Service vehicle in the event I discovered something that would prompt a sudden return to duty. But my Scout was a hell of a lot more fun to drive in Mud Season.

Because of the tall pines that shadowed the road, it felt to me as if night were falling all over again. Down along the river, the snow had largely melted, but high in the uplands, the white carpet might not melt before Memorial Day. Even with the heat blasting, I felt a chill.

I hadn't seen or spoken to Pulsifer in months, but he seemed different. More than that, he seemed transformed. He was still a wise-cracker extraordinaire, but at the Boom Chain he had showed flashes of vulnerability and restraint: two qualities I would never have used to describe the man.

He had let slip that the probably alcoholic father of the dead CO, Kent Mears, resided in Pennacook. Aside from his having been a brutal sadist, I knew nothing about the younger Mears. If I didn't have other matters concerning me, I might have liked to meet the father, if only to satisfy my curiosity. Maybe I could ask Dani about the family. She had to have known them.

By the time Pulsifer and I reached the turnoff to Webb Lake, the sun had finally cleared the summit of Mount Blue. The frozen lake was big but shallow and ringed around with seasonal camps and cottages. Generations had summered along its shores, drawn by the scenic vistas of the mountains that rose in every direction, their names almost ridiculous in their quaintness: Tumbledown, Spruce, Blueberry, Jackson, and Little Jackson. Not to mention Blue itself: neither the tallest, nor the most spectacular, and yet somehow the defining prominence of the range, perhaps because of the signature fire tower at its summit, a landmark in every sense of the word.

Continuing on, we crested the heavily wooded ridge that marked the watershed between two valleys. To the south, the streams and brooks emptied into the Androscoggin; to the north, the tributaries fed the farms along the smaller Sandy River. Having crossed over the divide, I noticed a subtle change in the landscape. I became aware of how the friendly cottages around Webb Lake had been supplanted by isolated homesteads, set far back in the conifers, often with signs at the foot of their drives warning trespassers of prosecution and dangerous dogs.

At a fork in the road, Pulsifer veered off to the left onto a poorly maintained track that seemed to consist of nothing but ice-filled craters. Then the pavement dropped off hard. The half-frozen grit sucked at my tires until I could hear the pebbles banging around the wheel wells.

We passed through a thick grove of sugar maples, every one of which had been spiked with a steel spile and connected by an arterial system of blue tubing to some distant pumping station. I'd never seen such a sophisticated sugaring operation before. This network of sap-sucking pipes must have been the sugar bush Pulsifer had described.

The best weather for sugaring is mild days and below-freezing nights, neither of which we'd consistently had. It would be a bad year for the maple syrup makers. I hoped Mary Gowdie had pumped out plenty of moonshine from her still.

I hailed Pulsifer on the radio. "How much farther?"

"A couple more miles. How's that glorified sports wagon of yours handling the road?"

"Fair."

"Are the tires studded at least?"

"So the road ahead is shitty, is what you're saying."

"Ever hear of the La Brea Tar Pits?"

Soon we were climbing through a storm-blasted grove of dead-falls and widow-makers, up the steep southern face of Number Six Mountain. As we gained altitude, the sky finally opened overhead—a perfect robin's-egg blue—and I felt a pressure building between my jaw and my eardrum. I wondered what poor soul was charged with driving a snowplow up this series of switchbacks.

The house came into view little by little. The stunted pines and leafless gray trees prevented a good look at it from below, but it seemed to be a structure unlike any residence I'd ever before seen. The derelict wooden building was more tall than wide, with sharply pointed arches, scrollwork trim, and a square turret at the center that rose four floors above the foundation.

We turned into the clearing that surrounded the place, which had once, no doubt, been much more extensive before the willows, birches, and poplars had begun their slow and steady encroachment. The only vehicles in sight were a flatbed Ford outfitted with a snow-plow and an ATV parked under a carport-type assemblage.

I pulled up beside Pulsifer's truck and got out. The temperature was well below freezing at this elevation, although there was no hint of a breeze. We stood side by side and gazed upon the grotesque house.

"It's something, isn't it?" Pulsifer said.

"I'll say."

Its original color was impossible to discern as the paint had flaked off decades ago. There were many windows, some of them tall, grand, and intact. The rest were covered with sheets of plywood. Two great chimneys rose at either end of the hillbilly castle, but smoke only drifted from one of them.

An architectural term I hadn't heard since college came into my head: Carpenter Gothic.

The first bird of the morning appeared, a mute robin. People associated the species with springtime renewal. But flocks of robins remained in Maine all winter, feeding on crabapples and winterberries instead of earthworms. They were harbingers of nothing.

Just then a woman's voice boomed from behind one of the pillars on the front porch.

"I hope you ain't here to tell me that creature's dead!" She pronounced *here* as *he-yuh*.

Pulsifer raised a hand in greeting. "Not yet, Mary! Not yet!"

She let out a piggish grunt. "Hate to think I went to all that bother for nothing. He would've made a hell of a rug if I'd only just waited."

"It was good of you to call us," I said.

Alcohol Mary Gowdie emerged from the shadows of the porch into the daylight. She wasn't fat exactly, although she carried a lot of weight. Rather she was barrel-chested in the way opera singers always are in cartoons. She looked as if she'd be right at home onstage, dressed in a Viking helmet, clutching a spear.

But instead of a winged headpiece, she wore a man's fedora, and instead of a Valkyrie's breastplate, she wore a cotton dress under a buffalo plaid coat that was splashed with mud at the bottom. On her feet were shearling-lined duck boots with leather uppers and rubber bottoms.

"Who's the fancy-pants with you, Gary?"

"This is Mike Bowditch. He's a warden investigator."

She squinted at me from beneath her hat. "Bowditch? You ain't Jack's son!"

"I am."

Under my shirt and "executive" bulletproof vest I was wearing his army dog tags. If she had needed proof.

She made a grunting sound that might have signaled acknowledgment or displeasure. "Heard you was the one who killed him."

"My father killed himself."

"So you say." Her tone suggested his suicide was somehow a matter of interpretation and still up for debate. "I used to sell 'shine to your old man. What a rogue he was, let me tell you. The last of the genuine outlaws. And not bad to look at neither."

Up close, I could see that she had blond curls that couldn't have been natural. The brassy hair contrasted with a face that made me think she subsisted off nothing but tobacco, alcohol, and red meat.

"Well, are you going to come in or not?" she asked as if we had already resisted several invitations.

I glanced at Pulsifer, and he gave me a wink. We entered the house.

With so little light filtering in through the unbroken windows, the space was as murky as a cow barn and had something of the same smell. The curtains were of red or purple velvet, gone gray with dust. The wall-to-wall carpets were scarred with burns from dropped cigarettes.

Alcohol Mary seemed to be a collector—*hoarder* might be the more accurate term—of antique bottles. Every flat surface was packed with glass containers of all colors and shapes that had once held patent medicines and other elixirs.

"Would either of you wardens care for a pick-me-up?"

"I don't drink on duty," I said.

"Come on, Gary. I know you'd like a tipple."

He squared his shoulders, drew a breath. "I've given it up."

"Once a drunk always a drunk."

He took a moment to collect himself but responded with a smile that seemed genuine. "People can change, Mary."

"Like hell they can." She turned her squinty gaze on me. "How about you, Warden Bowditch? Did you inherit your old man's thirst along with his baby-blue eyes? I can give you the ten-cent tour if you'd like. Samples are free. There ain't no one who comes up here who doesn't want a look at my potent potables."

This was some sort of personal test, I realized. She was trying to determine whether I was some kind of hard-ass who might cause her problems with the state.

"I'm sure if I worked for the Bureau of Alcoholic Beverages, I'd find it fascinating. But being a warden, I'm only interested in seeing where you found the wolf."

"That's a pretty answer." She pushed up the brim of her fedora and examined me, with one eye open and the other half-shut. "How old would you say I am?"

Another test.

This time I tried a smile. "My mother taught me never to guess a lady's age or weight, Mrs. Gowdie."

Her expression became one of elaborate disgust. "Your ass must be pretty jealous of all the shit that comes out of your mouth."

"Excuse me?"

"If you're scared of an old bat like me, you can't be much of a warden."

She might as well have been prodding me with a spear.

"You're sixty-one years old, Mrs. Gowdie."

Her chapped lips parted. "How the fuck did you know that?"

"Lucky guess."

In my peripheral vision I saw Pulsifer staring at me, slack-jawed.

After a tense moment, Mary let out another of her guttural coughs. "Are you sure you're Jack Bowditch's boy? How come you don't talk like him? You got his face and muscles, but there's something off about your comportment."

"I mostly grew up with my mother."

"Down in Portland, I bet."

"Scarborough actually."

"I knew you was a flatlander," she said as if she'd bested me in a parliamentary debate.

Having put me in my place, the big woman led us down a darkened hallway lined with photos of a Scottish terrier, through an ill-smelling kitchen where a Walmart boom box was playing a song by Elvis Presley, to a mudroom that hadn't been mopped since the previous fall. The ancient door at the end stuck when Mary Gowdie tried to open it. She threw her brawny shoulder against the frame and nearly shattered the glass panes forcing it ajar.

Behind the house, the ground was dappled with snow and mud. The white-and-brown pattern brought to mind the coat of an Appaloosa. Mary had arranged a series of planks so she could hopscotch from the house to the woodshed without wading through the mire. The boards sank under my weight as I made my way to the roofed, unwalled structure.

The firewood was neatly stacked, and there must have been five or six cords of it. I removed my SureFire from my pocket, and I shone the flashlight at the wet wood chips covering the ground. Shadow's blood was visible as tacky brown spots on the clumped sawdust. I crouched down on my heels like a baseball catcher and moved the beam around.

"When did you find him?"

"Last night, about ten, when I came out to get a load of wood for the stove. Thought he was a bear at first, he was so big and black. Scared the everlasting shit out of me, let me tell you."

"Do you have livestock here?"

"Chickens."

"How about pets?"

"Chickens."

"What happened to that little dog of yours?" Pulsifer asked.

"None of your beeswax!"

She then explained that the henhouse and fenced yard were on the far side of the building. The chickens might have drawn Shadow to the property initially, since they would have made for easy meals, but it didn't explain why the injured wolf had sought out this wood-shed to die.

"So you hadn't seen him around before?"

"I didn't, but Zane did."

"Who's Zane?"

She had a craggy laugh. "Zane Wilson. Calls himself my apprentice. Came up here one day asking if I could teach him how to boil sap and make 'shine. He moved up to the valley with his girlfriend, both from Brooklyn. I thought we were done with those foolish people back in the seventies, but now there's a new crop of wannabe hippies."

"Did he happen to mention if the animal appeared to be injured?"

"Not to me, he didn't."

"Did he happen to say anything about seeing a second canine nearby? This one would have been gray."

"He didn't."

"I'll need his number."

"No, you won't."

"Excuse me?"

"You won't need it because Zane and Indigo don't own a phone. Not to mention the kid should be here any second. Today I'm going to have him char the insides of my oak barrels. Heh, heh."

I straightened up, careful not to knock my head against the ceiling timbers. "There's been one particular question on my mind. Why did you call Warden Pulsifer and not your district warden, Ronette Landry?"

"Fuck her and her French family."

"I'm half-French." By which I meant Franco-American. My mother's family had hailed from Canada.

"Good for you."

"I am required to ask this, Mrs. Gowdie. I hope you won't take offense, but it's a routine question and not meant as an accusation. I need to know if you own a crossbow."

"Who do you think I am, Maid Fucking Marian?"

"I had to ask."

"If I'd shot that animal, why would I phone the fucking game warden to bring it to the animal hospital?"

Her argument was watertight. But I'd had no choice except to ask the obvious question. In criminal cases, unvoiced assumptions are what always sink you at trial.

When I failed to respond, she threw up her gnarled hands. "No, I don't own a crossbow! I own a fucking AK-47, plus this little number." From her coat she produced a blued Smith & Wesson Model 10 revolver. "And I'm a keen shot, I'll have you know."

"Probably best to put the gun away," said Pulsifer.

"I'm just making a point to you numbskulls." She shoved the heavy handgun back into her coat. "Now are we done? I've got real work to do—unlike certain state employees I could name."

I always got a kick out of criminals who prided themselves on their work ethic. We watched her plod off to an outbuilding across the yard. It had a steel pipe for a chimney. I assumed the wood structure contained her still.

The wind had begun to blow from the northwest. Pulsifer tucked his hands under his ballistic vest for warmth.

"I'm surprised she didn't kick us off her land," I said.

"Give her a minute."

"I'm going to follow these tracks."

The snow had repeatedly melted to mud, then repeatedly refrozen every night. But the canine trail wasn't hard to follow. It led across the mottled yard in the telltale pattern of a wolf—in a direct line or what trackers called registers—until it disappeared into the budding saplings and thornbushes at the edge of the clearing. I wasn't dressed to go bushwhacking down the mountainside.

My supervisors would never allow me to pursue an official investigation into the shooting, however heinous. Under Maine law, the killing of a coyote was encouraged and the reckless shooting of a stray dog was a minor offense. With only four investigators in the Warden Service, I already had a full workload. But my hope was that my boss wouldn't object to my conducting an off-the-books inquiry in my free hours. Most wardens had pet projects they pursued in their spare time.

Pulsifer came across the yard, heedless of the muck in his rubber-soled boots. "Quite a view, isn't it?"

I'd been so focused on my forensic work I hadn't appreciated the vista. There, below us, was the Sandy River Valley. I saw a patchwork of brown fields and pastures that were empty of animals but looked the right size for sheep or goats. Beyond the valley loomed a range of snowcapped mountains, above which dark clouds were building. The largest of the peaks I recognized as Sugarloaf, the second-highest mountain in Maine and home to the state's largest ski resort. With the intermittent warm spells we'd been experiencing, their season would be ending soon.

"Do you know who owns those pastures there?"

He spat on the ground. "I already told you this isn't my district."

"Did Mary get under your skin?"

"If I'm being honest, yes," he said. "But I'm learning to let things go."

"You seem like you're in a good place, Gary."

"I am today, which is all I can ask for. On another topic, I never knew you were psychic. How did you guess Mary's age?"

"I didn't guess. Back at the Boom Chain, while you were in the bathroom, I ran her name through the system. She's got quite a record of fish and wildlife violations. It explains her hatred for Landry. It seems Mary Gowdie enjoys poaching almost as much as she does making maple syrup and moonshine."

15

A pair of ravens swept into view above the valley. The black birds were silent, but I identified them by their wedge-shaped tails, shaggy throats, and rowing wingbeats. Also they were soaring. Crows don't soar. Finally one of the two let out a scolding *quork*—directed at me it seemed—and they continued on toward the next town over, where ravens were said to have a special attachment to a professor who had spent his life studying them at his cabin in the woods.

I roamed the edge of the field pondering a mystery. Why had Shadow taken refuge in Alcohol Mary's woodshed of all places? He had been hemorrhaging blood, barely able to breathe, with an arrow through his lung.

He'd been raised by people, and maybe he still associated them with care and comfort, but he'd lived in the wild the past several years, avoiding hunters, bait piles, and snares. If he had been wounded by a human, it would have made sense for him to avoid all contact. How come he hadn't found a den as far as possible from his enemies to await the coming of death?

I would likely never know the answer. But surveying Mary's land, so near Tumbledown Mountain—a place frequented by snowshoers and cross-country skiers—made me increasingly certain that Shadow had been attacked at a lower elevation, somewhere in the valley below. Those visible pastures especially intrigued me. For reasons of his own, he had made the difficult climb up Number Six Mountain. Let no one tell you that nothing wounded goes uphill.

When I checked my phone, I found that I had a stronger-than-expected cell signal. There was a new message from Aimee Cronk:

> Our lawyer says this pardon thing is for real. It might take a
> few days though. When the docs think Billy's strong enough
> they're sending him to the Farm. They figure he'll be safer
> there from any buddies of Chapman or Dow looking for
> payback.

The Farm was the nickname for the minimal-security Bolduc
Correctional Facility on the floodplain of the St. George River, a
mile or so below the prison hilltop. The Farm had no fences. An
inmate could walk away from the jail, but since most of the prisoners there were nonviolent offenders facing imminent release, few
ever did. I doubted that the legendary Killer Cronk would have anything to fear from the check kiters and car thieves at Bolduc.

I replied:

> That's great news! Work's taken me to the Sandy River
> Valley but I'll swing by the hospital when I'm back there.

Aimee was online and her reply came fast:

> If you feel the need.

This much was clear: it was going to be a while before Aimee
Cronk let me off her shit list.

With a heavy heart, I tried the number of someone I hoped would
be happier to hear from me.

Kathy Frost answered with her usual salutation: "Grasshopper!"

"Are you ever going to stop calling me that?"

"Do you want me to?"

"No."

Kathy had been the first woman in the history of the Maine Warden Service. Then its first female sergeant. Less noteworthy from a
historic standpoint, she had been my mentor before a horrific gunshot injury had forced her into early retirement.

These days, she worked as a consultant to law-enforcement agencies across the country, teaching first responders how to train K9s
to become better rescue and recovery dogs. In her spare time she

traveled, as a volunteer, to disaster zones with her Belgian Malinois to search for missing persons.

"I heard about Billy Cronk. I was going to call you, but I've been . . . occupied."

She placed an odd stress on that last word, but this wasn't the best time or place for small talk. Given the unpredictability of cell phones, I cut to the matter at hand. "I'll catch you up about Billy later, but I need your help first. Do you remember that wolf dog I rescued a couple of years ago?"

"Shadow? Of course! Did something happen to him?"

"Someone shot him with a crossbow, Kath."

The pain in her voice couldn't have been any more intense. "Please don't tell me he's dead."

"The veterinarian says he will be soon."

"Mike, I am so, so sorry. Who's the vet taking care of him?"

"Lizzie Holman at the Pennacook Hospital for Animals."

"I've heard of her. She's got a good reputation. Have you identified the son of a bitch who shot him?"

"That's why I'm calling you. Shadow carried the shaft of the arrow inside him for days, until Holman removed it. I'm hoping there are fingerprints. Other than that, I don't have much more to go on."

"Was he found near Pennacook?"

"Further north. He showed up at a homestead on Number Six Mountain, next to Tumbledown. But my gut tells me he climbed here from below, from the Sandy River Valley. Intervale probably, but maybe he came from as far away as Phillips or Avon. I'm hoping you and Maple can backtrack his blood spoor for me."

The line gathered static.

"Mike, you know I would if I could. But I'm not even in Maine. I'm down in Rhode Island."

She had no relatives there, as best I knew. "On business?"

"Visiting a friend. You don't know him."

Kathy had been widowed before we'd met and unattached for years. She hadn't mentioned having met a man, let alone having begun a romantic relationship. I had gotten used to thinking of my friend as asexual.

"Can you recommend a local tracker?"

She paused again. "I could, but he'll just tell you the same thing."

"Which is what?"

"You're not going to be able to track Shadow to the place where he was shot. K9 handlers like to play up how amazing our dogs are. But most of the time, when we find a missing person or whatever, there's a lot of luck involved. Even my dear, departed Pluto, if I'd brought him up there, would have veered off course the second he crossed the scent path of a coyote. It might be different if you were running a track on a bear or a bobcat. I know it's hard to hear, Mike, but what you want is beyond the capabilities of any K9 I've ever encountered."

Frustration burned the back of my throat. "I guess it's Plan B then. I'll talk to Ronette Landry. See if I can get the names of the local crossbowmen. Find out which ones use Spider-Bite X2s."

"Whoever shot Shadow will only claim he mistook your wolf for a coyote."

"I've got to try, Kathy."

"I know you do, Mike. But for whose sake? Shadow's or yours?"

"Why does it matter?"

"It's something to ask yourself, is all I'm saying."

"I need to know what happened to the she-wolf, whether she was shot as well. If she's still alive . . ."

"What are you going to do?"

I understood what she was getting at: Was I honestly going to search the entire mountain chain for a single wild wolf? It hadn't been that long ago that a thru-hiker wandered off the Appalachian Trail near here, got lost, and died of exposure, thirst, and starvation. It had taken searchers two full years to find her corpse less than a third of a mile from the trail.

"If I locate the person who shot Shadow, I'll at least know if she's dead, too."

"I understand. Be well, Grasshopper. I'll be praying for the big guy."

More ravens appeared, flying in from the northwest, headed toward Weld. I wanted to believe the sight of these intelligent birds was an omen. Everywhere the two species coexisted, ravens and wolves had a symbiotic relationship. Ravens on the wing scout for carrion the canines can scavenge. In return the birds rely on the fangs of the wolves to tear open carcasses their own bills cannot penetrate.

Stacey and I had once attended a powwow on Indian Island in the Penobscot River. The gathering was meant to be a celebration of Wabanaki culture, but like most such events, the mood was one of cultural confusion. Food trucks served up Navajo fry bread and vendors sold Ojibwa dream catchers to a crowd that consisted mostly of white men and women who toured the grounds as if it were just another carnival.

But for all our arrogance, we had both succumbed to the role of cultural tourist. Stacey bought a beautiful little ash basket shaped and colored like a strawberry. It had, at least, been made by an actual Passamaquoddy artisan from eastern Maine. My souvenir, purchased in my near drunkenness, was a slate-gray T-shirt bearing the aphorism WHERE THE RAVEN FLIES, THE WOLF FOLLOWS. Only after I had gotten home did I discover the Made in China tag inside.

I heard a truck downshifting up the hill.

It had to be Mary's apprentice, Zane. She'd said he would be arriving soon.

I began to hopscotch on the patches of snow in a path toward the dooryard. I arrived around the corner of the house in time to see a Toyota pickup spinning around the driveway in a circle. It let out a sudden farting burst of exhaust and disappeared down the hill in a cloud of noxious fumes.

Gary Pulsifer had opened the door of his patrol truck, preparing to give chase.

"Why's he running?" I called.

"I have no idea. Should I go after him?"

I started forward through the slushy mud. "I'll go with you."

The road up had seemed slow and steep; the road down seemed precipitous. The switchbacks came one after the other, and around each corner loomed a tree thick enough to flatten the most rugged of vehicles. Pulsifer reached to turn on his pursuit lights, but I stopped his hand.

"I am afraid he's going to panic and go off the road."

"Too late for that."

Just past the storm-blasted field of deadfalls Pulsifer pumped the brakes, but still slid across a patch of ice until the studs kicked in and caught us.

We jumped out and looked down a hillside of snags and fallen timber. The plummeting path the Tacoma had taken showed itself in broken logs and flattened baby pines. The exhaust pipe was still smoking, but there was no sign of movement from the wrecked pickup, thirty feet below.

16

My first thought was that the poor bastard must be dead. Then I saw an arm emerge from the driver's window, and a moment later a bearded young man began crawling from the wreckage. His face was covered with blood as if with war paint. But he seemed to be moving well, with no signs of broken bones.

"Stay there!" I said. "We'll come to you."

He kept scrambling as if he hadn't heard me.

Pulsifer shook his red head. "The fool is going to impale himself trying to climb through the blowdowns."

"Better get a rope." I cupped my hands around my mouth. "Stay there, Zane!"

But the bloody man would not be deterred. From above, I saw that he was a little guy, so skinny that even dressed in a hooded work coat, farmer's overalls, and steel-toed logging boots, he looked like a kid wearing his father's clothes. He seemed to have modeled his hairstyle and beard on Jesus as depicted on the covers of books aimed at teenaged Christian girls.

Pulsifer's truck was a mess, and he was having trouble finding a belaying line. Unwilling to wait, I began picking my way down the obstacle course of logs. Sheets of ice were hidden under the dead leaves. I slid and skinned my knee on the first log in the path.

By then, Zane Wilson had almost reached my position. Even banged up and bleeding, he had clambered up that incline with the energy and sure-footedness of a goat.

Behind me, I heard Pulsifer return and utter an all-purpose curse, probably at having had to fetch a rope that was not needed, but perhaps out of exasperation with the morning in general.

"Take it easy, Zane," I said as he drew near my position.

It was almost as if he hadn't been aware of me before. He stopped short, wiped blood from his eyes, and shook his head the way a wet dog might.

"Are you all right?"

He tapped his head behind his ear and opened and closed his mouth.

"Zane?"

"Sorry, I'm on the fritz," he said in the blunted syllables of someone partially deaf. "Hearing aid's not working right."

"What the hell were you running for?" Pulsifer shouted from above. He'd raised his voice even louder hoping it would penetrate Zane's damaged eardrums.

The guy had enormous blue eyes like those of a cartoon rabbit drawn by Walt Disney. "Are you going to arrest me?"

"That depends." I tried to move my lips so that he could read them. "Did you commit a crime?"

I sat him down on the tailgate and checked his pulse. It was rapid-fire, but no more than one would have expected. Most of the blood was flowing from a horizontal cut along his forehead that resembled the initial incision a mad scientist would have made before attempting a brain transplant. Wounds to the skull bleed copiously and often appear worse than they are. This seemed true in the case of Zane Wilson, who, aside from his malfunctioning hearing aid, showed no signs of a concussion, broken bones, or internal injuries.

"Can you read lips, Zane?" I said as I applied a compression bandage to his dripping forehead.

"I haven't had to in a while, but yes."

I'd given Pulsifer the injured man's wallet to call in his driver's license to see if he had outstanding warrants or a criminal record that explained his escape attempt.

"What happened here? Why did you take off like that?"

"I came up the hill and saw the police and figured you were here to bust Mary."

"For bootlegging?"

"She's always said the law was after her and would drag her off to prison someday."

Standing this close to him, I became aware of how dirty his clothes were and how badly he reeked of body odor. But his teeth were so white and perfectly aligned that a skilled orthodontist had to have played a starring role in his dental history.

"Bootleggers aren't my concern. I'm Warden Investigator Bowditch and my partner is Warden Pulsifer. The reason we're here is that Mary discovered an injured wolf near her woodpile last night. Someone had shot the animal with a crossbow bolt. Would you know anything about that?"

He paused so long I thought he hadn't understood. "Is it dead?"

"Not yet."

"And it's an actual wolf, not someone's dog or something?"

"Mary told us you saw an animal that fit its description. Is that true?"

It was a simple enough question, but I noted how his gaze shifted from mine.

"I saw it in my headlights the other night as I was driving home. I didn't see it well."

"When was this?"

"Two, three nights ago."

"And did it look wounded? Like it might have been in pain?"

He fiddled with his malfunctioning hearing aid.

Pulsifer reappeared, waving Zane's driver's license between two fingers. "It's no mystery why he hightailed it. His license is expired. Also his truck hasn't been inspected in two years. Plus, he's got three arrests on his sheet for possession."

The injured man finally piped up, but his tone was respectful. "I shouldn't have run like that, but I panicked because of my history with the police. I've been apprenticing with Mary because my girl-friend and I want to open a legal craft distillery. Cannabis has caused me too much trouble, and it's only going to get taken over by agri-business anyway, so what's the point?"

Despite the grime and cloud of funk that hung about him, he spoke like a man who had received an excellent education.

Pulsifer leaned close to my ear. "What do you want to do with this character?"

I rubbed my unshaven jaw. "I think totaling his truck and losing a pint of blood is worse punishment than being arrested."

"I feel like a doc should have a look at him."

Where had this kindly man come from? Whoever he was, he certainly wasn't the Gary Pulsifer I remembered. "You're probably right."

"What do you say, Zane?" Pulsifer said. "How about I drive you to the hospital in Farmington. A doctor needs to stitch up that head wound."

"No, thank you."

"We can't make you go, but take it from me, you need a professional to treat that cut."

Zane produced an oil-stained bandanna from his pocket. With horror we watched him tie the dirty cloth over the gauze bandage I'd taped to his skull.

"It's just a scrape. I'm not worried about it. Besides, I've got to figure out what I'm going to do about my truck."

"How about we call a wrecker for you then?" Pulsifer asked.

"No, thank you. I can handle it."

Alcohol Mary appeared in the road near the top of the hill. Her coat was blowing open in the breeze revealing the faded dress beneath. "What's going on there? What did you do to my apprentice?"

Pulsifer answered before I could. "Mr. Wilson had an accident."

She dug her bare hands into her pockets and began marching toward us. "Accident? What kind of accident?" Then she spotted the skid marks where the Tacoma had left the road and launched into space. "Jeezum Crow, Zane! I'm not paying to haul your vehicle out of there. And you sure as shit ain't leaving it. I'm not one of those hicks who likes having junked cars all over my property."

"I'm sorry, Mary."

"Christ Almighty. You knocked your head, too? You already couldn't hear worth a damn."

"My hearing aid broke, but I'm all right. The other's OK."

"I won't be legally liable for your medical bills either, so you better not be planning on hiring some slick lawyer to sue me. I maintain this road in tip-top condition. You sue me, and I'll sue you right back."

"I'm not going to sue you, Mary."

"So are you going to sit there bleeding all day or are you going to char those barrels we talked about?"

I doubted that Mary Gowdie was the first person to mistake his hearing difficulties and imperfect articulation as a lack of intelligence.

"I have one last question for him," I said.

The woman put her hands on her hips. "You wardens are worse than the Spanish Inquisition!"

"Where did you say you saw the wolf, Zane?"

"Near the trees in back."

I dug out a business card, one with my private cell number on it, and gave it to him. "If you start having doubts and think you might have been mistaken or remember anything else of importance, you can reach me day or night."

He slid the card into his shirt pocket, where I was certain he would forget it. "I only saw it that one time at the edge of the field behind the house."

Misdemeanors aside, he seemed like a nice enough guy. Naïve, maybe. But nice.

So why was he lying to me about Shadow?

17

Pulsifer and I shook hands, and I thanked him for what he'd done to save Shadow's life, if only temporarily. He extended an invitation to visit him and his family on their farm, an hour to the north, and I sensed that it wasn't merely a gesture of politeness. As I watched him drive off ahead of me, I remembered the words he'd spoken to Mary Gowdie when he'd rejected her temptation of a drink: *People can change.*

I wasn't certain I shared that belief. But seeing a serene Gary Pulsifer had given me pause.

At the bottom of the hill, where the dirt road intersected the mountain pass connecting Pennacook and the Sandy River Valley, I had a choice to make. Turn right and return to the mill town on the Androscoggin where Shadow lay on his deathbed. Or turn left and begin collecting evidence that might lead me to the crossbowman and, with luck, the she-wolf.

I turned left.

The inquiry would have to be purely personal, done on my own time: Pulsifer had been correct that the Warden Service wouldn't sanction one of its investigators wasting his duty hours on such a minor matter that probably wouldn't even result in criminal charges. Fortunately, I still had a few days of vacation.

As it descended, Route 142 afforded me fleeting glimpses of the early-spring valley and the backsides of the ski mountains beyond. While winter reigned on the summits, at the lower elevations there were faint indications of life returning to the land. The evergreens, which became darker during the cold months, had a verdant brightness in their needles. Elsewhere the colors were softer and more muted: a landscape rendered in pastels. Ochers and khakis, dove grays and taupes. To newcomers, the hills and fields along the Sandy River must have appeared dead, or at least sleeping, but what I noticed was the arterial redness of the dogwoods and the first furry catkins peeking out from the branches of the aspens.

Adrenaline and caffeine had powered me through the night, but my body was beginning to crash. I wore my exhaustion like a lead-weighted coat.

I pulled over at a sideswipe in the snowbanks where the plows had cleared an arc to turn around and continue back up the mountainside. I had worried I would lose my cell signal once I reached the bottomlands, but I hadn't. I tapped out a text to the district warden, Ronette Landry.

What are you up to?

The answer came at once.

Just rolling and patrolling. RU in the area?

I'm in Phillips. But I don't want to drag you from work.

Please do! There aren't a lot of anglers along the Sandy 2day. Want coffee?

You read my mind. Where?

There's a place called The Bard. It's in Avon.

You're shitting me.

Coffee's good even. Can meet you there in 15.

Ronette and I weren't friends, but we had worked that hunting homicide on Maquoit Island together. In addition to being a patrol warden, she was a longtime member of the Maine Warden Service Evidence Recovery Team, an expert in DNA handling, blood-spatter analysis, and crime-scene photography. She did double duty as part of the Forensic Mapping Team, which utilizes high-tech data collectors to reconstruct crash scenes and determine bullet trajectories. As an investigator still wet behind the ears, I found myself intimidated by her breadth of knowledge.

While I had been texting Ronette, I had missed a call from Dr. Holman. Driving distracted, with one hand on the wheel, I hit the callback button and prepared myself for bad news.

"He's still hanging in there."

I swerved close to a snowbank. "Really?"

"His vitals are holding steady. He's one tough son of a gun." She cleared her throat in a way that reawakened the lepidoptera in my stomach. "I had one of my assistants do some reading about the laws concerning wolf hybrids. And I have a few questions I need you to address for me. They have to do with the clinic's responsibilities and liabilities."

"Go ahead."

"It's unclear whether he should be categorized as a wild animal or a feral dog. If he's a wolf, doesn't he legally belong to the state? That's my understanding of how Maine laws apply to wild animals."

"Yes, but Shadow was originally registered as a wolf *dog*. That makes him a domestic animal under the statute."

She paused to consider the ramifications. "How do you know his name? What is it you're not telling me?"

"I rescued Shadow from some drug addicts a few years ago. To the extent anyone can lay a claim to him, it's me."

"So what was he doing up on Number Six Mountain?"

"A few years ago, he got away from me in the woods near the Widowmaker Ski Resort and has been on the run ever since."

"Did you make an effort to relocate him?"

"Yes."

This was a complete lie. The truth was I hadn't known what to do about the fugitive wolf dog, and it had been easier and more self-indulgent for me to fantasize about his becoming a modern-day White Fang.

"I'm surprised we never heard anything about this from the state," Holman said. "If not from the Department of Inland Fisheries and Wildlife, then at least from the Animal Welfare people at the Ag Department."

"We thought announcing that a de facto wolf was on the loose near Rangeley Lake would cause a mass panic. We worried it might endanger domestic dogs, as well as coyotes."

In this case, the pronoun *we* consisted of just me, Gary Pulsifer, and a few coconspirators.

Holman paused to process my justification. "I feel like I should be in touch with someone at the Department of Agriculture, at least."

"That's really not necessary. As I said at the clinic before, I am willing to cover all of his medical bills. Put my name down as his owner."

"You're willing to swear he belongs to you then?"

"I am."

"I'm serious about this because I could lose my license for knowingly violating the law."

I took a deep breath. "I swear."

18

Never having visited the United Kingdom, I couldn't compare Stratford-upon-Avon to the rural Maine town that had borrowed the name of the English river. But I suspected that the high street of Shakespeare's birthplace didn't include a fireworks dealership, a marijuana grow shop, or an automotive graveyard. Maine's Avon consisted of little more than farm fields and two high-speed roads that ran parallel—one to the north of the Sandy River and one to the south—without a single bridge to connect them. You had to drive to the next town to cross the stream.

I found the Bard of Avon coffeehouse across the highway from a masonry school and down the road from an airstrip named for Charles Lindbergh because the celebrity pilot had set down there once in the 1940s. From the outside, the building appeared to be nothing special: another box of painted cinder blocks. But it sported an artful-looking wooden sign with an image of Will Shakespeare hefting a steaming mug of joe.

Somehow Ronette had beaten me there. Her black patrol truck was identical in every way to Pulsifer's except that it gleamed with a fresh coat of wax and wasn't dented and scratched from having backed into stumps and sideswiped tree branches. It was, notably, the lone vehicle in the lot.

The interior of the Bard was like a trip back in time to the Age of Aquarius. Folk music keened from unseen speakers. The walls were papered over with leaflets, posters, and flyers for upcoming contra dances and candlelight vigils protesting wind farms, and advertisements for practitioners of Ayurvedic Yoga Therapy and Rolfing.

Ronette Landry rose from a dark-stained table to give me a hug. She wore her olive uniform under a black snowmobiling coat with a gold badge embroidered on the breast. Around her throat was a black balaclava she could pull up to cover the lower half of her face when the temperature dropped.

"Hey, stranger!"

"It's great to see you, Ronette. Congratulations on winning Warden of the Year."

She gave a polite shrug of the shoulders in lieu of a response.

"We missed you at the awards banquet," I continued.

"Thanks, but we both know they gave it to me because I'm a woman." The light dimmed in her copper-colored eyes. "The political climate being what it is."

Ronette was a Franco who fit every physical stereotype. She had olive skin, brown-black hair, and a nose that couldn't help but attract your attention. She was graying, but her complexion was flawless. Like many of the women in *ma famille*—my mom being the sad exception—she would probably live to be a hundred years old.

I recalled that Ronette had given family illness as the reason for not attending the annual ceremony. "How's your great-grandmother?"

She sipped from a hand-turned clay mug. "I think it's a matter of weeks now."

"Is she in hospice?"

Ronette seemed taken aback by the question. "Oh, no. She's at our home with my mom and *mémère* playing nursemaid. What could be worse than to die in a stranger's bed, far from God?"

My own late mother, born Marie Cormier, had raised me as a good Catholic boy. I often forgot what it had been like, as a young child, to be part of a culture that put family first, or second, after the Church.

I remembered my grandparents, uncles, aunts, and numerous cousins with fondness, and it saddened me that my mom had estranged herself from them after she'd met my stepfather and married into money. She'd had no choice, she claimed. The same relatives who'd never wanted anything to do with her when she'd been hitched to my no-good father had suddenly reappeared in her life with begging bowls. They'd wanted her to invest in their self-storage businesses and their tanning salons, asked her to cosign on mortgages for houses they couldn't afford, and pleaded for loans to buy speedboats and snowmobiles.

As I began to sit down, Ronette said, as if in alarm, "You don't even have coffee yet!"

I looked around for a waitress.

"You need to order up at the counter. The baked goods come from Dough Business in Farmington."

At the register, I noticed a printed announcement for an informational meeting of the Maine Prisoners' Rights Association at the Bard the next week. I could only imagine the incendiary reaction of that group's members to the prison attacks. No doubt they would be anticipating a cover-up. Their fears were well-founded.

"What'll it be?" said the man behind the counter.

He had a full head of white hair and bushy eyebrows that would have required sheep shears to trim.

"Just a large regular coffee."

"There's no such thing as *regular* coffee. Do you mean dark roast? Medium roast? Light roast?"

"Medium." I inspected the glass case containing the baked goods. "Do you have any molasses doughnuts?"

"Try the maple-sugar bun." It was a command.

"What kind did you get?" Ronette asked as I returned with my plate and mug to the table. "Is it the Kenyan? Or the Ethiopian?"

"I'm not sure."

She reached out to tear a piece from my sugared pastry. "You know I'm dying to ask about what happened at the prison and the hospital. Everyone's talking about it. But I have a sneaking suspicion it has nothing to do with why you called me. So what brings you to my neck of the woods on this shitty April morning?"

What did I say about Ronette being a smart cookie? I appreciated not having to rehash the drama with Billy. Instead I started the story with the call I'd received from Gary Pulsifer, summoning me to Pennacook.

When I had finished, her eyes had grown wide. "I thought those wolf sightings were all bogus. I came to the conclusion that people were seeing big coyotes and assuming they were wolves. It's bizarre that an injured animal sought out Mary Gowdie of all people."

"I take it you and she are not the best of friends."

"Mary's the only person I know who hunts deer with an AK. The last time I pinched her for hunting without a license I thought she was going to use me for target practice. It's no wonder she called Gary instead."

"Having met her, I'm surprised she called anyone at all."

Ronette arched a black eyebrow. "I've always figured Mary has a soft side, especially when it comes to dogs. I've heard a rumor that she brought her last dog, a Scottie, to a taxidermist to have him stuffed, she was so unwilling to part with the little ankle-biter. She supposedly keeps him at the foot of her bed."

The ease with which the image materialized in my mind told me it had to be true.

"How about this Zane Wilson?" I asked.

"I know he and his girlfriend live in a yurt."

"A yurt?"

"They're millennial hippies. I've seen them around, at the farmers' market, other places, but haven't had a real conversation with them. Zane is quite the hottie, as my daughter would say. His girlfriend, Indigo, seems like a firecracker. My guess is it's her family's money they used to buy their little patch of Dogpatch. I've never heard a bad word about either of them, other than people scratching their heads why young people would want to move here of all places to start a farm."

Her description bolstered my generally positive impression of Zane Wilson. "I'd feel better about the guy if he hadn't lied to me. He first claimed to have seen Shadow two or three nights ago on the road in his high beams. Later, he said he saw him on the back side of the property, which is nowhere near the road. Hence Zane couldn't have seen him in his headlights."

"Maybe he was confused. You did say he hit his head."

"No, he was definitely lying."

"I doubt it was Zane who shot your wolf," said Ronette. "More likely it was a coyote hunter over a bait pile."

It was the logical inference. "Can you give me the names of anyone in the area who hunts for predators with a bow or crossbow?"

She shifted her hips on the wood bench. She studied the bottom of the mug in her hands. "I can think of a few possibilities. Gorman Peaslee's right at the top of the list. Maybe the Beliveau boys. Where do you think the shooting might have happened?"

"I saw some fields and pastures below Mary's property that intrigued me. They looked ideal for someone who might want to hunt predators from a blind. There were several farming homesteads with newly built houses all grouped together. Do you know who owns that land?"

Ronette made a wincing expression.

"Is that a yes?"

"Those farms are owned by our new Amish neighbors."

I paused in licking maple sugar from my fingertips. "There are Amish people in the Sandy River Valley?"

"Here's a piece of trivia for you. The Amish are the fastest-growing faith group in the country. And Maine's got the fastest-growing Amish population in the Northeast. Third fastest in the nation."

"I knew there were settlements up in Aroostook County—"

"And in Whitefield and Unity. Now we've got three families living in Intervale. Of all the places for them to settle, but I guess it makes sense. No one else wants to buy land there."

"What's so bad about Intervale?"

"It's where that asshole Gorman Peaslee lives, for one thing. It's never been a place I'm wild about visiting alone. Peter, my husband, hates it and always wants to ride shotgun. And I mean that literally. Do you know who else lives there? Zane Wilson and his girlfriend. Their yurt is over near Tantrattle Stream, not far from the Stolls. They're one of the Amish families I mentioned."

"What are they like, the Amish?"

"I haven't had many dealings with them, but they seem like good people. Some of the locals have complained about their horses and buggies in the road: the usual small-minded crap. I am not wild about driving onto their farms to interrogate them about shooting a wolf."

"Do you know if they even hunt?"

She chuckled. "The Amish might not be big on televisions and computers, but they do love their .22 rifles."

"How about crossbows?"

"If their faith permits them to use firearms, I doubt they're forbidden from using bows of any kind."

Finally, I had a lead.

19

When I opened the door of my Jeep, Ronette asked to see the crossbow bolt. She peered at the carbon-fiber shaft with a scientist's concentration.

"If this thing was inside a wolf for days, you're not going to get any prints off it. You understand that, right?"

"You never know."

"In this case I do know." She handed me back the plastic bag. "It would probably be better for the two of us to ride together into Intervale in my patrol truck. It's clearly a police vehicle. And when they see there are two of us inside, it'll get the message across not to fuck with us."

"Are you talking about the Amish?"

She had a big smile that seemed to engage every muscle in her face. "I'm thinking about several individuals, but notably Gorman Peaslee. I'm not looking forward to knocking on his door. We won't have any trouble with the Amish. Have you ever had any interactions with them before?"

"Not unless you count a five-minute conversation I had with a chair maker at the Common Ground Fair."

"And?"

"I was surprised by how normal he seemed. I wondered if he might be an impostor wearing a fake beard so he could charge a markup on his furniture."

"You're so suspicious of everyone."

We left my Jeep outside the Intervale Town Hall, where it was less likely to be broken into than if I'd parked it along the Rangeley Road.

"Someone would break into it in the middle of the day?"

"It doesn't take more than a second to shatter a window."

I climbed into her truck, which, predictably, was immaculate and somehow had a new-car smell.

I was traveling light: just a gun, a badge, my cuffs, and a knife. It occurred to me that if I couldn't crack this mystery by day's end, I would have to go home for supplies and several changes of clothing. I hadn't seen any motels, which raised the question of where I would stay upon my return.

From the flyspeck municipal center we traveled north. Ronette drove with a practiced casualness. She braked hard and accelerated fast. She paid less attention to the road than to identifying the drivers of passing vehicles and checking posted land for signs of trespassing. I'd begun to wish we'd taken my Jeep instead.

"So what's going on with you and Dani Tate?" she asked as if the question had recently occurred to her and she hadn't been waiting until the exact moment when I would be unable to escape.

"It's complicated."

"That's a term my daughter uses about boys on Facebook."

"You're better off asking Dani rather than me."

"If you haven't forgotten, I was the one who played matchmaker."

"I haven't forgotten."

"So should I be having second thoughts about you two? Relationships between LEOs can work—because you understand the stresses of each other's job—or they can be total nightmares." The acronym LEO stood for "law-enforcement officer." "On the other hand, there's a lot to be said for being married to a civilian. There are so many days I thank God I married a builder who doesn't have a clue about the scary shit I see and do every time I go on patrol. Peter's been so patient with me and such a good dad. He's even a great cook!"

"You're lucky."

"I prefer the term *blessed*."

Then, without any warning, Ronette swung a right onto a gravel road that lacked a street sign. As we careened around the corner, I glimpsed several cardboard squares floating in a black ditch between the trees and the graded surface. It took me a moment to recognize the sodden objects as real estate signs that had been uprooted, knocked over, and tossed into the half-frozen water.

I craned my neck, looking back. "Someone who lives here doesn't want anyone buying land, I take it."

"Peaslee."

The first mile or so of the road was the usual second-growth forest, which had sprung up after the woods had been logged to the ground. Most of it was soft wetlands, not fit for anything but alders and willows, but I suspected some good cedars had once flourished in this marsh.

Then the forest parted, and we were looking across a vast field of snow-broken cornstalks. Something like a hundred crows hopped about between the rows, oblivious to a scarecrow, whose shredded shirt flapped in the breeze, and whose sack head had mostly been decapitated by a shotgun blast.

"Peaslee," Ronette said.

Up ahead we saw the first road sign since we'd left the main thoroughfare. Fluorescent yellow, shaped like a diamond, it depicted the silhouette of a horse pulling a four-wheeled buggy. Someone had blasted holes through the sheet aluminum with double-aught buckshot.

"Peaslee?" I asked.

"Whatever in the world makes you say that?"

Ronette slowed as we entered a birch thicket. The land rose sharply to our left. A narrow drive led up the wooded hill. My inner compass told me this was the base of Number Six Mountain.

"Zane Wilson and his girlfriend, Indigo, live up there in their yurt," she said.

We continued on until the road was again passing through open cropland. I recognized these as the plowed fields and fenced pastures I had seen from above. In the first plot, three killdeers, having returned from their winter migration, ran hither and yon, unable to locate insects in the clumped soil. In the next, a small herd of mixed sheep nibbled whatever plant matter they had missed on their prior forages. As we passed the fence, a donkey approached to bray at us.

"Better than sheepdogs, my farmer friends tell me," Ronette said.

"Donkeys are naturally aggressive toward canines. They bite, stomp, and kick. If I were a coyote, I'd give these lambkins a wide berth."

Now the first farmhouse came into view. Immediately apparent, even from a distance, was its newness. The white clapboards reflected the sun like snow atop Sugarloaf. An enormous barn, carpentered from unpainted wood, rose behind it.

"This is the Stoll place," Ronette said. "Instead of driving onto the property, I think it would be more polite to walk."

The house had been built in the shade of a cluster of ancient red maples, all of which had been tapped for sugaring. Someone must not have informed the Amish that red maples don't yield the best sap even under ideal weather.

We had gotten out and were standing beside the vehicle when we heard the roar of a truck engine coming from the direction of the main road, behind us.

"Shit."

I didn't have to ask Ronette to elaborate on that remark. The Dodge Ram 3500 Laramie model was already among the largest pickups on the road, but this one had been modified with monster tires and a lift kit that raised the chassis another half foot off the ground. The driver must have returned from a mud run because the entire exterior looked to have been finger painted in dog shit.

The Ram stopped on a dime and the window slid down. The big man behind the wheel was not at all what I had expected. He had a face like a baked ham—his head was shaved—and he was wearing a blue blazer and a white button-down shirt opened at the collar to let loose an effusion of gray chest hair.

"What are you doing here?" he said in the voice of a man who enjoyed his whiskeys.

"And a good day to you, Gorman," said Ronette.

"It's my land and I've got a right to know."

"In fact, this is a public way, and our business is none of your concern."

"Did one of the neckbeards poach a deer?" The thought made smile lines radiate from the corners of his piggish eyes.

"I hope you're not referring to one of your Amish neighbors," I said.

"Excuse me, pretty boy, I ain't talking to you."

I had heard a lot of insults, but that was a new one.

"Game warden investigator." I raised my badge. "You call me that again and I'm going to pull you down out of that truck."

"Ooh, scary."

Ronette waded into the fray. "Why don't you move along, Gorman."

"Because I have a right to be here. You said it's a public road."

"A public road you happen to be blocking," I said.

"But it's OK when the neckbeards drive their little carts down the middle of it?"

"I warned you about using that term," I said.

"This town is being overrun by religious fanatics, and I'm the bad guy." He pitched his voice high in mockery of someone, perhaps me. "'Oh, but the Amish are peaceful people who want to be left alone.' What happened to my rights? How come my personal liberty matters less than the Children of the Corn? My family founded this damn town."

"When we're done here," I said, "we'll be visiting your house, so don't go anywhere."

"Not without a warrant you won't be."

He scanned the inside of the truck, rummaged around (for a moment I feared he was reaching for a gun), and held up a thin white booklet. He waved it in the air.

"You might want to read this sometime. Schools used to teach it. But now it's considered politically incorrect."

He tossed the slim pamphlet at my feet. "Don't come onto my land. I'm not even joking."

Then he lifted his foot from the brake and slammed it on the gas pedal. The Ram shot forward, leaving us choking in a cloud of exhaust.

I squatted down on my heels to retrieve the booklet from the mud. It was a pocket edition of the U.S. Constitution.

20

Not until Gorman Peaslee had driven off did I notice that a young boy had come down the road from the farmhouse and was standing in the gap in the fence.

He was wearing a blue shirt, high-water black pants held up by suspenders, clunky boots, and a broad-brimmed straw hat. His head was square shaped with wide-set brown eyes like those of a herd animal of the savanna. His hair, the same hay color as his hat, had been cut in straight bangs that fell below his eyebrows. In his small hand he clutched a switch he'd made from a ruddy birch branch. I guessed him to be about ten although he might have been short for his age.

"Good morning." He had the faintest trace of a Teutonic accent.

"Good morning," Ronette said for both of us. "What's your name?"

"Samuel."

"Samuel Stoll?"

"*Ja*. Who are you?"

"I'm Warden Landry, and this is Warden Bowditch. We're game wardens. That's a kind of police officer."

"I know what a game warden is."

"Are your parents home, Sam?" I asked.

"Samuel." His face had remained empty of emotions. "*Datt* went to town with Uncle Ike. I am supposed to watch the sheep."

"What about your mother?" Ronette said. "Is she here?"

"*Mamm* is making pies with Indigo and my sisters."

I recognized the name of Zane Wilson's girlfriend. "Can you get her for us?"

He pointed the switch at the flock in the pasture. "I am supposed to watch the sheep."

The child's lack of affect unsettled me. "I bet your donkey can protect them while you're gone."

"Not if the black one comes back."

"The black what?"

"The black coyote. He killed Little Amos and dragged him away before *Datt* could get his gun."

Ronette and I exchanged glances.

"Little Amos was another of your family's donkeys?" I asked as if the answer weren't obvious.

The boy bit his lower lip so hard I saw his upper teeth and he whipped the branch back and forth as if it were a cutlass.

"Would it be all right if we walked down to the house, do you think?" Ronette asked.

"If you are police, as you say."

"We are."

"Then you are welcome."

Ronette locked up her vehicle. Samuel stepped aside to let us pass. I wanted to make a new start with the blank-faced child. I squatted down on my heels. "I am very sorry about what happened to Little Amos."

But, of course, the boy didn't understand why I felt the need to apologize for what a wild animal had done.

"Strange to see a house without power or cable lines, isn't it?" Ronette said as we drew near the farmstead.

"At least their lives don't stop every time a storm knocks out power to the grid."

Most of the first-floor windows were dark, but several at the far end were illuminated by lantern light. I took that room to be the kitchen.

The young woman who answered the door wasn't remotely Amish. She was thin with honey-brown dreadlocks and a stud in her nostril. She wore blue jeans and a loose gingham shirt from which tattoos were peeking out at the wrists and above the neckline. On her feet were a pair of purple gardening boots. She smelled of marijuana.

"You probably don't remember me," Ronette said.

The woman wrinkled her nose. "Did you arrest me once?"

"No."

"Then, sorry, no."

"I'm Ronette Landry and this is Mike Bowditch. We're with the Maine Warden Service. We'd like to ask Mrs. Stoll a few questions."

"About what?"

"Can you get her for us, please, Ms. Mazur?"

From behind the young woman, a female voice said, "Let them in, Indigo. No need to be rude."

Nearly identical black coats hung from hooks along the wall of the mudroom. Where the hallway met the kitchen stood a woman wearing a homespun dress, a white apron, and a heart-shaped bonnet made of some sheer fabric. Her hair was the shiny brown of a model's in a shampoo commercial, but her skin was ruddy with untreated rosacea. If I had to guess, I would have said she was somewhere in her late thirties, a full decade older than Indigo Mazur.

"I am Anna Stoll," she said in the same slightly Germanic accent as her son's.

"We saw you out there talking to Peabrain," said Indigo.

"You know how I hate it when you call him that."

The hippie chick rolled her bloodshot eyes. "The man's a tool, Anna."

Anna Stoll wiped her flour-covered hands on her apron and beckoned us forward. "Please, come inside where it is warm."

Warm was an understatement; the kitchen was so hot that they had been forced to open the windows. The air smelled of woodsmoke from the stove and of kerosene burning in the lanterns mounted along the walls. More subtle odors drifted on the moving air: cinnamon, nutmeg, lemon. They were making pies.

In my utter ignorance of their culture, I had been under the impression that Amish women were forbidden to speak with strange men, but Anna Stoll seemed poised and confident.

Still, it was Indigo, the blunt Brooklynite, who took the lead. "Are you here about the coyote?"

"It was too big to be a coyote," Anna said. "It was someone's pet dog."

"That's what Zane keeps saying. I bet it belongs to Peabrain. He breeds some kind of super-aggressive watchdogs. We can sometimes hear them barking at our place, and that's like two miles from his house. If it was his dog, he should be punished for letting it run loose."

I turned from Indigo to address Anna Stoll. "What can you tell us about the animal?"

"It slaughtered their burro!" said Indigo. "His name was Little Amos!"

She seemed pretty well baked to me. The cannabis had brought her emotions close to the surface.

In the far door I spotted two little girls peeking at us. Both of them were brown haired and wore bonnets like their mother's. I waved awkwardly, and they ducked, terrified, behind the door frame.

"We'd prefer to get the story from Mrs. Stoll," said Ronette. "When did you first see this animal?"

Indigo Mazur puffed air out of her mouth and sat down in the corner on a stool that looked to have been designed for milking cows.

The Amish woman began, "A week ago, my husband and his brother Isaac were coming home from town after dark. They have a furniture shop along the main road. Down near the swamp, the horses became very nervous. Then behind them a black animal crossed the road, just out of the light of the carriage. They thought it must have been a bear."

Ronette had an easy way with these women. "Have you seen bears here?"

"Once last summer, a mother and cubs. But we had bears in Pennsylvania."

I thought of taking out my notebook, then reconsidered, not wanting her to stop talking. "How soon after your husband saw the animal did it attack your donkey?"

"The next morning. My husband thinks it was after one of our sheep. But Little Amos was very young, and he didn't know that this big dog couldn't be frightened away like the coyotes. It was quite horrible. My son saw it happen and came and told us, but when my husband ran outside with his gun, the dog was gone, and he'd taken Little Amos with him in his jaws like one of my daughter's dolls."

"Did your husband pursue the animal?"

"Yes, but he couldn't follow him through the swamp."

"Do you know if he fired his gun?"

"He didn't have a chance."

"What about your brother or your neighbors?" asked Ronette. "Did any of them encounter this animal?"

"No."

"Are you sure?"

"Yes, because the men were all talking about it again this morning, before they went to town."

I thought of Samuel Stoll, alone out there with nothing but a switch. I found myself admiring his parents for letting him play outdoors. They hadn't felt the need to keep their son inside as so many modern people would have done. The world held its share of dangers, but it was highly improbable "the black dog" would return to make a meal of the child. Their attitude seemed to be that a boy needs to be a boy if he is to grow up to be a man. But I was probably projecting my own mind-set on these anachronistic people.

"I have another question. Have you or any of your neighbors seen signs of a second large dog roaming the area?"

"You mean there are two of those monsters?" Indigo nearly knocked over the stool as she rose to her feet.

"No, we haven't," said Anna. "Are my children and our animals in danger from these beasts?"

Ronette and I spoke at the same exact instant.

"No," I said.

"Maybe," she said.

"Are they rabid?" Indigo asked. "Is that why they're attacking livestock?"

"There is no evidence to suggest that," said Ronette.

"This might sound like a strange question," I said, "but does anyone in your family own a crossbow?"

"Like a slingshot?"

"It's a kind of mechanical bow and arrow."

Her voice rose noticeably. "We don't have anything like that in this house."

"What about your neighbors?"

"I think I would remember that kind of contraption if I had ever seen them using it."

Indigo ran a hand along her face, almost as if to calm herself. "Is it dead?"

"Excuse me?"

"From what you're saying, it sounds like someone shot the black one with a crossbow. Why else would you have mentioned it? There's something you're not telling us."

As stoned as she was, the young woman was quick-witted.

"You are so distrustful, Indigo," said the Amish woman. "It makes me sad."

"It makes me sad that you're overly trusting."

Anna Stoll shook her head. "Would you like some pie before you go?"

Ronette and I exchanged hopeful smiles.

21

The pie was a variety I had never before tasted. It was very sweet—predominantly molasses flavored—with a hint of ginger and cloves in addition to the cinnamon and nutmeg I had smelled on the warm air. Anna served it to us with big glasses of unpasteurized milk from a literal icebox.

"Is this shoofly pie?" Ronette asked.

The Amish woman gave us a delighted grin. "You have had it before?"

"Not like this."

"It's delicious," I agreed. I had always been a sucker for baked goods flavored with molasses.

Indigo Mazur excused herself before we had finished cleaning the last crumbs from our plates. She said she had chores to finish back at home, but I knew she had concocted the excuse to get away from us. Habitual users of intoxicants don't make a practice of hanging out with law-enforcement officers. I had to wonder what had happened in her history to make her so reflexively cynical. By contrast, Zane Wilson had come across as a naïf, which made me question the future of their relationship.

We had just said our goodbyes to Anna and her peekaboo daughters when we heard Gorman Peaslee's truck roar past again. This time, he was headed out.

"I guess he was serious about not wanting to be interviewed," I said to Ronette.

"Gorman wouldn't have spoken to us in any case. The only authority he acknowledges is his own."

I removed the dirt-stained Constitution from my pocket. "What about this?"

"Didn't you hear? Gorman Peaslee was that document's sole author. And the sole arbiter on its legal interpretation."

I put away the pamphlet. "Does anyone else live down that way?"

"Not this time of year. There are a couple of seasonal cabins, all for sale. The buyers didn't know what it meant to have Gorman for a neighbor. Not until it was too late."

I recalled the vandalized real estate signs at the corner. Unconsciously, I found myself looking around for Samuel, but the boy must have tired of playing shepherd and wandered off to pursue some new adventure.

"I'd like to have a look at Peaslee's house, anyway," I said.

"What for?"

"Because he doesn't want me to."

The sky was growing darker. It wasn't all that late in the afternoon, but heavy clouds had begun to descend on the summits of the taller mountains to the north, giving them an almost bisected appearance, as if they had been chopped down to the exact same elevation. The likelihood of a snowy drive home weighed upon my mood.

We passed the two other Amish farms. One of the families kept dairy cattle. The Holsteins paused in their cud chewing to turn their wide, empty eyes in our direction.

"I find it hard to believe that Anna Stoll has never heard of a crossbow," I said.

"That did seem odd."

When I didn't speak again, Ronette filled in the silence. "Now you understand why I called Indigo Mazur a firecracker."

"How does someone like her end up living in a yurt in the middle of the woods?"

"How else? Love."

"Should we have told her about Zane's mishap with the truck?"

"I'm surprised you didn't—knowing the delight you take in mischief making."

"Who says I take delight in it?"

"A certain state police trooper, for one."

I needed to keep in mind what close friends Ronette and my girlfriend were. I hadn't communicated with Dani since she'd left my house the day before. How was she interpreting my prolonged silence?

I had always attributed my successes in life to my ability to focus in the midst of chaos, but that same focus inclined me to self-involvement and a careless disregard toward the people around me. The moment was wrong for a phone call, but I needed to reach out to Dani as soon as I was alone again, if only to explain about Shadow.

The vacant cabins Ronette had mentioned began to flit past, one after the other.

"In a way it's kind of impressive that one man could drive away so many people," she said. "Awful, but impressive."

I didn't find Peaslee's tactics unusual. I had encountered plenty of men, and women, in the Maine woods who'd borrowed the same playbook. The prisoner Billy Cronk had killed, Trevor Dow, had been one of the worst offenders. For years, he and his redheaded clan had bullied an entire community into keeping mum about their multifarious crimes.

"Is Peaslee married?"

"Why get married when his money attracts an endless supply of girls? How that middle-aged creep manages to keep persuading young women—I was going to say it was a mystery, but the truth is it's not mysterious at all. There will always be frogs willing to carry scorpions across the river."

"Is he gratuitously hateful or does he have an actual reason for acting like a shit heel?"

"I'm no psychologist, but I think he's terrified people are going to discover he's not the big man he pretends to be. My priest would probably say Gorman's fear has made him a slave to sin."

For Ronette everything came back to faith. I envied the comfort it obviously provided her. For me there had only ever been doubt.

The road dead-ended at Peaslee's property, running headlong into a wooden gate that bore a resemblance to a colonial-era stockade. Made of heavy logs, sharpened to points at the top, and secured with a chain big and strong enough to haul an eighteen-wheeler out of a ditch. Dual security cameras focused, like the binocular eyes of a carrion bird, on the entrance. Gorman would have a video record of our visit to review when he returned to his fortress of solitude.

The fence continued in either direction from the gate, hiding the portion of the yard immediately behind it, but the house itself sat upon a low rise and was visible above the toothed barrier. The three-story cabin was made of the same orange-stained logs used to build the palisade. It wasn't difficult for me to imagine Lord Peaslee in his rough-hewn castle, surveying with rage the farm fields of the religious zealots.

Even before we stopped, dogs began to bark from inside the enclosure. To my ears they sounded large and hungry.

"Rottweilers?"

"Rottermans. They're a Rottweiler/Doberman cross. Gorman breeds them and sells the puppies for a thousand bucks apiece."

Shadow and the she-wolf would have given the Rottermans a wide berth, needless to say.

"How does Gorman make his money, aside from running a puppy mill?"

"Guys like Peaslee always have some racket going. He and his brother own a snowmobile and ATV dealership in New Sharon. They make most of their money by financing machines to people who can't afford them and then reselling the high-interest loans. They also run a rent-to-own franchise in Wilton. More recently, the Peaslees opened the first payday-loan business in Franklin County."

"The way you described him, I didn't expect the blazer."

"I guarantee you he was carrying at least three handguns on him and probably had a fourth pointed through the door at you. I don't know about you, but the sociopaths I've met are usually well-dressed."

Ronette rolled down her window and waved at the security cams.

With the glass down, I listened to the hostile dogs massing on the opposite side of the gate. Even above their barking, I could hear the collisions of their big bodies against the logs as they sought to scramble over the high fence, their claws digging into the wood. I expected any second to see them come slobbering over the palisades, a vicious pack of hellhounds.

"Seen enough?" Ronette asked.

"No. But it'll have to do for now."

We had passed the Amish farms and were entering the birch thicket when I put a hand on Ronette's forearm.

"Pull in here." I indicated the steep muddy track leading up through the ghost wood to the hidden yurt.

"What else do you need to ask Indigo about?"

"She seemed in a hurry to leave when the topic turned to Shadow."

"She might just dislike cops."

Call me crazy, but it seemed Indigo had been expecting us. She met us in her vehicle halfway down the deeply gouged dirt road. The car was a mid-aughts Subaru Baja. The eccentric design—a station wagon with an open truck bed—reminded me of the "Fiji mermaid" that P. T. Barnum had constructed by sewing the top half of a monkey to the back half of a fish.

She exited the idling car as we slowed to a halt. Since we'd last seen her, she'd put on a long woolen pullover I associated with the Peruvian Andes. It was striped in multiple colors, from red to yellow to blue, with a hood she wore over her dreadlocks. Her face was shining with perspiration.

"Headed out?" I asked through the window.

"I was on my way to Farmington. I didn't expect to see you again."

To be sociable I stepped from the truck. "I realized I had a couple more questions for you."

"For me?"

"I didn't have a chance to tell you before, but I met Zane this morning."

"What? Where?"

"Up on Alcohol Mary's mountain. He's not having the best day, but I'll leave it to him to tell you about it."

She tried not to react to this frustrating nondisclosure, but I saw a vein pulse in her temple. "That's not a question."

"The animal that killed Little Amos wasn't a coyote and it wasn't a dog. It was a wolf."

She opened her mouth, revealing a stud in her tongue. "You're shitting me."

"Mary found it seeking refuge under the shelter where she stacks her firewood. It had an arrow in it."

"That's why you asked about crossbows. But I still haven't heard a question."

Ronette leaned against the warm hood of her truck, content to listen to the clashing of our lances.

"Zane tells us he saw that wolf on her property a few nights ago. I'd like to hear what he told you about it."

"Why don't you ask him?"

"I did."

"What did he say?"

"That he'd glimpsed an animal in his headlights up on Number Six Mountain. How did you react when he told you about it?"

She danced easily out of my trap. "Who said he did?"

"It seems like the kind of thing he would mention."

"You can keep trying to outfox me or you can come out with the real question you want to ask. To hell with it. I'll do it for you. Why didn't I mention any of this back in Anna's kitchen?"

I couldn't help but offer a congratulatory smile on her quickness. "You've asked the question. Now, how about answering it?"

"You mentioned a second wolf—which I thought were extinct, by the way. I could see Anna was getting worried because her girls were listening. I decided to leave before I blurted something out that got them even more agitated. What are you accusing me of, exactly? Being polite and discreet?"

"I'm not accusing you of anything."

"I can tell you I've never killed an animal in my life."

"What about Zane?"

She had a healthy, hearty laugh. "That man makes pacifists look like warmongers. He's the one responsible for turning me— someone whose favorite food used to be steak tartare—into a vegan. You didn't notice that I passed on Anna's pie on account of the lard?"

I actually *had* noticed. So why was she bothering to learn to bake?

"If you think Zane is a killer, you've got him all wrong. The guy *live traps* mice in our yurt and releases them in the woods."

"You'd prefer more extreme measures, I take it?"

"I believe every creature has a right to live, but that doesn't mean I want to die from the hantavirus. He won't even allow me to have a horse because he says we don't have the right to imprison another creature."

A gust of wind rattled the birch branches. I thought I tasted snow on the air.

The Subaru was blocking the patrol truck from driving up the hill. "How about we continue our talk back at your place?"

"I need to get to town before the bank closes. Can't you just say what's on your mind?"

"I believe Zane lied to me about when and where he saw the wolf."

"He was probably blazed."

"I didn't have that sense."

"I mean when he saw the wolf. Give him a fatty and he'll tell you it's Thursday when it's Sunday."

I glanced at the hillside behind her where the birches were swaying in the gusting wind. "This isn't my home territory, but I think I have a decent sense of direction. That's Number Six Mountain behind you."

"So?"

"Mary's house couldn't be more than two miles straight up, as the raven flies."

"A mile and a half. Zane cleared a trail last fall for his 'commute' when the weather improves. And don't think I haven't noticed you're still playing games. What is the exact crime you are investigating and what role do you think Zane and I had in committing it?"

"Finding out who shot the black wolf isn't my primary interest. I'm trying to find out what happened to the gray one."

I had spoken with more passion than I'd intended, and Indigo had heard the change in my voice.

"Why?"

"I'd like to save her life if I can."

It had taken saying those words aloud for me to understand my own motivations. Whatever I had once believed about wild wolves coexisting with humans in Maine, seeing Shadow shaved and anesthetized on that cold table had convinced me otherwise. Too many people with guns and bows would fear them, resent them, and want their pelts as trophies.

"You said 'her.' How do you know the second one's a female?"

She was a sharp one, this Indigo Mazur. Baked or not.

"Zane has my card. Remind him to call if he remembers anything that might help me save the other wolf."

2 2

We drove in silence for five solid minutes. Then Ronette said, "So what are you thinking? That if you find the other wolf alive, you'll be able to trap her somehow?"

"I don't know."

"Mike, this is my district. I like to think I know these mountains better than anyone. The chances of locating a single canine on the move . . ."

I turned my face to the window. "The chances are slim. I get that."

"Can I make an observation?"

"Why not?"

"It's obvious how personal this is for you. Even Indigo saw it. But none of what is going to happen—either with Shadow or this other animal—is in your control."

"You sound like Gary Pulsifer."

Now it was her turn to bristle. "I've never been accused of that before!"

"His new mantra is 'Let it go.'"

"That seems like good advice."

I was tired and, despite knowing that Ronette had only the best of intentions, was in no mood to be psychoanalyzed. "I'm going to come back here in the morning with some supplies."

We drove along in silence.

"It's a hell of a way to spend your vacation. I can't think of a worse month to tramp around in the woods here. What isn't frozen solid is a quagmire."

"Can you recommend a clean, cheap motel?"

Ronette was done asking me what I hoped to accomplish with

this mad mission of mine. Now she looked at me in mock surprise. "You want clean *and* cheap?"

"Cheap then."

"There's nothing much open this time of year between Farmington and Rangeley. I can recommend a nice bed-and-breakfast over in Strong, though."

"I'm not sure a B and B suits me. I expect to be keeping odd hours. And I might be returning to the room pretty dirty, as you noted."

She eased up on the gas. "How do you feel about rustic accommodations?"

"Rustic I can deal with. I'll take a drafty lean-to over a sleazy motel any day of the week."

"Then have I got a place for you."

She refused to tell me where we were going. Back in downtown Avon, she dropped me at my Jeep and told me to follow her. As soon as she took the second turn off an already-dodgy road, I began to worry. To call this overgrown trail of mud, potholes, and fist-size rocks "unimproved" would be to oversell its condition. With the trees pressing in so closely, I couldn't imagine how we could possibly turn around if we reached a deadfall or other unforeseen obstacle.

I had to laugh in amazement when Ronette's brake lights came on and stayed on as she put the truck into park. An actual steel gate was up ahead, as if the dirt track itself weren't enough of an impediment to entry. From the warmth of my Jeep, I watched her get out with a ring of keys that would have made a high school janitor feel inadequate. It took her a minute to find the one she wanted and another to heave the metal gate open on its rusted axis.

She idled her pickup through the entrance, and I followed, leaving the gate ajar behind me.

Deep in the woods, higher up, and in the near-constant shadows of the mountains, a hard pack of frozen, melted, and refrozen snow remained on the ground. It provided better purchase for my tires than the ice had. The road bore the tread marks of snowmobiles and ATVs, which entered where a designated sled trail crossed. The weight of those vehicles had further tamped down the snow.

After several minutes, I began to glimpse, through the evergreens to my right, a gray-and-white expanse that could only be a pond with an eggshell coating of ice. Then the shadow of a small wooden cabin, perched on the edge of the water, loomed in Ronette's high beams. The surrounding trees had been cleared to create a dooryard wide enough for us to park side by side. We had arrived at our destination—wherever the hell we were.

When I stepped out, I could see my breath like my spirit leaving my body. The temperature was at least fifteen degrees colder than it had been in the bottomland.

I pulled on a pair of gloves. "If you brought me out here to kill me . . ."

"Don't make jokes about things like that."

"I wish I could say that I knew what body of water that is, but I don't have a clue."

"It's Tantrattle Pond, and I'm not surprised you've never heard of it. It's so shallow that it freezes down to the mud during hard winters, meaning it's a bad place for fish. The state built this cabin back in the late 1980s to house a crew of trailblazers who were going to build a new hiking path up Mount Blue. But then the economy went to shit, and the old Bureau of Parks and Lands was strained maintaining the existing system."

In the failing light, the cabin looked solidly built. The chimney, straight and square, bore the handprints of an experienced mason. The roof shingles, or what I could see of them peeking out from beneath the snowcap, didn't appear to be warped.

"What's the deal with all the snowmobile and ATV traffic on the way in?"

"Some riders have taken to detouring over from Route 89 of the Interconnected Trail System to have a look at Tantrattle. This cabin used to be quite the place for parties. It was getting vandalized every winter, until my husband, Peter, and his crew made the building harder to break into. Would you like to have a look inside, or have you already decided it doesn't meet your delicate standards?"

"What are you talking about? This is my dream cabin!"

Ronette reached back into the door well of her Sierra for a Maglite. I removed my little SureFire from the pocket of my coat.

We circled around the side of the building. Quite a few bootprints showed in the remaining snow, no doubt from intruders looking for a way in to steal whatever there was to steal.

Ronette straightened up. "Damn it!"

In the beam of her Maglite I saw the cabin door. More precisely, I saw the rectangular hole where the door had been battered, kicked in, and smashed to pieces. I followed a visibly irate Ronette into the dark void.

A sour odor overwhelmed me even before the flashlight revealed the source. Urine. The determined vandals, having rammed their way inside, had left yellow stains the way predators mark their territory.

"This was recent," I said.

Ronette was an experienced warden. She'd noticed what I'd noticed. "If it had happened weeks ago, there would've been wind-blown snow heaped inside the threshold."

"Exactly."

I stepped carefully and began sweeping the light around the interior. The first thing I saw was a couch with a broken back and an overturned easy chair. The cabinets had been ransacked, but Ronette said the entomologists who came to the pond to study dragonflies never left anything of value inside the cabin.

Under the circumstances I supposed it was lucky the sons of bitches hadn't burned the place to the ground.

I searched through the rooms and found damage to varying degrees in each of them. But one bedroom—containing nothing but a card table and a set of bunk beds—had been left entirely untouched. Ronette snapped some crime-scene photos, knowing nothing would come of them, that the vandals would never be identified unless one of them boasted to the wrong person, or the criminals turned on one another to avoid being prosecuted for a more serious offense.

My hot breath drifted from my nostrils. "I don't suppose you installed game cameras outside."

My question made Ronette smack her forehead. "How could I have forgotten?"

Almost every unattended outpost overseen by the Department of Inland Fisheries and Wildlife has hidden surveillance. Because these cameras are camouflaged and hidden by veteran wardens, such as Ronette Landry, they are remarkably hard for anyone but a true woodsman to locate.

Not hard enough, it seemed.

Around a handful of the local trees Ronette found severed cables lying like dead black snakes. The Tantrattle vandals had suspected cameras would be recording their actions and were woods-wise enough to find and steal them.

"That's a tough break, Ronnie."

When she turned, I spotted a gleam in her coppery eye. "We're not finished yet. Can you give me a lift up?"

She motioned to a birdhouse mounted under the eaves above the door. The weathered wooden box had white guano stains that suggested it had once hosted a nesting pair of chickadees or nuthatches. Only upon reconsideration did I understand why Ronette had reacted with such enthusiasm.

She stood on my shoulders while she pried the box loose from the logs. When she had it down on the frozen ground, she popped the back open with a hunting knife. Inside was an expertly hidden Bushnell game camera.

I fingered the white paint she had dabbed on the birdhouse. "The fake guano was a nice touch."

"The real hard part was hiding the openings of the motion sensors. That took some trial and error."

She unlatched the camera case until she could see the little screen inside where you could review the photos or videos you had taken. She clicked through a number of shots until she came upon the incriminating pictures.

"Got you, bastards!"

She angled the screen so I could have a look. I glimpsed the shadowy outlines of three men with what looked like impressive heads of hair.

"You recognize them?" I asked doubtfully.

"They're the Beliveau brothers. They're trappers, and they all wear beaver hats. It's their signature headwear. It wouldn't surprise me if they shot that wolf of yours."

"I hope some of your pics are in better focus."

"I'll take this home with me to have a look on the computer. I've got an Ultra HD monitor that I use for my forensic work. But I already know what it's going to show me. Those are the Beliveaus all right. Tomorrow I'm going to go bust their skinny little asses."

During our day together, talking about faith and doubt, anger and forgiveness, I had forgotten what a tech whiz Ronette was. She was a woman of many talents and even more interests.

I zipped up my coat. "I'd better pack my toolbox when I get home. This cabin's going to need a lot of work to make it halfway habitable."

My comment seemed to float about us like a balloon on the air.

Then she turned to me with a secretive smile. "We'll see about that."

23

Ronette said she would have a set of keys made and showed me where she would hide them, under a pulpy log outside the gate. Then we said our goodbyes. After what had been a brutal day, I was eager to get on the road, and Ronette was pumped up to pay a visit to the Beliveau boys.

Out of curiosity I checked to see if I had a cell signal, but my phone might as well have been dead. I could play solitaire on it or use the flashlight to light my way to the outhouse, but I wouldn't be engaging in pillow talk with Dani Tate from my cot.

The clouds were falling on the valley now like curtains after a play. I had spent enough time as a warden living outside in all weather to know that I was in for a wild ride back home.

The highway carried me downstream. I passed again the Bard of Avon coffeehouse, closed for the evening, and the airstrip named for Charles Lindbergh. Off to my left the Sandy River looked more like the muddy river, so brown was it with run-off from the farm fields and sheep pastures.

I finally got a four-bar signal when I crossed the border into the unusually named town of Strong. Maine was famous for its weirdo place names. The state probably had twenty municipalities that had been christened after foreign countries and capitals: Peru, China, Mexico, Norway, Paris, Poland. The list goes on. It was no wonder tourists described my rural state as "quaint." They might have re-thought their adjectives if I introduced them to men such as Trevor Dow, Gorman Peaslee, and the Beliveau boys.

Or Billy Cronk, for that matter.

Among the messages I had missed was a call from the man of

the hour. Someone in the Department of Corrections must have decided that they couldn't deny a soon-to-be-pardoned prisoner the use of a telephone. Billy's call was time-stamped midafternoon.

"Hey, Mike. I wanted to thank you for paying for my family's motel. You've always looked out for them while I was inside, and I won't forget it. They're transferring me to the Farm this afternoon. The docs think I won't die if I take my antibiotics and hold off on doing crunches a few days."

I couldn't be sure if that was a joke or not.

"Could you talk to Aimee for me? She still don't believe this is for real. She thinks the governor's promise is for shit and he's going to screw us over as soon as the camera lights go off. What do you think about that? Should I be worried? I'm trying not to get my hopes up."

I'd been planning to drive straight home, to give myself time to pack for an extended stay at the luxurious Tantrattle Cabin and get some much-needed sleep. But hearing my friend's bearish voice made me wish to see him again in person. I checked the clock. No way was I going to make it back to the Midcoast in time for visiting hours at the Bolduc Correctional Facility. But again, maybe Billy's heroism and provisional pardon had earned him special treatment.

The other messages weren't urgent or important.

I had hoped for an update from Dr. Holman concerning Shadow. I was doing my best to manage my expectations about his survival. The clinic was surely closed now, and while the veterinarian had given me her personal number, I was loath to call lest I hear bad news.

It also worried me that I'd heard nothing at all from Dani.

I had been reckless, letting our relationship get physical so quickly, assuming she would be content with an extended period of no-commitment nights together while I got Stacey out of my head. But Dani had been clear that she couldn't continue with the status quo. I knew she would want to hear about Shadow, but I wasn't ready to give her an answer about my feelings, if the conversation took a turn in that direction. I would call her when I got home, I decided.

Coward.

As I crossed the bridge and entered the outskirts of Farmington,

I spotted the gun shop Pulsifer had mentioned over breakfast. My plan was to canvass the area hardware and sporting goods stores in the vain hope that my unknown archer had purchased the bolt locally. But for a variety of reasons I was reluctant to step through the doors of Fairbanks Firearms.

A few wet flakes of snow landed on my windshield as I pulled into the parking lot. The faux log cabin was ringed by concrete Jersey barriers to prevent a determined thief from doing a smash-and-grab. A large orange banner across the door shouted WELCOME ANGLERS! A smaller one pasted inside a dusty window whispered BUSINESS FOR SALE BY OWNER.

I had never visited my uncle's shop, but I had heard from one of my informants that Denis Cormier was not fully following federal and state laws pertaining to gun sales.

A buzzer sounded as I entered. The store resembled any number of backwoods businesses catering to fishermen and hunters. There were racks of spinning and bait casting rods, some as tall as the ceiling. Camouflage clothes for men, women, and children on hangers. Rifles and shotguns cabled together along the wall behind the counter. The room smelled of the bait tank bubbling in the back of the room: algae and fish.

"We're about to close," said a deep voice from behind a display case of hunting and combat knives.

"Uncle Denis! It's Mike."

"Who?"

"Your nephew. Marie's son."

He peered out from behind the register: a short man with narrow shoulders, an olive complexion, silver hair, and a black mustache. If there was a men's petite clothing size, he was wearing it. This shrimp was my mother's oldest brother.

I hadn't seen Denis since her funeral. After the burial, at the reception held at the Prouts Neck Country Club, he and my other uncles had gotten drunk enough to send my mom's tennis friends running for the exits. Next they had surrounded my hapless stepfather and begun arguing that my mother would have wanted her birth family to share in her bequest—never mind that the terms of her will explicitly excluded them.

"What do you want?" asked Uncle Denis, keeping his distance.

"I was in the area and thought I'd stop in and see your new business."

Like all the Cormiers he had delicate bones and moody brown eyes. My mother's had been as bright and lovely as opals. His were the color of unpolished agates. "You just missed the grand opening."

I think I must have blinked. "Really? When was that?"

He glanced at the "Time to Fish" clock on the wall. Then he turned to me with a stone-cold expression. "Two years ago next month."

Denis and his brothers had once worked high-paying union jobs at Madison Paper Industries. Then, like the mill in Pennacook, the papermaking factory had shut down. Suddenly the Cormier brothers—who had never saved a penny in their lives—found themselves in the unemployment line. Gary Pulsifer had been the one to tell me that Denis had opened a gun shop. Gary had also informed me about an illegal sideline he'd heard my uncle was involved in.

A paperback book lay on the counter; clearly my uncle had been reading it in the long intervals between customers. His choice of titles surprised me. It was *Green Hills of Africa* by Ernest Hemingway, one of my favorite authors.

"How are you liking that?" I asked, trying to shift the conversation onto a smoother track.

"The guy doesn't know shit about guns."

I could see how this was going to go. In a way, no longer having to work at being courteous made it easier. "I saw the 'For Sale' sign out front."

"You want to buy the place? I happen to know the owner."

"Actually, I'm looking for a crossbow. What do you recommend for coyote hunting?"

"A rifle."

"But if someone wanted to use a crossbow?"

"Still a rifle."

Denis carried three brands of crossbows, and only one of them—the Blood Eagle Tactical—took sixteen-inch bolts. It was secured by a bicycle cable to a standing rack. I lifted it from the hook on which it was hanging, and my fingers came away dusty. "You sell many of these?"

"Hell, yeah. Dozens and dozens. We can barely keep them in stock."

In a bucket at my feet were crossbow bolts, fletching side up. I picked out a Spider-Bite X2 identical to the one that had pierced Shadow's lung. "How about these?"

"You want to tell me what you're really doing here, Warden Bowditch?"

"I'm looking for the names of anyone you might have sold sixteen-inch Spider-Bite X2 bolts to."

He leaned his scrawny ass against the glass case holding used revolvers. "You think I keep those kinds of records?"

"I think you have a good memory and always have."

"Flattery."

"I'm serious, Denis."

"So am I. How long do you think I'd be in business if it got around I was ratting out my customers to my nephew the game warden?"

"It looks like you're going out of business as it is."

"Touché."

The man was such an unrepentant wiseass. He always had been. I had never met a person who wielded humor as a rapier the way he did. You left every encounter bleeding.

"Rumors have been going around about you, Uncle Denis. There's been a lot of gossip."

"It's all true," he said, unsmiling. "I really do have a ten-inch dick."

"The thing I keep hearing is that, for the right price, you're doing illegal modifications to AR-15s for customers who want full autos."

"So now you're trying to bully me into helping you?"

"I'm just sharing the gossip I've heard. If there's any truth to it, you might consider turning your talents as a gunsmith in a direction that doesn't lead to federal prison. But I'm not here to report you."

To my surprise Denis crossed the room. For half a second I expected him to punch me in the crotch. Instead he fishhooked a finger inside his mouth to reveal a dental bridge where several of his molars should have been.

"Do you remember how I got this?" he mumbled, finger in mouth.

"I'm afraid I don't."

"No surprise since you were running around in a diaper that night. Your dad did it to me when we were camping over at Long Falls on the Dead River back before they 'cleaned it up.' He accused me of having scratched his truck when I opened my door. But that was a lie. That scratch was already there. Jack was looking for an excuse to beat the shit out of someone because he was bored. He shattered my cheekbone, broke my jaw, and knocked out three of my teeth."

"I'm the last person to defend my father's actions. And you weren't the only one he assaulted."

"Says his defender in chief. I should have known Jack Bowditch's boy would grow up to be a bully. Like father, like son."

"I was hoping you'd willingly help me out."

"And what made you think that?"

"Because we're family."

The intensity of his laughter provoked a full-body coughing fit. "I've got to close up," he said after he'd finally caught his breath.

24

I had made the turn to Augusta and home, with that feeling of having escaped the mountains and their cruel weather.

Then the snow squall ambushed me from behind.

One second, the road ahead was clear, the next, a heavy cape of ermine had fallen across my windshield. Moments later, my Jeep was buffeted by a gust of wind so strong it nearly pushed me into a ditch. Heart hammering, I clicked on my headlights and hazards and pulled over onto the shoulder to wait out the microburst.

This was April.

The cruelest month? More like the most sadistic.

I thought about my mean-spirited uncle. The state was full of men like Denis Cormier. In the past decade alone, seven papermaking facilities had closed, forcing thousands of people out of work. Most of these proud hardworking individuals had painfully learned that running pulpers and after-dryer machines were not marketable skills in the so-called information economy. Consultants advised them to go back to school and learn coding or nursing—middle-aged men who might never have even graduated high school but had been collecting six-figure paychecks since they were in their twenties.

I had to remind myself that Denis had been an asshole even before he lost his job at the mill.

The bucket of arrows in his store intrigued me. Spider-Bite was a popular brand but not so popular that their products were available in every Walmart from here to San Diego. Also, most modern crossbows used longer bolts than sixteen-inchers since lengthier shafts offered greater accuracy in the field. That Denis stocked sixteen-inch Spider-Bite X2s suggested that the crossbowman had been a customer. Perhaps even a regular one.

Now if I could only persuade my scumbag uncle to give me a name.

After fifteen minutes, I saw the flashing yellow lights of a snow-plow in my rearview mirror. Because the snow hadn't accumulated more than a few inches, it wasn't plowing so much as sanding and spraying the asphalt with brine. I followed the big, flashing truck for the next twenty miles until we came to a stretch of road the squall had bypassed.

Twenty miles back it had been blizzard conditions.

But here the asphalt was dry, the moon was rising, and it was a smooth ride all the way home to the Midcoast.

The Bolduc Correctional Facility had been opened during the Great Depression as a farm barracks to feed the prisoners housed in the old penitentiary. Over time, it had expanded to become one of the largest beef and dairy farms in Maine. There was still a silo and fields where the inmates grew broccoli, tomatoes, and squash for sale at a roadside stand.

These days, though, most of the minimum-security prisoners held work-release jobs in the communities—as construction workers, road-crew flaggers, even firefighters—and returned to the prison to eat and sleep. The Farm was famous for not having fences. Yet every once in a while, some inmate with only weeks left on his sentence would walk off into the night. Inevitably these convicts would be recaptured and returned to the main prison, with years tacked onto their sentences for their brief, inexplicable flights of fancy.

It was after eight P.M. when I pulled into the lot. Two other ve-hicles—a black SUV and a small hatchback—were parked under the pole lights. The main building resembled an elementary school more than a penal institution. There were even picnic tables on the brittle lawn. The contrast with the state prison up the hill couldn't have been more stark.

I had already concluded I had little chance of being admitted.

Hero or not, Billy was subject to the rules of the institution. When it came to visiting hours, jails never made exceptions.

Or so I assumed.

The guard behind the admittance desk responded to my request with exasperation. "You'll have to wait. There's already someone with him now. I swear to God we've never had a more popular inmate than Killer Cronk."

"Who is with him?"

"I'm not at liberty."

"Is it his attorney?"

"I told you I'm not at liberty. If you want to wait, be my guest."

He gestured toward a row of chairs against the wall. I had barely settled my butt down before an interior door opened and through it stepped Novak Rancic. The suspended correctional officer was dressed in a black leather jacket, gray jeans, and motorcycle boots. His unshaven jaw was blue with stubble.

He froze when he caught sight of me. I rose to my feet. With the cold-blooded intensity of a cobra being stalked by a mongoose, he watched me cross the room.

"Officer Rancic."

"Warden."

"What are you doing here?"

His tone remained flat. "Extending my best wishes to your friend. He's quite the hero. Pardoned and everything."

"You disapprove of the governor's decision?"

"It's not my place to approve or disapprove."

"I was under the impression you were on administrative leave, pending a decision by the attorney general on whether the shooting was justified."

He smelled of cologne, and not the cheap stuff either. "That's right."

"Watching you at the hospital, it seemed to me you were pretty quick on the draw."

"Chapman was a murderer. He'd already cut up that nurse. He would have cut you if I hadn't discharged my weapon."

"You might have hit her or me."

"What can I say? I've always been a good shot."

"Where are you from, Rancic? Not from Maine, I'm guessing."

"What gave me away?" He exaggerated his New York accent. "I've lived here a while. Not that it's any of your business."

"How long have you worked in corrections?"

He smiled for the first time—if you can call an infinitesimal up-turn of the lips a smile. "Have a pleasant evening."

He retrieved his keys from the guard at the desk and continued outside. I followed him as far as the door and watched through the reinforced window as he remotely started the engine and lights of the SUV at the end. As the big vehicle pulled forward, I thought I caught a glimpse of someone in the front passenger seat. Whoever it was must have been waiting there in the dark and seen me drive in.

"You're up, Warden," said the admittance guard. "You know what to do with your sharp objects."

Billy was waiting for me in a small, glass-enclosed classroom that seemed to host the prison's group-therapy and AA meetings. The books on the table had titles such as *Living Sober* and *Relieved from the Bondage of Self*. The volumes looked as if they had never been opened.

He just about leapt to his feet. "What are you doing here, man?"

"I thought I'd look in on you."

"It's been a parade all day." He hugged me so hard I thought I heard one of my ribs crack.

"Are you sure that's a good idea—hugging people? I have this vague memory of your having been stabbed in the gut thirty-something hours ago."

He actually patted his abdomen with one of his big hands. "They stitched me up pretty good."

Incredibly, I seemed to feel more tired than he did. I dropped into a cushioned chair as he returned to the head of the table.

"So I met Rancic on the way in. I didn't realize you two were on friendly terms."

"We're not."

"So why was he here?"

"Beats me. He said he wanted to shake my hand and thank me for coming to Dawn's aid."

"Now you and she are on a first-name basis?"

"Nothing like that. I actually expected her to come by today. People say she's out of the hospital. But I haven't even seen her since the ER."

I was taught that it's polite to thank someone for saving your life. "Maybe now you can tell me why you wanted me to investigate her background."

"I wasn't thinking straight. I thought she was coming on to me, if you want to know the truth."

That possibility didn't strike me as remotely delusional. I had known many women who lusted after Billy Cronk. Why shouldn't the sergeant be one of them?

"It's got to have been more than that."

"She said she could make my life inside better than I could ever imagine. When I told her I loved my wife, she got all offended. Actually, she kind of threatened me. She told me I would prefer to be her friend than her enemy. I figured it was because I hurt her feelings, until Mears started hassling me, big-time. He reported to the sergeant so I figured the payback was coming from her."

"I still don't understand why you said it was a matter of life and death."

"I guess I was confused."

It seemed to me that Billy wasn't so much holding back the suspicions that had caused him to summon me. Instead—in light of what had happened in the prison laundry room—he had convinced himself that he had been as paranoid as I'd accused him of being.

I leaned my elbows on the table. "If she was such a bitch to you, why did you protect her from Chapman and Dow?"

The answer seemed so obvious to him it was as if he hadn't heard my question clearly. "She's a female."

"Yeah, but—"

There was no deeper meaning to Billy's response. The man clung to outdated ideals that were either chivalrous or sexist, maybe both, maybe neither. If a person was being assaulted by someone stronger than she was, he felt a moral duty to step into the fray.

"It won't be long until you're free."

"I'm counting the minutes. Aimee—you know how she can be—she says she'll believe it when she sees it. Thanks again for putting them in that motel."

"It's the least I can do."

"I've never blamed you, Mike. Almost never. I guess I did for a while. But I always understood that you had a duty to tell the truth about what happened. That's why I respect you so much. I've never respected anyone more, my brother."

"Gee, Billy."

"It's the truth, so help me, God." He put his hand on one of the sober-living paperbacks on the tabletop.

Exhausted as I was, I was in danger of choking up. I needed to change the subject.

"So who else has come by to visit?"

"Aimee and the kids. Our lawyer. The chaplain. A friend you don't know who I used to share a cell with who got out last year. Some of the COs. That detective, Klesko. Deputy Warden Donato."

"I bet he had a shitload of questions."

"Yeah, but my lawyer said not to answer them. Donato was ripshit when I told him that. He's being set up to take the fall for what happened in the laundry room. They're going to fire his ass, and he's doing everything he can to save his job."

"Was Pegg one of the officers who visited?"

"Someone told me they'd seen him outside, but he never came in. I don't know what his deal is. Why do you ask?"

"He seemed troubled when I talked to him at the hospital."

"Pegg's a good kid. He reminds me of a guy in my platoon in Iraq. He put on a tough act, but you could see that, inside, he was too sensitive to be a soldier. He didn't make it."

We talked a little longer. I told him about Shadow, and he gave me some technical information about crossbows—about the draw weight, which is the amount of tension on the bowstring. He told me that a sixteen-inch bolt was typically paired with smaller youth models. A serious hunter who pursued larger game and wanted the most penetrating power was unlikely to have used arrows shorter than twenty inches.

Eventually, a guard appeared to kick me out. Billy bear-hugged me again. I promised to look in on his family.

25

On my way home, I detoured through Rockport and slowed as I approached the Happy Clam Motel where I had paid to put up Aimee and the Cronklets. Lights peeked out from under and around the curtains in their rooms. I told myself the purpose of my visit was to see if they needed anything, but the truth was, I was curious to learn more about what was happening with Billy's pardon.

The Cronk family occupied the two end units overlooking Clam Cove. The inlet was well named. At low tide, the water receded, leaving an expanse of mud bubbling with bivalves.

Aimee answered the door with Emma clutched, almost upended, under her strong arm. The girl was a big-eyed blonde whom you could tell would grow up to break hearts.

"Oh, it's you," Aimee said.

"I got pulled away all day on an investigation in the Sandy River Valley and wanted to see how you were doing."

"Aren't you supposed to be on vacation?"

I was still standing in the doorway because I was afraid of tracking in mud, not that the carpet wasn't already sullied in just about every way possible.

"It's kind of a personal investigation."

"That seems to be a hobby of yours." She dropped the child beneath her arm, who somehow managed to land on her bare feet, like a cat. "You want a Mountain Dew? We had pizza for supper, but there ain't none left. The kids just about ate the box, too, the little goblins."

"Pizza and soda? I thought you were all about healthy eating."

"I figured the kids deserved some junk food after everything that's happened, and there's only so much meal prep I can do with a microwave and a bathroom sink."

The televisions were on in both rooms, turned up loud and tuned to different stations. Aimee had been watching a documentary on Marie Curie, while, through the other door, Homer Simpson's voice was droning on about an extraterrestrial roaming Springfield's forest.

"Emma, why don't you go annoy your brothers."

The little girl shot off like a bottle rocket into the next room.

Aimee muted the volume on her TV, then closed the pass-through door. The walls were thin as cardboard, and I could hear every word of *The Simpsons*.

"This looks like a nice enough place. How do you like it otherwise?"

"The manager took one look at us and asked if we'd ever had bedbugs. Other than that it's peachy."

I felt my neck grow hot. "What?"

"I guess we don't fit the profile of his usual customers."

I reached for the doorknob.

"He's gone home for the night and there's a lady on behind the desk. Don't go venting your wrath on that poor woman."

"Do you want to move to another motel?"

"What for? We've already been insulted. And who's to say the next place will be any more welcoming? I've always hated motels. Now sit down and have a Dew. It'll cool off that famous temper of yours."

Aimee had to clear aside the empty pizza boxes—six of them!—for us to have room to set our drinks down on the ridiculously tiny table. It was a testament to the stress she felt that she'd broken down and bought her kids this fast-food dinner. She hadn't yet pulled the shades on the back window, so the view was a reflected version of us, projected on black glass. My face looked like the ugliest version of me.

"The manager had no cause to insult you like that."

"Mike, look at us. You don't think it's the first time someone asked me if I'd checked my kids for head lice? We're trailer trash. That's how the world sees us, anyhow. You need to let it go."

I grasped for a response that wasn't falsely reassuring or tainted by well-meaning condescension. Instead I changed the conversation.

"I just came from visiting Billy."

Her happiness at this news made the world right again. "That's wicked cool. I'm *so* glad you went to see him. That man looks up to you like you wouldn't believe."

The sentiment embarrassed and confused me. I was the last person I would have recommended to be anyone's role model.

"You'd never know he'd nearly died yesterday," I said.

"The man's always been a regular Rasputin."

Why did Aimee's self-taught erudition keep surprising me? I was nearly as bad as the judgmental jerks who kept putting her down.

"He told me you'd been by, also your lawyer. I guess a couple of guards came to visit, too?"

"There are a few nice ones at the prison. The trouble is, the good guys all leave when they get a whiff of the shit piled up in there."

Out of an abundance of caution I decided against sharing my encounter with Rancic with her.

"How are you doing with all this?"

"Me?"

"You said you can't quite believe it's happening. I understand your skepticism. I share it. But aren't you a little hopeful?"

"Prosecutor Hildreth was all over the news earlier saying how Billy Cronk is a menace to society, and how he was convicted by a jury of his peers, and how letting him out is just a political stunt—which it is."

"Meanwhile you have to keep up a brave façade."

She narrowed her eyes and lifted her chin. "I can see why the ladies like you, Mike Bowditch. You may be as clueless as any man about the female sex. But at least you know your limitations."

I wiped the condensation from the soda can on my pants. "Thanks. I guess."

"Yeah, I got to be strong for the kids' sake. But also on account of Billy. The man's terrified of coming home again."

"That's common among people getting out of prison, I've heard."

"I've got more confidence in him than he does in that regard. Hell, I was there when he came home from his last deployment, and that wasn't no picnic. But that's not what's got me rattled. The thing that kept me up all night was what really happened in the prison laundry room."

"The police think it was simple revenge against Dawn Richie for throwing those two guys into solitary."

"So what did the remark mean about her being a rat? Billy told me what Dow said when he attacked her."

"Maybe she had gone to the higher-ups with suspicions they were engaged in something. Drug smuggling would be my first guess." I declined to share with Billy's wife what he had told me about Dawn Ritchie's propositioning him in exchange for protective services.

"How is that *ratting,* though? That's a term you'd use for another inmate. Richie is a CO. It's her job to snoop out the convicts dealing inside the walls."

"I doubt Trevor Dow or Darius Chapman possessed a sophisticated lexicon, Aimee. You may be reading too much into things."

"Says the pot to the kettle."

At that moment the door to the other room burst open and one of the boys—Logan, maybe? I always got them mixed up—came rushing in. He was shirtless, despite the chill in the rooms.

"Ethan's puking!" he said with delirious excitement.

"He ate enough pizza. Is he getting it into the toilet at least?"

"The bathtub!"

"Darn it!" The mother of five sprang into action, no doubt for the hundredth time that day. "Gimme a couple of minutes, Mike. You can change the channel on the TV if you don't like these historical shows."

I sat watching the beads of condensation slide down the Mountain Dew can. I'd spent hours trying to solve the puzzle of who had shot Shadow and what had become of his mate. Evaluating the merits of Aimee's suspicions concerning Dawn Richie was beyond the power of my sputtering neurons.

When Aimee returned, I was standing by the door with my coat buttoned.

"You leaving so soon? This is the time of night when things get all wild and interesting in the Cronk household."

"You don't need to tell me. I've babysat for you. I need to get home before I pass out behind the wheel from lack of sleep."

"At least your house ain't too far. You need to have us over for a combination housewarming, welcome-home-from-jail party. I'll bring the yellow ribbons."

"It's a promise."

As I stepped out into the night, she called to me in a softer, more vulnerable voice than the one she'd been using. "Mike? There's something wrong with that Richie woman. Not just wrong but bad. I got a sour feeling this ain't over for Billy—not as long as he's still locked up and at the mercy of those punishers."

"I've learned to trust your intuition, Aimee."

She thought about my response for a moment, then cracked a smile. "Aw, hell. It's probably just gas pains from that shitty pizza. Poor Ethan got his brain from his dad. But he got his sensitive stomach from me."

26

The first thing I noticed when I arrived home was that someone had driven down the long driveway to my house. The mud had thawed in the sun and then hardened again after dark, and the narrow treads showed clearly in my headlights. The marks had been left by small tires, not far from bald. The car had been a front-wheel-drive model. I couldn't think of anyone I knew who drove a vehicle that fit the description, but it could have been a census taker, a pair of Jehovah's Witnesses, or some lost person. Since the little car had turned around and headed out again without stopping, I felt no sense of alarm.

On my way inside, I gathered an armload of firewood from the two cords I'd had delivered to see me through the spring. My woodpile didn't have the benefit of a roof to shelter it from the rain and snow, so I'd been forced to cover it with a series of blue tarps and ropes that tended to come loose no matter how well I'd tied them down. I'd come to believe that nimble-fingered gremlins must live among the logs.

After I'd started a fire, I sat down at the kitchen table and thought about Aimee's experience at the motel. There was simply no way she and her family could continue staying there after what had happened. I didn't care if she was used to shoddy treatment.

I checked my phone for messages and found a single text from Dani:

> It hurt my feelings to learn about Shadow from Ronette
> Landry. But I guess if you were reluctant to reach out to

me, then I have my answer. You don't need to respond to
this. I'm on patrol.

Reading those words took me back to my first months as a game
warden, when, in my intense focus on my work, I'd failed to respond to the many messages left by my live-in girlfriend. Here I
was repeating a pattern I thought I had put behind me years earlier.

How could it be possible that I was both a quick study and a
slow learner?

At least I knew better than to obey her injunction.

You're right to be upset, Dani. I will call you tomorrow and
fill you in on everything that's been happening. Xoxo Mike

It was the first time I'd used the shorthand for hugs and kisses.
At least guilt hadn't suckered me into signing the text with *love*.

In my mailbox I also found an email from Angelo Donato, of all
people. I hadn't anticipated the deputy warden of the Maine State
Prison joining my list of pen pals, especially after our battle royal
at the hospital. I skimmed down to the relevant section:

I tried to reach you by phone earlier but the call kept dropping. I wanted to
apologize for the tone I used with you yesterday. I was upset about what had
happened to my officers and frustrated that our security protocols had failed so
spectacularly. There will be a reckoning here in the coming weeks. I might even
be among the casualties. You have no reason to help me but I believe you might
have information you don't realize is important that might help save my job. I
would appreciate a call back at your earliest convenience.

Aside from the bizarre politeness of the letter, what kind of
important information did Donato believe I possessed? My exhausted brain couldn't conjure an answer to the question.

I trudged up the stairs to the bedroom. Somehow I managed to
brush my teeth and strip off my muddy clothes before falling headlong into a sleep so bottomless it came close to being a coma.

* * *

I hadn't gotten around to hanging curtains in my bedroom's east-facing window. As a result, I always awakened as soon as the sun poked above the treetops. Even as a teenager, I had preferred rising at first light.

For that reason, I was stunned to open my eyes and see the room filled with sunlight. It was nearly nine o'clock.

I took a quick shower, shaved, and ate a banana for breakfast. I had much to do if I wanted to get back to the Sandy River Valley before noon.

I hauled out my collection of topographical maps and found the quadrangle that included Number Six Mountain and Intervale and Tantrattle Pond and spread the curling paper across the kitchen table, using my coffee mug, my gun, and my elbow to keep the corners pinned. Seeing the geography translated into print for the first time—the rises in elevation marked by rings, the blue streams wriggling downhill, the paved roads and the Jeep trails—I was finally able to plot several possible routes Shadow might have taken from the valley to Alcohol Mary's mountain. I circled the Tantrattle cabin and used an X to mark the pasture where the wolf had killed the donkey and another X for where the road dead-ended at Gorman Peaslee's house.

I had worried yesterday that Shadow might have wandered for miles before he finally collapsed beside Mary Gowdie's woodpile, but looking closely at the map, I had a powerful intuition that he had been shot somewhere within a three-mile radius of Number Six Mountain, somewhere to the north or east. The steep cliff faces to the south and west would have closed off access to all but the most determined bow hunters. And no serious outdoorsman would pursue his quarry using a youth crossbow and a cheap bolt.

Given the condition of the road into Tantrattle, I decided to drive my personal vehicle back up to the Sandy River Valley. Taking my Scout would also help if I was called to explain myself to the Warden Service brass. It would be much easier to portray my actions as personally motivated if I seemed to be on vacation.

I made a practice of keeping my Scout loaded with everything I might want for an impromptu weekend in the woods. I had a tent, tarp, sleeping bag, reflector oven and cooking supplies, ax, come-along, chain saw—anything and everything I might conceivably need. To this I added a toolbox, two-by-fours to repair the door, as well as a mop and a bucket to clean up the filth.

When I saw it was close to ten, a brainstorm came into my head.

"I want you to check out," I told Aimee when I reached her by phone.

"I told you to let it go, Mike. Besides, where are we supposed to stay?"

I was about to tell her that I would find them another motel when the invitation erupted from my mouth. "You can stay at my house!"

"Your house?"

"I won't be here for the next few days, and there is a lot of space for the kids to play outside. It will give you a place to lie low from reporters after Billy is granted his release. Besides, didn't you tell me you've always hated motels?"

"You're not afraid of us trashing the place?"

"Not at all," I lied.

I followed the sun west until I reached the state capital of Augusta and saw the Kennebec River in full flood and pushing free of its banks.

When I was young, there had been a dam here, but it had been taken down to free the river for salmon, alewives, and other seagoing fish to return and spawn in upstream tributaries. Now the head of tide was twenty miles to the north, in Waterville. Looking down from the high eastern bank, I saw standing waves and whirlpools where the fast-flowing current collided with the surge of salt water. Whole trees, torn up by their roots, were being carried along, their branches like skeleton arms outstretched for help. I hadn't heard if any of the towns along the river downstream had been swamped, but it wouldn't have surprised me to learn that the streets of Hallowell and Gardiner were underwater.

A bald eagle flew overhead with nesting materials gripped in its talons like a quiver of arrows and an olive branch. Our national symbol is a waterbird that prefers to nest in a huge tree with a commanding view of the ocean, a lake, or a large river such as the Kennebec. I'd read about an eagle's nest in Ohio that was supposedly twelve feet thick and more than eight feet in diameter. Charley Stevens had once told me how, as a boy, he'd climbed fifty feet to the top of a pine and spent the night in an abandoned nest after the eaglets had fledged.

And people accused me of being foolhardy.

Following the river south, I made my way to the wooded campus that houses the Maine State Police Crime Laboratory. I entered the building through the back sallyport. To prevent tampering with evidence, the lab has a complicated series of rules for how and when it receives materials for testing.

I ignored them. One of the technicians owed me a favor.

"Why are you doing this to me, Bowditch?" Paul Panagore asked when I presented him with the crossbow bolt. He was a bulging, thick-fingered man with a natural monk's tonsure and a constant air of being put-upon.

"I'll never ask for special treatment again."

"That's what you said the last time." He squinted through his reading glasses at the arrow in the bag. "You do realize that if you don't fill out the paperwork and submit this through channels, you're going to break the chain of evidence? Whatever I find will be useless in court."

I had no intention of bringing this matter to a prosecutor, but I decided to stay mum.

Instead I put my hand on his soft shoulder. "I want to know if we have the archer's prints in the system. Dust this and tell me what you find."

"Someone here is bound to notice that I'm freelancing."

"You won't be caught."

"How do you know?"

"Because you're the best there is. Any chance you can get me the results by the end of the day?"

Panagore removed his readers and pinched the bridge of his nose between his fingers. "You know what your problem is, Bowditch?

You dwell happily in a state of constant chaos. It doesn't occur to you that some of us are just trying to get through our days without being fired or arrested."

"Text me when you have something."

27

From Augusta it took me a solid hour, traveling through leafless forests and across fallow fields waiting to be plowed, to reach Pennacook. I crossed the bridge over the thundering Androscoggin and hung a right on Main Street, which took me through what remained of the downtown.

In the stark noonday light, I counted the boarded-up storefronts. There were fifteen, not including the shops with dusty windows and CLOSED signs that might or might not have been abandoned. Dani had told me that since Atlantic Pulp and Paper had decamped for South America, leaving the grand blue ruin of the mill behind, Pennacook had become one of the nexuses of the opiate scourge.

The temperature wasn't more than a few precious degrees above freezing, but a shirtless young man was arguing with a very pregnant girl on the sidewalk. Both of the disputants had the visible facial wounds, unhealed sores, and unbandaged scrapes that are common among addicts.

The girl, who was wearing pajama bottoms, fuzzy slippers, and a hoodie, had her hands tightened into small fists. "Shut up! Shut up! Shut up!"

I pulled to the curb and cracked my window. "Are you OK, ma'am?"

The man inexpertly flicked his cigarette in my direction, where it exploded in an orange burst on the road.

The girl snarled, "Fuck off, perv."

I turned the next corner and began climbing through a neighborhood of handsome clapboard homes dating from the nineteenth and early twentieth centuries, but even these houses seemed in need of paint or new roofs, and most had election signs in their yards with the Penguin's name on them.

Dani had never told me the name of the street where she had grown up. Nor had I met her mother or brother. Her father resided in the town cemetery overlooking the Androscoggin.

The parking lot of the Pennacook Hospital for Animals was so filled I had to park on the street. However tough times got, people cared for their beloved pets. They might not visit doctors or dentists themselves, but they would take their dog to the vet at the suspicion of a bad hip.

The young woman with pink hair sat behind the welcome desk. On one side of the room, a young Lab was lunging against his collar to get at a coon cat that had climbed atop her owner's shoulders to escape.

The veterinary assistant sprang to her feet with a radiant smile when she saw me. "You're back!"

"I can see you're busy here, but I wondered if Dr. Holman had a moment."

"I know you want to see Shadow."

I was doing my best not to interpret the woman's effusiveness as good news.

She told me she would be a minute and disappeared through a door behind the desk.

"He's trying to be friendly!" the lady with the Lab assured the man with the coon cat.

The man grimaced as the terrified cat jabbed her claws deeper into his shoulder.

The young woman popped back through the door. "Dr. H is finishing up a procedure but she said I could take you in." She peered past me at the waiting pet owners. "Will you two be all right for a sec?"

"Oh, yes," said the dog lady. "We're all friends here!"

The cat man had begun crying tears of pain.

The veterinary assistant led me past the surgery and around a corner to a door to the back side of the building. The sign said RE-COVERY.

One side of the room had stainless steel cages in three stacks. In the top row a little calico with a patch over her eye hissed at me. A tom the size of a bobcat turned away from us with what looked like disinterest but could have been contempt. Down below, a mixed-breed dog slept under a blanket with its tongue lolling out of its mouth.

The assistant foresaw my question. "We couldn't keep Shadow here because he wouldn't fit into any of these kennels—and he was kind of freaking out the other patients."

We passed through a second door into a large storeroom that was evenly divided between racks of supplies and several oversize crates. In the cage farthest from the door lay Shadow. He appeared to be sleeping. Aside from having acquired a blanket, he looked no different from when I had last seen him, the day before.

"Are you still sedating him?"

"God no. We want him to be active."

"So why's he out cold?"

"He's running a bit of a temperature. But we're giving him antibiotics and keeping a close watch on him."

"That sounds like it might mean he has an infection." I heard the anxiousness sneak into my tone.

"Dr. Holman will explain the details. I need to get back out front. You can wait here if you'd like."

After the young woman had left, I knelt down beside the kennel.

"You don't look so hot, buddy. How are you doing?"

When he opened a slitted yellow eye, I nearly fell over in surprise.

Dr. Holman opened the door, wearing her usual scrubs, but with her hair bound by a headband. You could have learned facial anatomy by studying the bones showing through her skin.

"He just woke up."

She arched a thin eyebrow. "Really?"

When I turned around, I saw that his eye was closed again. His rib cage rose and fell rhythmically. Had I imagined his waking up?

"Your assistant told me you're treating him with antibiotics."

"Running a fever after surgery doesn't mean he has an infection.

But I've got him on enrofloxacin to be safe. He had that arrow in him for a long time. I cleaned the wound as best I could, but he's still at risk of sepsis."

"How long until he's out of the woods?"

"Every hour gets us closer to a positive outcome."

"The truth, Lizzie."

"I'd only be guessing. That arrow did more than puncture his lung. I can't be sure of the nerve damage he might have sustained."

I nodded.

"A state trooper named Dani Tate called me this morning, asking about him. I was surprised since I thought this was all supposed to be on the q.t. I hope you don't mind my talking to her."

"You know Dani?"

"She brings her cat here, Puddin."

As the vet escorted me to the waiting room, she asked, "Any luck tracking down the other wolf?"

"I may have found a few leads."

"Do you know yet whether she's alive?"

"No."

Dr. Holman clutched the crucifix around her neck. I wished it were that easy for me to find comfort.

As I was returning to my vehicle, I remembered what Gary Pulsifer had told me about the father of Kent Mears. The old man, he'd said, resided in Pennacook, and from what Pulsifer had implied, I figured him for a recovering alcoholic.

I texted Dani:

> What do you know about the Mears family? The guard who was killed grew up in Pennacook and I wondered if you knew him. He would have been ten years older than you. His name was Kent Mears.

I waited ten minutes for a reply, but Dani must have been asleep. I proceeded to Plan B.

Older people are reluctant to part with their landlines. On a whim I checked the telephone directory. Only one Mears was listed.

First name also Kent. He lived up the street and just around the corner.

Rather than call first, I decided to get some exercise and fresh air. As a warden investigator I spent far too much time indoors. When I wasn't cooped up in my office, I was loitering for hours inside courthouses, waiting to testify in cases that required me to be on the stand for fifteen minutes tops. I spent even more time behind the wheel of my Jeep.

God, how I missed the woods.

The address I'd found was a triple-decker tenement. During the heyday of the mill, these apartment buildings had been alive with children, running up and down the external staircases, with lines of laundry stretching across alleyways from one block to the next. There had been kitchen gardens and sandboxes and men sitting around card tables, playing gin rummy and busting each other's balls.

Those days had died long ago. The firetrap that remained was peeling paint. The gravel lot between it and its neighbor sparkled with bits of broken beer bottles. Indeterminate pieces of litter tumbled about on the wind.

Mears lived on the first floor. I pressed the button beside a speaker.

There was no answer.

I pressed again.

"Knock it off!" came a voice.

"Mr. Mears?"

Again there was no answer.

Out of the corner of my eye I thought I saw movement in a window. A blind peeled away from the frame.

I pressed the button again.

"What do you want?"

"My name is Mike Bowditch. I'm a game warden investigator. I knew your son."

One lie out of three seemed an acceptable ratio.

"He's dead! Haven't you heard?"

"Yes, sir. That's why I am here. Would you mind if I came in for a few minutes?"

"What for?"

"To talk about your son."

I thought I'd lost him with that, but after a minute, the reinforced outer door opened, and one of the largest human beings I had ever seen filled the threshold. He had a mostly bald head and cauliflower ears and a nose that had been broken and reset so many times it was almost beautiful in its grotesqueness. His chest and stomach were one. He clenched a smoldering cigarette between fingers the size of breakfast sausages. He smelled strongly of beer.

"How'd you know my boy?"

"From the prison."

He clearly had no intention of letting me inside. Nor did I want to be trapped in a room with the still-muscular old giant.

"So what's this, a condolence visit?"

"I would have brought flowers, but I didn't know what kind you liked."

The utter ballsiness of my response caught him off guard and he came near to smiling. "I can tell from looking at you that you wasn't his friend."

"What did his friends look like?"

"They had big tits and fat asses."

"That doesn't describe Dawn Richie. Wasn't she his friend?"

He flicked his cigarette away. "Show me your badge."

I produced the shield for him, and he studied it closely, although I doubt his aged eyes could read the embossed words without the help of glasses.

"I wanted to make sure you wasn't a reporter. I've gotten calls from a few of them. Fucking vultures. So you want to know about Richie, huh? Well, I can tell you this much. She got my son killed."

"My understanding is Kent was stabbed by a man named Darius Chapman."

"But it was Richie who got him involved in whatever scam she was running. I don't have to guess how she lured him in either. Kent was a walking hard-on. I always figured he'd knock up one of the female inmates or get hauled into court on a rape charge. But getting stabbed in the neck, protecting some conniving bitch who never gave two shits for him? Pathetic."

"Did your son ever tell you what Richie had him doing?"

Mears took a step onto the concrete stoop. He was wearing Indian-style moccasins that had probably been manufactured in the country of India. He scanned the ground as if searching for something he'd just dropped. After half a minute, he located it. He pointed at the dirt where a used syringe waited for some child to pick it up and stick himself.

"Drugs?"

"I doubt she had him preaching the Good News of the Kingdom of God."

"Can you confirm that she had him dealing?"

"Not directly."

"Then why do you assume the two of them were smuggling in narcotics?"

"When Kent told me he applied to work in the prison, I told him he was a sap. 'You're going to be poor all your life,' I said. 'Why not come to work in the mill and be useful and make something of yourself.' When he mouthed off, I boxed his ears. Six months later I got my pink slip. I guess we were both saps."

He seemed to realize that he had wandered off track.

"I got an email from him a couple of months ago with photos attached. He wanted me to know he'd just bought a new truck. It cost fifty grand. He wanted to rub my nose in how much it cost. I told him he was an idiot going into hock to buy a vehicle he couldn't afford. He said he had a side business. He said, 'Why should I be the only one here not earning?' I didn't have to think too hard about what that meant."

Mears let out a mild belch, for which he didn't apologize. "I don't know who you are, Warden, or why you're here or what you're really after. But I will tell you this. My son got what he deserved."

28

I followed the same road over the mountains that Pulsifer and I had taken the day before. As I passed the turnoff to Alcohol Mary's distillery, I weighed stopping. I had an idea of backtracking Shadow's blood spoor myself—or trying to—but the blanket of new snow would have hidden whatever prints the wounded animal had left behind.

I wasn't sure how to feel about Mr. Mears. Unlike Gary Pulsifer, he hadn't managed to stay sober, and I pitied him for that. On the other hand, he had raised a son who was, by all accounts, a sadistic bully. I had never believed that a son should be punished for his father's sins, but I was less sure about the other side of the coin.

Mears hadn't exactly been forthcoming, but he had disclosed more than he intended. It sounded as if Richie had come to the prison to continue a drug-smuggling operation she had probably begun at the Downeast Correctional Facility. She had tried to use sex and money to recruit Billy into her operation, but when he'd rejected her proposal, she had settled for Kent Mears as her bodyguard. Billy had mentioned a spike in inmate overdoses that corresponded with the months since she'd arrived from Machiasport. The attack in the laundry room could have been retribution for disrupting some rival smuggler's operations.

Only as I was turning down the Tantrattle Road did I realize I had left my topographical map at home.

What was Pulsifer's new mantra? *Let it go?*

It wasn't the worst advice.

Over the winter, the top few inches of the road had melted into mud during thaws and refrozen into ice during cold snaps. But underneath remained several feet of permafrost. As long as the rock-solid substrate remained, the road would be passable. Once we got the first warm spell of the season, all bets would be off. The mire would start swallowing vehicles whole, never to be seen again.

For now, the Scout's raised suspension and oversize tires made easy work of the potholes and exposed rocks. I found the bouncy, jostling ride exhilarating.

Fresh nicks were on some of the roots that snaked across the road, caused by the underside of a low-riding vehicle, perhaps a heavily laden truck. Someone else had been into the camp this morning.

I was within a mile of my destination when my phone began to buzz and vibrate in my inner pocket. It was Charley Stevens. I was surprised that I had any kind of signal in the shadow of the mountains.

"Hello?"

"Yeah, Charley, I'm here."

I hit the brakes and turned off the vehicle. The hot engine continued to tick beneath the hood, but the quiet made it easier to hear the old pilot's voice.

"There's some wicked static on my end."

"I'm up near Tantrattle Pond in Intervale. I'm headed in to the warden cabin there."

"I know it well!"

That came as no surprise. Having spent three decades in the service, including as a patrol warden in the same district now assigned to Gary Pulsifer, he knew every owl's nest and bear's den in the forest. Charley was the best woodsman I had ever known.

"We'd better talk fast before the call drops," I said.

"So I checked into this Dawn Richie for you. Don't start whining about it. You wouldn't have asked me about her if you didn't want me nosing into her past."

The old geezer understood me too well.

"Not many people around Machias knew her. She wasn't much of a social butterfly, it seems. Nor active in the community. Her ex-husband, though . . ."

"She's divorced?"

"Widowed. Her husband committed suicide a year ago. Carbon monoxide poisoning in his garage after getting liquored up and stuffing wet socks in the tailpipes of his BMW M4."

"How come I didn't find a mention of this online?"

"Newspapers still believe suicide is a private tragedy."

"She should have shown up in his obituary, though."

"She did—under her first name, Janice. Dawn is her middle name."

Why hadn't it occurred to me to widen my search? "A BMW M4 is a fancy car. What did this husband of hers do?"

"Owned and operating a trucking company. People who worked for him were shocked he killed himself. They said he was an up-beat, high-energy businessman. Always talking, always on the go. Maybe too much so."

"As in he used cocaine?"

"How'd you get so cynical at such a young age? But yes, that's what I reckon. Freight transport being an industry that—"

There were two beeps and the call dropped.

I tried redialing but couldn't connect.

Instead I restarted the Scout and backed down the rocky, root-crossed road until I could turn around. Then I barreled back to the paved way.

When I tried again, Charley picked up. "There you are."

"I'm not sure how long we'll have a signal. The coverage in this valley seems spotty even by Maine standards. So you're always warning me against making assumptions, but it seems like you're having a hard time following your own advice here. What are you thinking? That someone murdered the husband and made his death look like suicide?"

"The state police considered that possibility, but there was no evidence and no suspects they could identify."

"What about Dawn?"

"She was on duty at the Downeast Correctional Facility when her husband took his life. Hard to beat being in prison when it comes to an ironclad alibi."

"Maybe she had an accomplice."

"The detective who investigated Mr. Richie's suicide came up dry when he looked into that theory. She collected a decent payday from the life insurance and the sale of her dead husband's business."

"So why is she still working as a prison guard risking her life every day and making forty grand a year?"

"I've been asking myself that very same question."

I let the possibilities tumble around my skull.

"Mike?"

"I'm still here. Charley, if it's not too much to ask, I wonder if you could make one more inquiry for me."

"You want to know if any other guards from Machiasport got hired at the Maine State Prison along with Dawn Richie?"

I nearly slapped the steering wheel in delight. "How did you know that's what I was going to ask?"

"Ora says you and I suffer from the same mental affliction. OCD—obsessive curiosity disorder. I'll make a few more calls and see what I can find."

I warned the old man that I was likely to be out of range when he phoned back, so we set a time later in the day for me to drive closer to civilization and attempt a call.

As I headed into the woods, again, I weighed the information Charley had given me. Trevor Dow had called Sergeant Richie a "rat" before he slashed her, as if she had exposed a conspiracy—maybe a smuggling operation that included both guards and inmates. Perhaps her decision to turn informant wasn't motivated by high-mindedness but by a desire to take over the drug trade inside the prison walls. It was one way of getting rid of the competition.

I remembered Dawn Richie's sangfroid at the hospital and grew increasingly anxious. She had seemed to shrug off being slashed across the face and watching her fellow CO die violently in front of her. The coldness of her reaction had bothered me at the time, but I had chalked it up to the shock of what had happened. Now I began to wonder if the woman might be a sociopath. Billy Cronk was getting out of there just in time.

The gate to the cabin was open when I drove up. Nonetheless, I got out, searched for the keys Ronette had promised to leave me, and found them in the agreed-upon hiding place. Then I continued on to the camp at the edge of the half-frozen pond.

The whine of a saw pierced the air with the loud insistence of a cicada. When it stopped, I heard nails being hammered into wood.

I had been correct in inferring that a loaded pickup had scraped the roots snaking across the road. But I had undercounted the number of trucks. Two identical white Ford F-250s were parked in the dooryard outside the cabin. They both bore the same name on their mud-spattered doors: HUNTER MOUNTAIN BUILDERS.

Sawdust lay upon the dead leaves and patches of trodden mud like a beige snowfall. A door made of brighter yellow wood leaned against the logs, waiting to be hinged into place. The shutters were all raised, and new windows, tacky with fingerprints, gleamed in the former voids.

One of the carpenters—a burly, bearded man—looked up from his portable table saw. I recognized him as Ronette's husband, Peter. Now it was clear why she'd told me I shouldn't worry about needing to repair the cabin myself. She had recruited—or more likely dragooned—Pete Landry and his crew into making the building habitable for me.

"Ronnie was hoping to surprise you!" he said, wiping his dirty hands against his Carhartt coveralls.

He wasn't any taller than his wife, but the bones in his wrists were thick as two-by-fours. I clenched my teeth when we shook hands. I bet he could have crushed a walnut in that big brown palm.

"Who's paying for this, Pete?"

"Aren't you?"

He had such an effective deadpan that my heart seized up. Then he swatted me on the back.

"Just joshing with you. Ronette said she can arrange for me and the boys to use this place as a hunting camp next fall. You know how she is: always looking for a win-win. The cabin gets fixed up and she gets me out of the house for a couple of weeks. And if it helps you find that she-wolf . . ."

I might have cautioned Ronette against sharing the details of my private obsession with Peter, but it would have been presumptuous.

Who was I to tell her what she could say to her husband? But I suspected that the two men working for Peter now also knew about the other wolf. I had no reason to expect them to be discreet with the information.

He introduced me to his employees, then took me by the arm and guided me around the exterior of the cabin, pointing with pride at the work they'd already done and explaining what they still needed to do. Next, he escorted me inside through the frame where the door would soon be hung. I didn't recognize the place as the same vandalized structure I'd seen the day before.

"You can thank Ronnie for cleaning things up. She and her mom were over here at the crack of dawn. Frenchwomen are human dynamos. But you already know that, being half-frog yourself."

The last thing my Franco-American mother had been was a cleaning dynamo. My only memories of her lifting a broom were from my early childhood when we had dwelled in cabins smaller, draftier, and dirtier than this one. She didn't so much clean a room back then as attack it with fury at her miserable life situation.

"I stopped in your uncle's place a couple of weeks back, before the end of ice-fishing season," Pete said. "Same old Denis. He acted like I was inconveniencing him by wanting to buy some shiners."

I had forgotten that Peter Landry and I had once been distantly related. Denis had been married to Pete's aunt, a coal-eyed, jet-haired woman infamous for her frequent public infidelities. For years my uncle had worn his suffering on his sleeve—he thought he was the only man who would put up with her affairs—only to have her leave him for another sucker.

"You know he sells crossbows and arrows there?" Pete said.

"I do."

"I'm not saying he sold the one that was used against that male wolf."

"I've already had a conversation with him. He denies all knowledge."

Pete grinned. "My aunt used to say Denis Cormier had a Ph.D. in denial. I hope you don't mind my saying that, him being your uncle."

"We've never been close."

Pete nodded sagely, wanting me to know that he saw our es-
trangement as a good thing.

"What can I do to help?" I asked.

"Go find the man you're looking for."

"Seriously."

"I am serious. We've got a rhythm to working together, my boys
and me, and you'd just be in our way. Come back before dusk for
the grand unveiling. We'll have a little toast to celebrate. Ronnie said
she's bringing over some food and beer for you."

I couldn't say I was disappointed having my schedule wiped
clean. Enough hours were still left in the day for me to poke around
the Amish farms, since they were the last place where Shadow had
been seen. With luck I might find something—wolf tracks, a donkey bone—that would help fill in the gap between the bloody events
in the Stolls' sheep pasture and Shadow's turning up injured at
Alcohol Mary's house.

As I was putting the Scout in reverse, Pete looked up from his
table saw and hurried over. I cranked down the window. The crisp
air smelled of newly sawed wood.

"Ronnie said I should tell you that she paid a visit to the Beliveau
boys. She pinched them on trespassing, vandalism, breaking and
entering—the whole shebang. I begged her to bring along a couple
of Franklin County deputies as backups. It's good she did because
she needed help transporting those three stooges to the jail in Farmington."

"I'm glad it went smoothly."

He scratched his beard, dislodging some wood chips. "She did
leave a message for you, by the way."

"Yeah?"

"She said to forget about the Beliveaus as suspects in the attack
on your wolf. She and the deputies didn't find so much as a broadhead when they searched the house. She called the place a shrine to
modern sporting rifles. Those hillbillies are too in love with their
black guns to pick up a weapon that went out of style in the Middle
Ages."

29

The perforated sign warning about the presence of horses and buggies swayed in the wind that had begun blowing down from the hills. Even by the demented meteorological standards of New England, the weather in the Sandy River Valley seemed freakish and nasty.

A half mile along the road, I overtook a horse-drawn carriage with a reflective orange triangle affixed to the back. The buggy was black, box shaped, and being pulled by a bay horse that trotted along at an impressive speed. I eased my foot off the gas, concerned the animal might spook as I approached, but it must have been accustomed to motor vehicles and continued on without breaking stride.

The buggy had rearview mirrors—salvaged from an auto junkyard—mounted on either side, and in the one on the left, I could make out a man's face and beard beneath a black hat. To my knowledge Intervale's Amish community had only three adult males. I was eager to speak with each of them, but it seemed rude for me to pull over a man in a moving carriage for no good reason.

Instead I let the distance between us grow. When I came to the tire-track road leading up to Zane and Indigo's yurt, I swung a left. I could always catch up with the carriage driver later.

Clumps of fresh straw that hadn't been there the day before lay in the road.

Under normal circumstances, I wouldn't have thought twice about this. The young hippies were living on a hardscrabble farm they had carved out of the birch woods. What else would you expect to find in such a place?

But Indigo had mentioned that Zane had argued her out of owning a horse and, presumably, other herd animals. I supposed there must be other uses for straw and hay on a farm. Maybe they stuffed their mattress with the dried-out stalks or used it to thatch roofs. Possibly they'd piled bales around the outside of their yurt as insulation against the hard winter weather. Maybe they made their own scarecrows.

But if there was one thing I had learned as a game warden, it was to notice the object out of place, the item that had been disturbed, the detail that didn't belong. Although I couldn't have told you why at the time, the newly scattered straw bothered me.

Where the trees opened up and the road entered a smallish field, still not entirely cleared of glacial rubble, I came upon a sign planted in the ground: FOREST FARM II. YOUR GOVERNMENT IS NO LONGER MINE.

So this homestead was a sequel to another whose name I didn't recognize. The confrontational motto surprised me, I had to admit. It seemed like a proclamation Gorman Peaslee would have shouted from his barricades.

At the far end of the field stood a hooped greenhouse made of torn plastic sheeting. With every gust, the tattered structure would fill with air, then, as the wind leaked out, it would contract again. The potting shed seemed to be breathing.

Indigo's Subaru was nowhere to be seen. Zane's truck, I assumed, was either still perched precariously on the side of Number Six Mountain or had been hauled away for repair or demolition.

I had never set foot inside a yurt before. The Mongolian structure sat upon a raised wooden platform. Stairs led up to a single, impressively carpentered front door, engraved with artful images of storks and carp. The house was round with a conical roof. The walls were made of a fabric like sailcloth. The heavy fabric seemed to be stretched tightly over hidden ribs that provided structure to what was, in essence, a glorified tent. The windows were of translucent plastic. Curlicues of woodsmoke issued from a metal stovepipe jutting from the top.

Around the property I saw assorted sheds. One looked to be a sugarhouse; another was perhaps Zane's attempt at building his own distillery. Some were equipped with solar panels, but none had a thatched roof. Nor were any hay bales in evidence.

The bearded farm boy must have heard me drive up because he came around the greenhouse with a root chopper in his hand and a wary expression. After a moment, he managed to summon a smile. I had hoped no one would be at home so I could snoop around in private. As a game warden, I was not bound to obey property lines, woodland fences, or even NO TRESPASSING signs under certain circumstances; I suspected, however, that the assistant attorney general who advised our department would have said that none of those conditions applied to this particular freelance caper.

Zane wore a bright white bandage on his head wound, but it was the only clean thing about him. His hair and beard were matted, and he reeked of perspiration with a hint of weed, but all it would have taken was a shower and a shave for the handsome dude to win a modeling contract.

"I didn't expect to see you here." I had forgotten about his hearing difficulties until he spoke in that telltale monotone.

"Where did you expect to see me?"

He didn't realize it was a joke until I cued him with a smile of my own.

He played with his erratic hearing aid. "Any news about the wolf?"

"Still alive."

"Really? That's amazing!"

"He's not out of the woods. When I saw him this morning, he was unconscious and running a fever. Dr. Holman is worried about sepsis."

Zane glanced in the direction of the tree line and dabbed at his eyes, trying to hide the pain this news caused him. I found it hard to dislike the man. His feelings ran so deep.

"What's the status of your truck?"

"Not good. I snapped both axles. I'm going to need to buy a replacement, it looks like."

"So you're stranded here, in other words. Where's Indigo?"

"Farmington. She had a doctor's appointment."

"Listen, I was hoping you had time to answer a few quick questions for me."

"What about?"

"The wolf."

"I've told you everything I know already."

"Pretty often in my line of work, I discover that people know more than they realize. And I'd love to see the inside of your yurt if it's not too much trouble. I've never been in one before."

Zane Wilson, I had seen from the moment I'd met him, was a polite, accommodating man—perhaps too accommodating. While he might have been willing to stonewall me concerning Shadow, he was too well-mannered to resist my request to see the inside of his one-of-a-kind dwelling.

"I don't want to impose," I added with false graciousness.

"No worries, man."

I followed him across the piazza of mud.

"I noticed you call this place Forest Farm II. Where was Forest Farm I?"

"That was the Nearings' place in Cape Rozier. Scott and Helen Nearing. You ever read *The Good Life*?"

"No."

"It's essential reading."

"I was struck by the motto on the sign, about your government not being my government. What's up with that?"

His high cheekbones took on a pinkish tint. "That was Indigo's idea. It's one of Scott's quotes. Kind of like his mission statement. She feels the same way about things, I guess."

"But you don't?"

"I'm more into compromise and reconciliation. Restorative justice. That kind of thing."

The yurt consisted of a single circular room, larger than I had expected, with a king-size bed at the center. The rest of the furniture was minimal: a folded futon, a table with four chairs, a couple of bureaus and end tables. An opaque skylight at the apex of the roof let in some grainy light. The floors were all of varnished pine except where Turkish carpets lay scattered about. The woodstove, which doubled as the cooking stove, was kicking out some serious heat. An old-time icebox and a sink with a hand pump rounded out the décor.

"This is a beautiful space," I said, genuinely impressed.

"It took a lot of work."

"I bet it did."

Instead of kitchen magnets or to-do lists, the icebox had a hand-lettered plaque attached to the door.

OUR COMMANDMENTS

We wish to set up a semi-self-contained household unit, based largely on a use economy, and, as far as possible, independent of the price-profit economy which surrounds us. We would attempt to carry on this self-subsistent economy by the following steps:

1. Raising as much of our own food as local soil and climatic conditions would permit.

2. Bartering our products for those which we could not or did not produce.

3. Using wood for fuel and cutting it ourselves.

4. Putting up our own buildings with stone and wood from the place, doing the work ourselves.

5. Making such implements as sleds, drays, stoneboats, gravel screens, ladders.

6. Holding down to the barest minimum the number of implements, tools, gadgets, and machines which we might buy from the assembly lines of big business.

7. If we had to have such machines for a few hours or days in a year (plow, tractor, rototiller, bulldozer, chain saw), we would rent or trade for them from local people instead of buying and owning them.

"Those commandments are different from the ten the nuns taught me at St. Sebastian."

He smiled. "Oh, those are from the Nearings, too. From *Living the Good Life*. It's funny, you know. I was the one who introduced Indigo to them, but she's become a lot more hard-core about this stuff than me. She wants everyone to hear the message."

I sat down at the table without Zane inviting me to do so. He stood with his arms hanging at his side, unsure. The warm air rising from the stove created currents that circled the room and fluffed the hair on my head. "Could I trouble you for a glass of water?"

"Absolutely. You want to try some of my 'shine? Mary won't share her secret recipe, but I've been watching her, and people say my stuff isn't half-bad. Indigo and I want to open a real distillery and tasting room out on the main road next year."

"I can't drink alcohol on duty." Even though, technically, I was not on duty.

"How about a kombucha? Indigo and I make it ourselves."

"I think I should stick with H_2O."

"No worries."

He pumped two stoneware mugs full of well water and sat down across from me at the table.

"Something's been bothering me, Zane. I could beat around the bush, but I'm going to come out and say it. I can't understand why you lied to me about seeing the wolf."

I saw his Adam's apple bob beneath the fringed beard. "I don't think I lied."

"First you told me you saw it in your headlights in the road. Then you said you saw it in the back field. Which was it?"

"Both."

"You saw it twice."

"Yes."

"Why didn't you say so?"

"I guess because I was feeling guilty."

I rested my forearms on the table, wondering if this was the start of a confession. "Why would you feel guilty?"

"Because I saw it was injured, and I didn't tell anyone except Mary. And so it was suffering for days on my account. You keep calling it a wolf, but I could tell, from the way it looked at me, that it was a dog. In my head I had this idea that it had escaped from the person who owned him. Someone cruel like . . ."

"Gorman Peaslee?"

When Zane nodded his head, he put everything into it. "We always had dogs when I was a kid. I loved them so much. But then I read Peter Singer and realized pets are animal slaves. I refuse to confine living creatures in cages. It's an ethical thing, you know?"

If this were a college dorm room, I might have argued that dogs and cats have done an effective job training humans to feed and shelter them. In many houses I'd visited it was unclear who the real master was.

"I'm going to share something with you, Zane. You were right about the injured wolf dog. He's a hybrid—mostly wolf, genetically speaking—but he grew up in a human's house. He slept on couches and beds and ate dog food for years before he escaped into the forest. His name is Shadow."

"I knew it! Sometimes you can sense things."

"I need to ask you another tough question, and I need you to be honest with me. You knew that Shadow attacked and killed the Stoll family's donkey before he showed up at Mary's place. How come you didn't mention that yesterday?"

"I thought I did."

"Nope."

"Are you sure I didn't?"

"Positive."

He batted the mug around the tabletop with his filthy hands, even spilling some water. "I guess, maybe, I didn't think it was relevant. And I was still kind of shaken up from wrecking my truck. Maybe I was a little high, too."

"You know who shot Shadow, don't you?"

He reacted as if I had called his good character into question. "No!"

"Maybe you have a strong suspicion."

"I said I didn't."

"All right. Indigo must have told you that Shadow hasn't been alone in the mountains. Game cameras have captured him with a large female canine that is almost certainly another wolf—a real one. It might sound like I'm looking to punish someone for shooting Shadow. But what matters most to me right now is finding out what happened to the she-wolf, whether she is alive or dead. Can you help me find her before she's killed, too?"

He looked at his strong dirty hands cupped around the mug. "Maybe."

"Have you seen her?"

"No, but Samuel Stoll told me he did."

"Any chance you might be available to ride over there with me now? I have a feeling he'd be more likely to open up to you than to me."

"What about Indigo?"

"Leave a note for her. You can blame me for twisting your arm. That should get her off your case."

"No offense, Warden Bowditch, but you don't know her. Sometimes I wonder how such a small woman can have such a big temper."

30

The Amish boy Samuel Stoll was guarding the sheep again. He sat perched on the split-rail fence at the edge of the pasture with a new switch he'd fashioned from a thorny blackberry branch. He wore the same outfit as the day before except that his mother must have made him put on a black coat before he'd ventured out into the gusty afternoon.

"Hey, Samuel," said Zane through the passenger window.

"Hello, Mr. Wilson."

"You don't need to call me that. You and I are buds."

"My dad says I do." Then Samuel grew alarmed, as if he'd unintentionally uttered a curse word. "I mean, my *datt* says I do."

Even Amish children, I gathered, were not immune to cultural homogenization.

Zane climbed out of the Scout as I turned off the engine. "Warden Bowditch is hoping you can show us where you saw the other wolf."

From the boy's reaction it was apparent he hadn't expected his friend Mr. Wilson to violate their secret. Samuel glanced at the farmhouse as if he expected to see one or both of his parents storming down the lane to punish him for confiding in two outsiders.

"I am not supposed to leave the sheep."

Zane gestured at the surviving donkey. The animal was watching us with ears up and swiveling. "I think Mose can keep the flock safe for a few minutes. Show Warden Bowditch the bite he gave you on the shoulder."

Samuel Stoll would not be removing his coat and shirt to show me his tooth marks.

"You said you saw the gray one across the road, right?" Zane said.

"*Ja.*"

"Did I tell you I was carving a shepherd's crook for you?"

"Really?"

With someone other than Zane Wilson, I might have assumed that this was a ploy to manipulate the child, but I detected no hint of dishonesty in the farmer's voice.

The little boy had his mother's oversize smile. He dropped off the fence and started forward along the gravel road in the direction of Peaslee's house. After a hundred yards, he hopped over a watery ditch and entered a tunnel in the leafless bushes. Zane followed, and I brought up the rear. Being taller and broader than the others, I had to stoop and fight my way through the entwined branches of the willows and alders.

"Wait up," I said.

I plucked a grayish clump off a thorn. It resembled deer's hair, but the fibers were not hollow.

"Is this where the black wolf dragged Little Amos?"

Samuel looked at me in wonder. "How did you know?"

I showed him the tuft and pushed it around my open palm. "Do you know what a deduction is? It's when you draw a conclusion based on bits of evidence. This hair looks to me like it came from a donkey. I deduced that this path is where the wolf dragged Little Amos. How about I go first from here?"

The ground was soft and springy with patches of ice that collapsed beneath my boots and plunged me ankle-deep in muddy water the color and consistency of a frozen coffee drink. The surface, being coated with small multicolored leaves and having frozen and thawed multiple times, was hard for me to read. But I found more donkey hair and, finally, a few wisps of black fur.

In the distance, I heard the brisk clippety-clop of hooves. One of the Amish buggies was headed back up the road.

A rock face reared out of the tangled bushes, eight feet tall, made of lichen-crusted sandstone. Shadow had been stronger than I'd imagined. There was no missing the claw marks he had gouged in the moss as he'd hauled the burro, a hundred pounds or more of dead weight, up and over the crag.

When I turned to point out the marks to my junior guides, I noticed Samuel staring through the trees in the direction of the road with an upright alertness I associated with prairie dogs. My ears caught the rumble of a truck engine that became a roar as it drew closer. It might have been an aural illusion, but it sounded as if the pickup was accelerating.

The boy took off through the shrubs so fast he knocked off his hat and left it lying in a puddle.

Not thirty seconds later, we heard the crash. Wood shattered and snapped. The truck skidded on loose gravel to a halt. The horse let out a scream that became a series of guttural whinnies.

Now Zane and I were both fighting our way back through branches that whipped at our faces. By the time we stumbled out to the flooded ditch, Samuel Stoll had nearly reached the scene of the crash. The same black buggy I had encountered earlier lay on its side in the matted grass. Falling, it had snapped a fence rail and torn off a spoked wheel. The panicked bay horse, still in her harness, was trying and failing to rise. Her iron shoes tore at the wet topsoil.

An Amish man, jettisoned from the wreck, lay limp in the field.

Gorman Peaslee had not emerged from his truck. Cleaned of mud, the vehicle was a bright fire-engine red. Plumes of blue rose from its chrome tailpipe.

While Zane sprinted toward the crashed buggy, I pulled my phone from my pocket. Thank God, I had enough of a signal to call 911. I identified myself to the dispatcher as a game warden and called for immediate assistance.

Then I, too, began to run.

Samuel was pawing at the shoulder of the motionless man, who lay almost perfectly spread-eagled on his back. "Ike? Uncle Ike?"

Zane stood over the boy, arms loose, fingers spread, seemingly at a loss what to do.

"Check on the horse!" I said. "Get it loose if you can."

I took the boy by the arms and, as gently as I could, lifted him clear of his injured uncle. "Let me look at him, Samuel. I'm trained in emergency medicine."

A blood-smeared bone jutted through a torn coat sleeve. Compound fracture of the radius. How white it looked. I reached under Isaac Stoll's bristly jaw until I located the carotid artery. His pulse was weak, whether from shock or a blow to the head, I couldn't be certain.

"Isaac? Mr. Stoll? Can you hear me?"

He made no response.

Plenty of rocks, some as big as fists, protruded from the damp earth around us. Chances were good he had hit his head against one. A concussion was probably the best-case scenario. What I feared was that he had broken his neck or back.

Out of the corner of my eye I saw the mare rise. Zane had gotten the animal loose of her tack. Impossible to believe, her fragile legs seemed unbroken. She might have internal injuries, but they weren't severe enough to stop her from galloping across the field. I had been prepared to put the horse down.

"Should I go after her?" Zane asked.

"I need your help here."

"We're not supposed to move him, right? That's what they told us in Outward Bound."

"It depends on whether he has a spinal injury or not. As long as he keeps breathing steadily, we should leave him where he is until the EMTs arrive. The danger is if he starts to vomit. Then we have to find a way to ease him onto his side. If there's damage to his vertebrae, we could snap his spinal cord."

Tears had run rivulets through the dirt on Zane's cheeks. "Shit, man!"

"Samuel?" I said to the boy. He had lost his own hat, but he had retrieved his uncle's and was clutching it to his chest. "I want you to run back to your house. Tell your parents what happened. Tell them I have called an ambulance. Have them bring me blankets. This is important. We need to keep your uncle warm until the emergency medical technicians arrive."

The kid nodded and took off. He was more composed than his adult neighbor.

"Here's what I need you to do," I told Zane. "Kneel down beside me. You don't want to block him from getting air. You need to be close enough to listen to his breathing. If you hear him start to have problems—"

"What kind of problems?"

"Gasping. Gurgling. Anything that sounds like he's in distress. If his breathing changes at all, yell for me. Of if he wakes up."

Zane's blue eyes widened. "Where are you going?"

I jerked my head toward Peaslee's idling truck. "To arrest that son of a bitch. If he's lucky, that's all I'm going to do to him."

31

Peaslee must have been watching in his rearview camera because, as I neared his truck, he cut the engine and stepped out. He squared his shoulders to meet me. His clean-shaven face and scalp were red and shone with perspiration. He was dressed as he'd been the day before: in a blazer, open-collared shirt, and gray slacks. I spotted the bulge of an ankle holster on his lower leg and assumed the coat was covering another hidden firearm. He might even have had a derringer in his pants pocket.

"The idiot was driving down the middle of the road," the big man said preemptively. "He wouldn't move over."

"And for that you drove him into a fence?"

"The horse spooked."

"Like hell she did. That mare is accustomed to being around motor vehicles. Ike Stoll is unconscious with a compound fracture of the forearm and God only knows what internal injuries. Were you ever going to get out of your truck to check on him?"

"I was calling 911."

"How about handing me your phone then?"

"Why?"

"So I can check your recent calls to confirm you're telling the truth."

"I'm not violating my own Fifth Amendment rights."

"You know what, Gorman—"

"You and I are not friends. You will address me by my last name. And put a *mister* in front of it."

"You know what, Mr. Peaslee? That man over there might not even live until the EMTs arrive, and I haven't heard a contrite word come out of your mouth. What am I supposed to make of that?"

"Do you want to know who I called, hotshot? I called my fucking lawyer."

"And what did he tell you?"

"He told me not to say a word to the cops. I'm not going to help you assholes build a case against me. I take it that's your Scout parked back along the road."

I ignored the comment. "Are you carrying any weapons, Mr. Peaslee?"

"What business is it of yours?"

"Turn around and bend over the hood with your hands straight out behind you."

"You're going to cuff me? Why?"

"I'm stopping you from fleeing the scene."

"What?"

"Your failure to exit your vehicle combined with your refusal to provide aid makes you a flight risk in my opinion."

His fat hands became fat fists. "Fuck you."

"Don't make me tell you again."

"Fuck off."

With that, he turned toward the open door of his truck, daring me to stop him.

It was a foolish move. Dani, the black belt, had been teaching me some jiujitsu takedowns.

As he raised his right boot to mount the running board, or nerf bar, I lunged into him and wrapped my arms around his waist, my head pressed flat against his lats, my hips lower than his. I pulled him backward, he stutter-stepped, and I pressed my right foot against his heel, causing him to totter over. As he lost his balance, I fell to my side, swinging him around with me. He landed hard on his enormous chest. As he tried to reach around at me, I snapped a cuff on his right wrist and gave the chain a twist. He cried out in pain from the torque, and I took the opportunity to snap the other cuff onto a strut supporting the nerf bar.

Gorman Peaslee was on the ground, manacled to his own pickup. The whole move had taken less than five seconds.

Before he could blink, I had pulled three firearms off him: a Smith & Wesson engraved 1911 in a shoulder holster, a Ruger .38 at his ankle, and a Beretta Pico in his blazer pocket. Plus an illegal dagger stuck in his sock.

He pawed at his chained hand with his free one. "Asshole! You nearly broke my wrist."

"Tell your lawyer to file a complaint."

"Don't think I won't!"

The lit screen of his cell phone glowed from where he'd dropped it. I snatched it up and pressed the phone icon and recent calls. Peaslee had reached out to someone in Portland. No doubt his lawyer. But the son of a bitch hadn't phoned 911 as he'd claimed.

"That's an illegal search under the Fourth Amendment!"

"Relax, Mr. Peaslee. I was picking it up for you. Here, I'll put it inside your truck where it'll be safe."

I tossed the phone onto the passenger seat. From his position on the ground, there was no way he could ever reach it.

I removed a laminated card from my wallet and read him his Miranda rights. Prosecutors preferred we read the statement verbatim as it closed off a line of attack from the defense at trial: the possibility we'd omitted an important phrase.

Meanwhile Gorman exhausted his entire vocabulary of four-letter words at me.

When I was certain he wasn't going anywhere, I headed back to the ruined carriage where Zane Wilson continued to kneel above the unmoving Isaac Stoll.

Hurrying up the road were a pack of people, all dressed in black coats. A man whom I presumed to be Mr. Stoll was in the lead, along with his son, Samuel. The women and girls, in their plain dresses and nineteenth-century shoes, couldn't keep pace.

The husband was at least a decade older than his wife and his brother. He was tall and rail-thin with a long face, a long nose, and a long beard the color of corn silk.

"Is he dead?" Of all the Amish I had met, he had the most pronounced accent. *Dead* sounded more like *debt*.

"No, he's still alive. We've called an ambulance, which should arrive shortly."

Anna hurried to the side of her brother-in-law. Samuel held his uncle's black hat tightly to his chest.

Stoll glared in the direction of Peaslee and his truck. "That man ran Isaac down?"

"Mr. Peaslee claims your brother wouldn't move aside."

"*Lügner.*"

"He says the horse spooked, causing Mr. Stoll to lose control and crash through the fence."

"That horse doesn't 'spook.' Anna says you are an officer of the law. You are arresting him?"

"I'm still tallying up the charges."

"Did she tell you that he killed our lambs?"

Stoll reached into his coat pocket and produced what looked like a steel ball bearing, about half an inch in diameter. "Samuel has found these in the field, near the dead animals."

"You think he was using a slingshot?"

Peaslee had to have excellent aim if he could kill a lamb from the road with such small-bore ammunition. It occurred to me that a hunter who used a weapon as primitive as a slingshot might also have a predilection for other antiquated armaments. Crossbows, for example.

A moment later a boxy ambulance appeared, its red and yellow lights flashing. Behind it came another vehicle: a late-model Jeep Grand Cherokee. Because of the glare coming off the windshield, I couldn't identify the driver.

The EMTs wore blue shirts and blue pants: a uniform that brought to mind the inmates at the Maine State Prison. For the briefest of instants I thought of Dawn Richie, the alleged black widow and drug-smuggling mastermind. Then the ambulance driver, a burly man with a graying blond beard, was standing before me while his partner rushed to assist the injured man. The driver looked familiar; I was certain we had met on a mountain rescue or at some other emergency scene.

I explained that Ike Stoll lay where he had almost certainly landed and that we hadn't moved him out of fear that he had suffered a spinal injury. Nor had he so far awakened.

"Did you need to stabilize his breathing at all?" the emergency medical technician asked in a voice at once deep and gentle.

"No."

"That's good. I can't pretend we didn't expect one of these incidents was coming. We've talked about the possibility around the station ever since these Amish folks moved up here. What happened to the horse?"

"She ran off, uninjured."

"If that isn't a miracle!"

As he left to assist his partner, the driver of the unfamiliar Jeep finally emerged. It was Ronette, and she must have had the day off. She was wearing a roll-neck sweater and blue jeans under a gray puffer coat from Patagonia.

"How is he?"

"Bad."

"Did you see this happen?"

"No, but I heard it. Peaslee ran Ike Stoll off the road. I doubt he did it for any reason other than he's wanted to since the Amish moved in."

"That son of a—" She stopped herself from uttering the full curse. She was a good Catholic woman. But I had never seen her so enraged. "Where is Gorman?"

"Handcuffed to the bottom of his truck. He resisted my commands and tried to leave the scene so I was forced to restrain him."

"Good. But I hope you read him his rights."

"I did."

"Good."

"He didn't even call 911, Ronnie."

She covered the bottom half of her face with her hand. Without looking at me, she said, "These people are never going to be safe as long as he's still living here."

One of the EMTs called across the windswept field, "Can you give us a hand, Warden?"

"Come on, Ronnie."

"The four of you men should be able to handle it," said Ronette. "I'm going to go keep Gorman company."

At the time, I thought nothing of this.

I went to help the medical technicians steady and secure Isaac Stoll's head in a brace so they could slide him onto a stretcher. Ike groaned and parted his eyelids as we lifted him out of the field. I had never studied head and spinal injuries, but I knew that a return to consciousness is never a bad sign. When we had carried the litter back to the road, the EMTs released the catch on the wheeled legs so they could roll him into the back of the ambulance.

"Tilda? Where's Tilda?" the injured man kept asking.

His sister-in-law squeezed his good hand. "She is uninjured, Ike. She was not hurt."

"Where is Tilda?" he asked as if Anna hadn't spoken.

32

Gorman sat on the road, his muddy knees drawn up, the back of his blazer against the side of his pickup, to which he remained cuffed.

Ronette came toward me. To my surprise, she seemed ecstatic in the religious sense of having been touched by a divine light. She held something in her hand. It was a silver object pinched between her thumb and index finger.

"Look what I found!"

The broadhead was meant to be screwed into the shaft of a hunting arrow or crossbow bolt. It consisted of four razor blades that met at a point like the sides of a pyramid.

"Where did you find it?"

"In the bed of Gorman's truck."

He let out a snarl. "I told you it ain't mine!"

I lowered my voice. "We don't have a warrant, Ronnie."

Of course, I hadn't had legal justification to search the man's phone either.

"It was in plain view. It couldn't have been any plainer."

"It ain't mine!" insisted the handcuffed man. "Somebody must have planted it. Everyone's heard that you're looking for a guy who owns a crossbow."

"And you don't?"

"Fuck no."

"What about a slingshot," I asked, thinking of the dead lambs.

His gaze went sideways for a moment. He had no intention of answering that question.

"So you're telling me someone randomly planted a Spider-Bite broadhead in the back of your truck."

"I'm saying it ain't mine, and I have no idea how it got there. And what's the big deal anyway? Suddenly the government doesn't want us to own bows and arrows either? It's not enough you're taking our guns?"

"No one's taking your guns."

"Damn right, you're not."

It was like listening to a radio and trying to argue with the talk show host.

"So where did you go today?" I said.

"I ain't telling you!"

"If someone planted the arrowhead, I'd like to know where it might have happened. Understand?"

"No place special. I drove into town to check on my businesses. I like to make sure the guys know I'm watching them. Grabbed lunch at McDonald's. After that, I had to stop at the hospital to settle a billing dispute. The fuckers overcharged me for my PT *again*. On the way back, I stopped in at Denny Cormier's place."

"You stopped at Fairbanks Firearms?"

"Yeah. Why?"

My uncle had a perverse sense of humor. He would know that Gorman was a person of interest and that he and I were bound to cross paths again soon. But why would Denis pull such a potentially fateful prank on a man he considered a friend?

"Can you help me get him up, Warden Landry?"

"Where are you taking me?"

"To the jail in Farmington for booking."

"On what charges?"

I recited the list. "I can add resisting arrest if you make this difficult."

"What about my truck?"

"Warden Landry is going to take some photographs of the scene here," I said. "We need to document where your truck was coming from and where the buggy crashed through the fence. The state police will want to do the same. After that, I'm sure someone can have it towed for you."

"You're going to impound my vehicle?"

"Well, we can't leave it blocking the road now. Can we?"

I thought he'd called me every dirty word in the dictionary, but he seemed to have kept a slew of them in reserve.

"You don't mind taking your free time to document this?" I said to Ronette when I'd gotten Gorman inside my Scout and chained to the D ring I'd had installed on the floor for occasions like this one.

"I'm going to leave this one to the state police crash-reconstruction team. Gorman and I have history, and I don't want to mess this up even a tiny bit. That dirtbag needs to go down for this, Mike, and he needs to go down hard."

The remaining members of the Stoll family milled about the field. It appeared that the father must have ridden in the ambulance with his injured brother. I glanced around for Zane, but he had vanished. Perhaps his emotions had gotten the better of him. The man's skin was as thin as rice paper.

I climbed inside the Scout beside my muddy, cursing prisoner. He wore a strong cologne that wasn't so powerful it covered the smell of fear in his perspiration.

"I gotta pee."

I started the engine. "You're going to have to wait till we get to the jail."

"I could always just wet my pants all over your nice seat."

"Don't push your luck, Gorman."

"I told you to call me—"

"And I said, 'Don't push your luck.'"

For the first ten miles or so, I thought Gorman Peaslee might actually have wised up and decided to heed his legal right to remain silent. Instead he had been using the time to think of ingenious ways to torment me.

"I bet it was that bitch Landry who planted the arrowhead in my truck."

He was bent over in his seat, his handcuffs fastened to the floor between his legs, so he had to angle his bald head to make eye contact.

"What?"

"It makes total sense, the two of you entrapping me like this. Because you know I'm in the clear on that crash."

My first instinct was to rush to defend my fellow officer (and to a lesser extent myself) from his slander. I couldn't think of a warden less likely than Ronette Landry to pull a stunt like that. The woman had studied the code-of-conduct book the way other people do the Bible. I had never seen her take an action that was even borderline unethical.

But Gorman Peaslee had succeeded in planting a seed of doubt. I felt ashamed for even entertaining the vile notion. Yet the improbable accusation stayed with me.

This is what sociopaths do. They trick you into distrusting your judgment. That's how a serial killer or a pedophile continues committing his crimes under the noses of people who sense that something is amiss but can't bring themselves to believe their kindly, personable neighbor is a monster.

For once, I did the smart thing and bit my tongue.

But Gorman wasn't finished poking me in the eye. "You know who my attorney is?"

"I don't know and I don't care."

He recited a name that made no impact on me whatsoever.

"Never heard of him."

"He's the best lawyer in the state! 'Always hire the best lawyer, the best accountant, and the best doctor'—that's what my old man used to say."

"Your father sounds like he must've been a font of wisdom."

That really riled Gorman up. "You want to know why I didn't help that neckbeard? I'll tell you why. Because I knew, no matter what I did, I was going to get blamed anyway. These days, you can't say a bad word about a black or a gay or a transgenerate, but a middle-aged white American like me? It's open season on us."

"I believe Isaac Stoll is also a middle-aged white American."

"He's a religious kook."

"As enjoyable as it is discussing politics with you, Mr. Peaslee, I won't object if you'd like to exercise your right to remain silent for the remainder of this drive."

"When I'm done beating this rap, I'm going to have my lawyer sue you and the state for false arrest and police brutality. I don't even care if I win as long as my suit forces you to pay for your own attorney. Do you want to know the best thing about being loaded? It's having the financial resources to take revenge slowly. *Drip, drip, drip.* That's the sound of your life savings going down the drain, Bowditch."

When we arrived at the Franklin County Jail, we entered through a series of locked doors in the rear of the building. In one of the anterooms, I was required to secure my sidearm in a special box. Then and only then were we allowed through the sallyport into the booking area.

I had been threatened in more sinister ways by more fearsome characters than Gorman Peaslee, so I didn't worry about his intention to bankrupt me. But I can't claim that the friendly way he was greeted by the county turnkeys didn't give me pause. They all seemed shocked to see the great man arrive at the facility in chains.

"Are you sure you want to go through with this?" asked the sergeant in charge of processing new prisoners.

"He nearly killed a man. So, yeah, I'm sure."

The sergeant, stooped and gray-haired, was so close to a Florida retirement you could practically smell the suntan lotion on his skin. "You said he was Amish, this fellow who drove off the road?"

"He didn't drive off the road. Peaslee forced him through a rail fence."

"You probably don't have any Amish where you live, Warden, so you wouldn't realize what a menace those horses and buggies are on the road. We handle multiple complaints about them."

The time-consuming intake process, as it is called, includes the taking of mug shots, the scanning of fingerprints, the logging of personal possessions and clothing, the invasive prodding of a strip search, the furnishing of the signature orange jumpsuit, and many other indignities.

"Do I need to bring this to the sheriff?" I said. "Or are you going to begin Peaslee's intake?"

"How about you stop telling me what to do?" The sergeant removed his granny glasses to ensure I had gotten his warning, then started in wheedling again. "Look, Warden, this Amish fellow, he probably won't even press charges. Those people don't think the way we do. They have their own laws and such. And Gorman is a respected member of the community around here. He donated a lot of money to the sheriff's last campaign. Have you spoken to the district attorney yet? It would be a shame for you to waste your time on this only to have the DA kick him loose."

"I appreciate your concern, but I'm willing to risk it."

The gray guard tried one last appeal. "He may not look it, but Gorman Peaslee is not someone you want to have as an enemy."

"So he told me."

"Don't say I didn't warn you."

PART 3

The Wild, Cruel Beast

33

When I left the jail, I remembered to check my phone after having forgotten it inside the Scout while I'd been dealing with Gorman Peaslee.

I'd missed three calls. I listened to them as I drove back toward the cabin. The sun had slipped behind the summits to the south and west. The northern peaks—Crocker Mountain, Sugarloaf, and Mount Abraham—remained in light, but a tide of darkness was moving down the valley.

The first message had been left by Paul Panagore at the Maine State Crime Lab. I'd asked him for test results before the end of the day, and the fingerprint wizard had delivered with an hour to spare.

"First things first. No matches. I lifted some partials from between the fletching but couldn't match them against anything in the AFIS database. There was an overlay of blood, plus smearing and extensive scratches. The size makes me think it was left by a kid. Maybe a small woman. I'm not sure if you noticed this or not, but there was a spot of glue residue on one of the fletches, as if someone had peeled off a sticker. It had picked up dirt and blood, so I'm guessing you didn't recognize it as an adhesive. It's acrylic glue, not rubber-based, if that makes any difference. The location of the sticker seemed potentially interesting to me, suggesting your arrow was sold as a single retail item. I made a call to Spider-Bite, and the person I spoke to said their arrows, including the X2s, are sold in multipacks. He suggested that a retailer might have made a bulk purchase of warehouse seconds—arrows that came in damaged packaging—and then sold them individually at a markup. The big-box stores and larger online dealers don't do that. I hope this information helps. I'm making a note to myself so the next time you try to sweet-talk me—"

The second message was from my self-appointed operative, Charley Stevens. "I've hit a dead end, young feller. The widow Richie was the only guard transferred from Machiasport to the state prison at the time of the closing. One of my informed sources tells me Sergeant Richie has hired a white-shoe lawyer from Portland to sue the state for negligence, and this attorney only takes cases he knows he can win."

The third message was from Dani. "I got your text. Why didn't you just call me? I didn't know Kent Mears but heard about him growing up. He and his friends used to hang out in the graveyard, and there was a story about a girl who made a shortcut through there and something happened. She was pretty screwed up afterward and got into drugs when she was older. Pennacook is my hometown. I might even be useful if you share your suspicions instead of sending me cryptic text messages."

Shadow, Billy, Dani—untangling the threads of my life was daunting. Too daunting to be done while driving along a shadow-draped road. What I needed was a chair beside a fire.

Not that long ago cell phones had played a small part in my day-to-day life. Maine seemed to be one giant dead zone. (Sometimes it still did.) Back then, I hadn't appreciated what it meant to be inaccessible. I mourned that lost epoch now. It had been easier to think, and think clearly, in those long lost silences.

The gate was bolted when I came to the end of the Tantrattle Road. I found Ronette's spare keys where I had tossed them in the center console, got out, knelt in mud becoming gritty with ice crystals, and unsnapped the padlock. The steel arm swung open with the faintest creak. Peter Landry had even greased the pivot for me.

On the final stretch, my high beams lit up the eyes of some fast-moving critter as it disappeared into the trees. It was too large to be a mink, too upright to be an otter, too dark to be a fox. Most likely it was a fisher, which many people thought was a kind of cat when really it was a supersized weasel. The fearsome hunter was on the prowl for sleeping porcupines.

The dooryard of the cabin was so heavily matted with sawdust and wood shavings it seemed to give off an ochre glow in the darkness. When my headlights touched the cabin itself, my jaw nearly dropped. That morning it had been a vandalized wreck. Now it was a perfect little cottage.

As cold as it was, the constellations told me that winter was coming to an end. For the past months I had seen Orion in the east. Now he and his two hunting dogs had crossed the sky to the west, where they would eventually disappear altogether, come summer. Orion always made me think of Billy Cronk, the best tracker of deer I had met since my father died.

I pulled my duffel from the back seat and hauled it with me up the steps. Peter Landry had replaced the propane tank and left the lines open to the glass lanterns hanging from the ceilings. I waved a match under the mantle of the nearest one until the silk mesh caught fire.

Peter had left me a dusty box of Sears, Roebuck–brand shotshells atop a stack of even older-looking flesh magazines. The periodicals had names such as *Oui* and *Nugget* and *Black Busters,* and the copious pubic hair on the nude models was a testament to the decades that had passed since their publication.

The accompanying note was brief and to the point:

> *Found these in the walls. Thought you might have some use*
> *for them if you get lonely. ;-)*

I did have a use for the magazines. I tore them into shreds and wadded them between two pine logs, sprinkled some wood shavings over it, and built a pyramid of kindling over the naked ladies.

The ancient porn magazines caught easily, then the edges of the kindling began to turn orange, and when I could see that I wouldn't need to return my fire-starting merit badge, I arranged three logs crosswise over the leaping flames. It was an old stove, this rusted

Ranger, but it drew well, and I sat back on my haunches for a minute to take pleasure in what I had built.

I put a match to every lantern in the cabin. I filled the place with light. No doubt the homey glow could be seen across the half-frozen pond, maybe even from the top of the nearest hill.

I found an old pail by the door. I trudged through the ankle-deep snow behind the cabin down to Tantrattle Pond. The ice hadn't entirely refrozen along the edges after a day in the sun. A haze was beginning to settle in over the valley. When I looked at the sky now, it seemed as if a sheet of gauze were stretched between the mountains, and only the brightest stars and planets showed as dull blurs through the canopy of clouds. Mars appeared as a small red stain.

I broke through the crust and dipped the pail into the inky water and hauled it back with me to set on the stove to boil. I spent five minutes listening for owls or coyotes, but the night was quiet, except for the wind sighing in the boughs. I might have tried calling them, but it would have been an act of profanity: like shouting in a cathedral.

The builders hadn't had time to sweep the floors, but they had left me a broom. Before I brought my sleeping bag and pillow inside, along with the rest of my gear, I busied myself brushing out the rooms. The last time I had felt this kind of childish delight was on some Christmas morning long ago.

I filtered the steaming water through a triple layer of coffee filters to catch the sediment and used it to cook some spaghetti. I stirred the tomato sauce in with the drained pasta and sprinkled on hot-pepper flakes. When I was done with dinner, I refilled the pail to wash my dishes. Then I added a couple of maple logs that would burn all night to the fire. I brushed my teeth with strained water from the pond and climbed, fully dressed, into my sleeping bag. After a minute I got up to open the window above my bed so I could listen to the wind in the trees.

I was settled. Nothing could touch me. It was a good place to camp.

I awoke to the sound of howling. I sat up with a start. The room was pitch-black. I checked my watch, but the luminous hands had faded. I reached for the little flashlight I had hidden under my pillow alongside my pistol and shone the beam on the dial and saw that it was five minutes until midnight.

I waited, unsure. Then the howling started again, and it was, without question, a wolf. I had listened to too many recordings—in the event I ever heard Shadow calling again—to be fooled by a dog or coyote. The noise was coming from somewhere high above and far away. It echoed across the natural bowl that contained the pond.

All of my life I have fought the urge to attribute human thoughts and emotions to animals, not only because I view anthropomorphism as a childish stage of brain development. It is my heartfelt belief that ascribing human traits to other species denies them their uniqueness and dignity as sentient beings. Why can't we just let wolves be wolves?

Despite these hardened opinions, the thought came to me as I listened to the eerie, searching sound that this wolf, presumably the female, was calling for her lost packmate. She howled and waited for a response, but the reply did not—and would never—come.

Let it go.

I laced my boots and went outside, where I was surprised to find luminous flakes of snow falling silently. The wolf continued to howl. My internal compass placed her somewhere in the general direction of Mount Blue. The night was calm except for those distant wails.

Feeling my own heart starting to break, I lifted my face to the sky, letting the flakes melt as they landed on warm skin, admitted my own arrogance and ignorance, and surrendered to the mysteries of a universe I knew I could never comprehend.

In time the female stopped or moved higher up the icy slopes where I could no longer hear her laments. The foolishness of my obsession to capture her overwhelmed me. By the time I returned with a culvert trap, she could be a hundred miles from here. I could only pray that providence would lead her north, farther and farther away from men with guns and bows and snares, and that she would lead a long if lonely life. These were presumptuous prayers, I realized. The wolf was free, and that meant her fate was also beyond my ability to control.

Too wired to sleep, I returned to the cabin.

As I was squatting beside the stove, I glanced into the woodbox. To assist me in fire building, Peter had brought over some newspapers along with kindling and firewood from his barn. I had presumed the papers had been old editions, but there was the front page of that morning's *Lewiston Sun Journal*.

In a photograph the Penguin stood at a podium looking flushed, sweaty, and full of rage.

GOVERNOR PROMISES "TOTAL ENEMA" AT MAINE STATE PRISON

Always a class act, our chief executive.

The Penguin had uttered these words in a speech at a breakfast meeting of some chamber of commerce. He said, "While it would be premature to place blame on senior prison officials," he seemed eager to do just that. Why wait for an investigation when there were political points to be scored?

I thought of Deputy Warden Angelo Donato, and the concerns he had expressed about his job being in danger in that oddly solicitous email. It seemed to me that his boss, the prison warden, would be more likely to take the fall. But the governor didn't seem to rule out slaughtering a whole herd of scapegoats.

A sidebar article dealt with the process by which the governor could unconditionally pardon any individual convicted of having committed a state crime. A lawyer on the chief executive's staff would need to draw up a pardon warrant for submission to the Maine secretary of state. In the case of a person who was still imprisoned, such as Billy, a second document—a warrant of commutation—also needed to be drafted and certified. Copies of those two official documents would then be forwarded to the warden of the institution in which the pardoned person was incarcerated, at which point the door would open and Billy Cronk, in this case, would walk free.

I was curious to learn how soon that might happen, but the story jumped to another section of the newspaper. I rummaged through the stack, but the pages were missing. I tried to find the answer on my smartphone, but there was no signal.

In choosing this cabin over lodging with modern amenities, I had hoped to escape the digitized, interconnected world and find some old-fashioned solitude.

Be careful what you wish for.

34

Despite the adrenaline in my bloodstream, I drifted off again and awoke at first light.

The new snow had reset the calendar and returned the forest to winter, or so it seemed from inside the cabin. When I ventured outside to visit the privy, I was surprised by the mildness of the air upon my skin.

The temperature was already climbing—into the forties, if I had to guess—and a mist was rising from the layer of slush underfoot and drifting off between the trees. The fog obscured the far side of the pond, but I could hear the otherworldly sounds the ice made as it began melting in the morning heat.

On the cast-iron skillet I made pancakes from a mix only to realize I had forgotten to bring syrup. Considering the hundreds of sugar maples I had seen nearby—from Mary Gowdie's operation to the more humble efforts of the Amish—my absentmindedness seemed all the more inexcusable. I had to content myself with a lather of butter.

Paul Panagore's voice mail had been tossing and turning in my brain all night. The bolt that had pierced Shadow's lung had been purchased individually and not as part of a pack. Someone had applied a price tag to the fletching. The only friction ridges on the shaft had been left by a person with small fingers.

Using water I heated atop the stove, I washed my crucial areas but didn't bother shaving. I put on a green chamois shirt over an oatmeal Henley, tin-cloth logging pants, and the L.L. Bean boots I wore every day during Mud Season. I attached my holstered P239 and badge to my belt along with my handcuffs in their clip-on case.

Then I buttoned over everything the last gift my mom had given me before she died: an expensive Fjällräven trekking jacket I would never have purchased on my own. I wore the raincoat as a reminder of her, just as I wore my father's dog tags on a chain around my neck in bittersweet remembrance of a man I had both loved and hated.

If anything, the fog had grown even thicker since I'd last ventured out. When I reached the gate, I realized I should have checked the woods around the cabin for new game cameras. Knowing Ronette Landry, she had installed a full complement, hidden in spots even a squirrel would be hard-pressed to find.

By the time I turned south onto the Rangeley Road, the morning commute—such as it was—had begun. The residents of Phillips, Avon, Intervale, and the upriver townships were headed into Farmington and perhaps as far away as Waterville and Augusta. It was Friday, I realized.

I arrived at Fairbanks Firearms mere minutes after my uncle Denis had opened the store for the day. As before, a buzzer went off when I pulled open the door. This morning, the shop smelled of dead fish.

I found my uncle in the corner using a broken-off pool skimmer to ladle dozens of dead shiners from one of the bait tanks.

"Did the aerator give out?"

"Either that or these fish committed mass suicide." He was wearing glasses this morning, shooting-style yellow specs. "What do you want now?"

"Just browsing again. Don't mind me."

"I have always minded you."

I made my way down the aisle with the bucket of arrows and the plastic containers of broadheads. The same model arrowhead Ronette had found in Peaslee's truck was on sale. I removed a three-pack for purchase. I did the same with three Spider-Bite X2s. Each of the carbon fiber bolts had price tags on the fletching. The stickers said the arrows retailed for five dollars apiece.

I called to my uncle from across the store. "Do you ever get the Amish in here?"

"Sometimes."

"What do they purchase?"

"Oh, you know, GPS receivers, fish finders, night-vision scopes—they're into all those high-tech electronic devices."

I brought my purchases to the counter and laid them down beside the register.

Denis was too sharp not to understand that my shopping trip was bad news for him. He wandered over, still clutching the skimmer, which now had a coating of slime on the netting.

"You're not going to let this go?" he said with a sigh.

I motioned to the bows and crossbows strung together on a bike chain, hanging off a rack. "I'd like one of those crossbows, too."

Without a word he unlocked the cable. I reached for the crossbow I'd handled on my prior visit. It had a black synthetic stock, an aluminum frame, cheap sights, and no mounting rail for a scope. The tag identified the piece of junk as a Blood Eagle Tactical.

"So what makes this a tactical model?"

"It's painted black. And it costs ten bucks more than the non-tactical version."

"Ring me up."

The total bill came to less than a hundred dollars.

"I don't suppose you'd like to sign up for our rewards program?"

"Only if you tell me who you sold these items to recently."

"I already told you I don't rat on my customers. I'm not sure why you thought buying this shit would entice me to open my mouth."

"I took that bolt to the Maine State Crime Lab to have it tested, Uncle Denis. I know it came from your store."

"Is that what passes for CSI work with you wardens?"

I felt the skin beneath my collar grow warm. "Look, I know you resent me—"

"Don't think that makes you special. There are lots of people in the world I hate."

"Including my mom?"

I expected a cruel remark, but he let out a gasp instead. "I never hated your mother."

"Right."

"Don't scoff at me. Marie was my baby sister. I would have done anything for her. That's God's honest truth. We were raised by my parents to believe there was nothing—*nothing*—more important than family." He pushed his shooting glasses up his nose. Smoothed the corners of his mustache. "Your mother broke our hearts. Not just mine but all of ours. You might not remember the little VW I fixed up for her when things were going to hell with your old man. But I bet you remember going to stay with your aunt Michelle in Portland when your parents split. How long did you two live in that apartment? Six months? Eight months? And your mom never paid her sister a dime for room or board. Instead, after she married your asshat stepfather, she treated us like dog shit she couldn't wipe off her shoe fast enough. Your mom was a selfish, spoiled person when she was a baby, and she was a selfish, spoiled person the day she died. If you have a problem with me saying that, we can go outside so you can kick my ass, like your dad used to do."

Whatever I had expected coming through the door, it hadn't been a cri de coeur. Now I was the one unable to sustain eye contact.

"Gorman Peaslee said he came in here yesterday," I mumbled.

"That's how you're going to respond? Have it your way. Yeah, Gorman is one of my best customers. He knows you're my nephew. Gave me no end of shit about it, too. He called me last night about the Amish guy crashing his buggy and your blaming Gorman for it. He said you nearly broke his wrist arresting him."

"News travels fast."

"Gorman Peaslee has a lot of friends around here, me included. Some of them are cops. Another is the commissioner who granted him bail."

So the sociopath is on the loose again to terrorize his neighbors or even come looking for me.

I felt that I should warn the Stolls until I realized that they would have seen and heard him as he returned home.

The buzzer sounded as the door opened.

"I hope I'm not interrupting a family reunion," said a familiar voice.

Gary Pulsifer stood inside the door in his usual posture: thumbs tucked under his heavy ballistic vest.

"Two wardens in one day," said Denis. "What did I do to deserve this?"

"I was passing by and happened to notice Mike's ride outside. There aren't too many rebuilt 1970 Scouts cruising around Maine."

I suspect that both my uncle and I were grateful for the interruption.

Pulsifer gestured toward the crossbow in my hand. "Are you taking up a new hobby?"

"Something like that."

"Ronette told me you're staying at the cabin on Tantrattle Pond," said Pulsifer.

"I spent the night there."

"It's a pretty spot. Hard to get a signal, if I recall. You probably haven't been keeping up with current events."

His unspoken message couldn't have been clearer. Something had happened. Something he didn't want to talk about in front of my uncle.

"I was just leaving." I turned to the small man behind the register. The sad self-pity was gone from his expression, replaced by the familiar dyspepsia. "Goodbye, Denis."

"Careful not to shoot yourself with that thing" were his parting words to me.

Pulsifer thought it best for us to drive down the road a ways. Whatever he had to tell me required real secrecy.

I followed his patrol truck to the empty parking lot of a church and then around back, where haze was rising from a small, melting graveyard. We pulled our vehicles together facing in opposite directions, as cops do, so we could converse through our driver's-side windows.

"What's happened?"

"Another state prison guard died last night."

"What? How?"

"Carbon monoxide poisoning. He and his mother and sister—they all died in their sleep. The news hasn't been released to the public yet, but the staties are saying it was a faulty furnace."

"Did you happen to catch the name of the guard?"

"Clegg maybe."

"Pegg?"

"Yeah, that's it."

I slumped back against the seat. I am sure I must have looked to Pulsifer as if I'd been poleaxed.

"You knew him, I take it."

"Not really," I said. "But he struck me as a decent guy. He was young and naïve, but he had a good heart. And they killed his mother and sister, too?"

Pulsifer pricked up his ears. "Who's the *they* in that sentence?"

"I don't know."

Rancic was the name in my head. But however much Gary Pulsifer might have changed in sobriety, he was still a rumormonger at heart. I couldn't trust him with my unconfirmed hunch.

"So I take it from the crossbow and arrows you just bought that you're pursuing a theory about who shot your wolf."

"It doesn't seem as important as it did a while ago."

"If it keeps you from meddling in active homicide investigations, I'm all for it. As your union rep, I recommend that you continue chasing your mystery archer. Which brings me to the other thing I want to talk to you about. I got a call from Kent Mears last night. He was drunk and pissed off. He's no Socrates, but he figured out how you came to knock on his door yesterday. The fact that we're both game wardens. It wasn't cool of you to do that, Mike. The program is supposed to be anonymous."

"I apologize."

He stuck his hand into the cold air between us for me to shake. "Just don't do it again."

"Do you really think people can change, Gary?" I wasn't sure who I had in mind with this question.

"I'm betting my life on it."

35

After Pulsifer had driven off, I placed a call to Steve Klesko. To my surprise, the detective picked up immediately. I had assumed he would be too busy for me.

"You must have heard about Pegg," he said.

A crow descended out of the mist to perch on a branch in the tree beside the graveyard. The wet black bird had a look of eager, deserving expectation, as if I might be inclined to toss it some food.

"All I've heard so far has been third-hand," I said, trying to ignore the beggar. "What's this about a faulty furnace?"

"I can't comment. You know that."

"If you're not going to talk to me, then why did you take my call?"

I could hear him breathing on the other end as he considered his response.

"What do you know about Pegg's connection to your friend Billy Cronk?" Klesko said at last.

"I know he tried to visit Billy at the Farm a couple nights ago, but got cold feet. I suspect he had information about the prison stabbings, who was really behind it, maybe."

"Maybe he did and maybe he didn't. All I can tell you is he got up the nerve to visit Cronk at Bolduc last night. It was the last time Tyler Pegg was seen alive."

"Why don't you ask Billy what they talked about?"

"I would, except he's not here."

I assumed it was a joke. "What do you mean he's not there?"

"I mean that sometime last night Cronk walked out of the Bolduc Correctional Facility and disappeared."

"What?"

"With all the talk of a pardon he must have figured he was free to go. The warden begs to differ, needless to say."

"Shit!"

Leave it to Billy Cronk to jeopardize his pardon by escaping from a facility from which he was due to be released any minute.

"Any idea why he jackrabbited?" Klesko asked.

"Pegg must have told him something."

"Like what?"

"That his family was in danger."

"You wouldn't happen to know where they are, by the way? Aimee and the Cronklets as you call them."

The crow stared at me through my windshield, which was growing mistier by the minute from my rapid breathing. "They may be staying at my house."

"May be staying?"

"I offered the place to them while I'm up in the Sandy River Valley. Whether or not they took me up on the invitation, I have no idea."

Klesko paused half a minute to process my statement.

Then he said, "We know that Cronk called his wife last night after he met with Pegg. So he knows his family is shacked up at your house. My impression of Mrs. Cronk is that she's not going to be inclined to share information with me. Would you call that a fair assessment?"

"More than fair. Look, Steve, the only reason Billy would have walked away from the Farm is that he is deeply worried for Aimee and the kids' safety. And given what happened to the Pegg family, I'd say his concerns are legitimate. Is there any way—?"

"I can't assign a trooper to watch them if that's what you're about to ask. I can, however, stake out your place since it's the most logical place we're going to find Cronk."

"So you're going to use his family as bait?"

"The man escaped, Mike. That's a felony. Maybe the governor will pardon him for that one, too, but in the meantime, we're going to put out a BOLO with his name on it."

"I get it."

"There are a few more questions I need to ask you. You're not going to like them, but I don't have a choice. From Billy's folder I know he worked as a caretaker at a mansion outside Grand Lake Stream. There's good reason to think he's familiar with the operation of furnaces—"

"You think Billy might have killed Pegg and his mother and sister?"

"His whereabouts are unaccounted for. And Pegg's Honda is missing."

"No fucking way."

"How can you be certain?"

"Because Billy Cronk is incapable of harming an innocent person."

"It's nice that you believe that, but I don't have the luxury. And since I can't ask Tyler Pegg what he told your friend, I have to pursue all possible theories about how those three people died. Which means my chief priority right now is locating Billy Cronk and taking him back into custody."

The crow had taken wing while my attention was elsewhere.

"Don't take this the wrong way, Steve, but go to hell."

"I told you you'd be pissed at me. And, buddy, I hate to have to say this, but as mad as you are at the moment, please don't call Aimee Cronk. There are prosecutors in the AG's Office who would like nothing better than to rope you in for aiding and abetting a fugitive."

The first thing I did after I hung up was try Aimee's cell.

I expected to get her voice mail at least. Instead I received an automated intercept message: "We're sorry. We are unable to complete your call as dialed. Please check the number and dial again, or call your operator to help you."

That clever, clever woman. Knowing her phone could be used to triangulate her location, she had removed the battery. Chances were, she had packed up the kids, left my house, and driven to meet Billy. Where did that leave them to run? The cops would be waiting at the apartment in Lubec.

What had Pegg told Billy?

When I talked with the young CO back at the hospital on the

day of the stabbings, he had clearly been scared, confused, and full of doubt.

Dawn Richie's husband had supposedly committed suicide by poisoning himself with carbon monoxide. That the Peggs had died under similar—allegedly accidental—circumstances couldn't be a coincidence. The similarities were either the work of a killer using a tried-and-true method to kill again or a deliberate attempt to incriminate Richie by making the connection almost comically obvious.

I couldn't think of a damned thing to do except wait. With luck, Aimee would reach out to me on a prepaid phone she'd bought at one of the bargain stores she frequented.

In the meantime there wasn't another soul who could help me.

No sooner had that thought passed through my mind than I realized what a dunce I was being.

She picked up on the second ring.

"It's about frigging time," said Dani Tate.

She had been finishing up her patrol when she heard about the horrific death of Tyler Pegg and his family. After clocking out, she had spent the past couple of hours on the phone and at a computer at the Troop A Barracks, bringing herself up to speed. She'd even learned about Billy Cronk going AWOL.

"They're keeping his escape quiet so far," she said.

"Why?"

"Bad press. It raises questions about the governor's judgment, pardoning him."

"Klesko told me they were going to issue a BOLO." The acronym, which stood for "be on the lookout," had replaced the old *all-points bulletin* everywhere except on television cop shows. "Something is seriously wrong with this, Dani."

"Gee. You think?"

"I tried to call Aimee, and it's pretty obvious she destroyed her phone to keep from being tracked. I guarantee when the cops get to my house, they won't find anyone home."

"You must have some idea where they'd go."

"They've both got relatives Down East, but Aimee's too smart to go where they'd be looking for them."

"You think she and Billy are together?"

"It makes sense that he called her from a pay phone asking to be picked up."

"The special statement I've seen says she's driving a blue 2006 Tahoe. Maine Purple Heart recipient plates. License number BB544."

"Billy would have swapped out the plates with something he pried off an unattended vehicle. I'm finding it hard to focus on the most important question here—who murdered Pegg and his family?"

"Maybe no one. People die of carbon monoxide poisoning."

"Pegg knew something about what really happened at the prison—the actual reason Richie and Mears were ambushed. And now the conspirators think Pegg shared his suspicions with Billy before he died."

"Is that your working hypothesis?"

"For the time being, until I can learn more and come up with another one."

"What are you scheming, Mike? I hope you're not planning on driving down to the Pegg house in Thomaston."

"It occurred to me."

"You have to realize the more you try to help Billy, the less anyone will trust you when the time comes for you to vouch for him again. The facts won't matter. You'll be viewed as unreliable and probably an accomplice to his escape."

"What am I supposed to do?"

"You could go visit your wolf. Lizzie Holman told me his fever's down and he's fully conscious. He ate an entire Smithfield ham."

"When did you speak with Holman?"

My tone must have transmitted some of the unease I was feeling at Dani's involving herself so deeply in Shadow's convalescence.

"I'm not butting into your life, Mike. She actually texted me because she couldn't get hold of you, and you'd mentioned we were friends. Check your messages, and you'll see I'm telling the truth."

I did, and she was.

"I heard the she-wolf last night," I said.

"Are you sure?"

"One hundred percent. She is still alive, Dani. I don't know for how long. She seemed to be up on one of the Mount Blue spurs. I'm still not sure if I should try to live-trap her or let her go, hoping she heads back into the Boundary Mountains."

"Trying to trap her would be an adventure."

"A futile adventure."

"Fun, though." Her tone was both excited and wistful. She missed being a game warden, I could tell.

At precisely this moment in the conversation I realized how much I wished we were having this conversation in person.

"You'd love the cabin where I'm staying. It's on the shore of Tantrattle Pond. Do you know where that is?"

"You keep forgetting I grew up over the gap in Pennacook. We used to ride our sleds over that way in the winter. There's an ITS trail that goes right past Tantrattle."

"Do you want to come up?"

"I have to work again in less than nine hours, Mike. I'm exhausted and not going to drive up for a quickie. It would make me feel cheap, for one thing."

She had wounded me with the accusation. "That's not what I had in mind. I want you to see the cabin because it's so peaceful and perfect. I know you'd love being there."

"That's sweet. But it doesn't make up for the fact that you were never going to ask me for help."

"I made the call, didn't I?"

"Finally."

"Better late than never."

"Not always." She went away for a while. "I've got to get some sleep. You weren't the only one who had a dramatic night. I busted a guy who'd been beating his girlfriend's son with a belt. And for once, the woman didn't even make excuses for the scumbag. Domestic violence cases are always so frustrating. This one feels different. I actually have hope."

"It sounds like you made a difference."

"Time will tell, I guess. If I were you, that's what I'd focus on today, making a difference. You can't help the Cronks, but maybe there's someone else you can help. We all need a friend in our corner."

She meant the rogue wolf, but she meant more than that.

36

As I drove north up the valley, I reflected on what my uncle had told me about my mother. I had so many things to occupy my mind, between the Peggs, the Cronks, and Dani. Yet it was Denis's words that echoed inside my skull: "Your mom was a selfish, spoiled person when she was a baby, and she was a selfish, spoiled person the day she died."

That assessment was false in all kinds of ways.

But I couldn't dismiss it.

Denis had been right about me, as well. Six years earlier, I might well have beaten him up for insulting me, just as my father would have done. But I liked to believe that I was a different person now.

Not until I had met Dani—a sane, stable woman who wanted a normal life—had I finally made the connection between the fucked-up example that my parents had set for me in childhood and my subsequent romantic failures. I hadn't believed men and women were destined to live happily ever after. Marriage in my mind was like sharing a cell with someone who started out as your best friend but who, over time, transformed into your mortal enemy. Was it any wonder I had sought a life of self-sufficiency despite knowing that such an existence would be lonely and miserable?

All of the counterexamples I had seen of loving, long-term partnerships—Ora and Charley Stevens, Aimee and Billy Cronk—had failed to disabuse me of my self-damaging beliefs. And my own misadventures with Stacey couldn't have helped.

When I reached Avon, I turned down the dirt road to the grassy strip of the Lindbergh Airport. There were no hangars, no landing lights, no control tower, just an open field with a couple of dripping wind socks and no one watching. With all the fog, I felt it was a safe place for me to conduct my scientific experiment.

I had noticed a stack of wet, moldering hay bales there on my prior visit: a poor backstop for a sliding plane. I removed an L.L. Bean fishing catalog I'd tossed in my back seat and brought it with me across the wet field. I slid the catalog under the baling wire to create an improvised target.

Then I screwed the broadheads onto the three Spider-Bite X2 bolts and snapped two of the arrows into the quiver on the underside of the mechanical bow. I slid my boot toe into the cocking stirrup, gripped the bowstring with both hands, and straightened up, pulling the length of waxed polyester until I heard a catch. The draw didn't take much strength—most crossbows and bows I had drawn strained muscles I didn't know I possessed. I fitted a bolt into the slight groove until the fletching was secured beneath the retention spring.

Then I paced off ten yards. I aimed, fired, and nailed the center of the catalog. The bolt penetrated the paper and the hay all the way to the fletching.

I paced off another ten yards and repeated the process. This time the bolt caught the upper corner of my target.

Ten more yards and the broadhead missed the catalog by a foot.

I'd been winging it thus far, trying to get a feel for the weapon. I hadn't been steadying myself and bracing my elbow as I might have in a genuine hunting situation where I was attempting to kill a big animal from a place of ambush.

I retrieved my three bolts—all fortunately intact—and paced out to fifty yards. While the Blood Eagle Tactical wasn't a toy by any means, I estimated its effective range to be as abbreviated as that of a BB gun.

I knelt on my right knee in the grass and braced my left elbow on my left kneecap. Without a log or branch to steady my aim, it was the best I could do. I breathed in and let out half a breath. Then I fired at my target. I reloaded and fired again. A minute later, I repeated the action for the third and final time.

I was a fair shot—not the best in the Warden Service, but not the worst either—and I had missed the hay bale, not to mention the target, by a country mile with every volley.

My experiment had proven two things. The first was that this particular bow was capable of being drawn and fired by a person lacking upper-body strength. The second was that, unless the shooter was a world-class bowman, he or she had to have been quite close to Shadow when firing the fateful bolt.

I secured the three sharp-pointed arrows in the attached quiver and set the unloaded contraption on the back seat of my vehicle.

Afterward, I headed off to the only grocery store in a fifty-mile radius. Dani's offhand remark about Dr. Holman's feeding Shadow an entire ham had helped me realize something I hadn't properly considered. From the start, I had assumed that the wolf had been drawn close to the shooter by the use of bait. Most serious predator hunters obtained their meat scraps through unconventional means: either by using deer or moose carcasses they had killed themselves or by purchasing unsalable beef and pork from slaughterhouses.

But this much I knew now: I was after an amateur.

I made a direct line to the meat counter at the rear of the market in Phillips, where I had a five-minute conversation with the butcher. By the time I exited through the automatic door, I knew the name of the person who had tried and failed to murder my wolf.

37

Being a vintage vehicle, my Scout didn't have a dashboard thermometer, but I could tell from the squishiness of the road and the fog drifting through the trees that the snow was melting in the mountains.

Isaac Stoll's wrecked carriage had been removed from the field. The Amish had even repaired the fence with new rails. The only reminders of the recent violence were the scars in the earth.

Outside the farmhouse, a buggy was drawn up, along with a handful of automobiles owned, no doubt, by well-wishers from the community who had come to offer support to their Amish neighbors. Indigo Mazur had angled her Subaru Baja outside the barn, where the Stoll family stabled its horse and donkey.

I glanced through the open door and breathed in the scent of hay. The wooden floorboards were cleaner than the "washed" plates in my dish rack at home. I heard the breathing of a horse somewhere in the dark and the swishing of its tail.

"Hello?" I called.

"Good morning," came Samuel's small voice.

His sisters were with him, along with three other girls. The girls hung back, but the big-eyed boy seemed glad to see me.

"How is your uncle Isaac doing?"

"He is in the hospital."

I had hoped for a more detailed description of his condition, but it made sense that Samuel's parents hadn't disclosed the extent of his uncle's injuries, especially if there was a prospect of paralysis or traumatic brain injury.

"How about the horse? Her name is Tilda, right?"

"She has a strained shoulder and cuts and bruises. *Mamm* made a poultice. We can give her apples, but not too many because they make her stomach sour."

"I see that Indigo is here."

"And Zane!" said one of the older girls, a preteen.

The young farmer appeared out of the shadows with straw in his hair as if he'd been playing hide-and-seek with the children. "Hello."

"I thought you were inside with the adults."

He pulled a thread of straw from his hair. "What's an adult?"

"I stopped by your yurt on my way in, but neither you nor Indigo were there."

"She's inside with the Amish and some concerned people from the community. They're discussing how to deal with Peaslee, now that he's free on bail. Indigo wants the Stolls to take out a restraining order."

"I actually came here looking for you."

"Me?"

"I have one last question before I let this matter go about the wolf. How about we go for a walk together?"

"OK."

A fox sparrow was scratching at the leaves under the big maple that towered over the dooryard. As on the other maples around the farm, a bucket hung from the trunk to collect sap. The warm spell would cause it to run better now.

"How is Isaac Stoll really doing? It didn't sound like the Stolls are sharing the details with the kids."

"Ike has a concussion and bruised bones in his back. And a broken arm, of course. I guess there were multiple fractures. Is that the question you wanted to ask?"

"You're a vegan, aren't you, Zane?"

He came to a halt. "You know I am."

"So why did the butcher at Edmunds' Market tell me you were in there last week buying three whole hams?"

The color drained completely from his bearded face.

"To donate them, maybe? Like to a food bank?"

"Which food bank?"

He contemplated his boots. "The one in Farmington."

"They must have really appreciated such a generous gift. I'm sure they'll remember your coming in clearly. But I have to ask, why would you, as a vegan, choose to support the animal industrial complex that way? I thought you had ethical issues about pigs being bioengineered, raised in confinement on factory farms, and then slaughtered with a bolt to the head?"

The gory image I had evoked brought a flush of anger to his face. "Not all of them die when they're 'stunned.' A lot of them die later in the scalding tanks. There's a video online. You should watch it the next time you think of eating a hot dog. You really should watch that video."

The foraging fox sparrow had been joined by two gray squirrels, whose drey, or nest of leaves, I'd noticed in the higher reaches of the maple.

"Zane, why were you putting out hams around Mary's property? Before you answer, I am going to suggest a reason. It was to draw Shadow in close, wasn't it?"

"I didn't shoot him."

"I know you didn't."

His eyelids began to flutter. He opened, then closed his mouth so that his lips disappeared.

What Zane Wilson hadn't noticed was that, in our seemingly directionless stroll, I had been leading him to his girlfriend's vehicle. I slowly moved my head so that he would follow my gaze down into the tail bed of the Baja.

A Spider-Bite X2 crossbow bolt lay on a small mat of straw.

He snapped his head up in alarm. "Indigo said she—"

"Got rid of the other arrows?"

Zane wasn't the brightest guy, but he was bright enough to know he'd given himself away.

"Here's what I think happened, Zane. I may have a few details wrong, but I am fairly confident about the big picture. After Shadow killed the Stolls' donkey Little Amos, Indigo got very, very mad. You yourself said she has a big temper for a small woman. So, being worked up, and with the killer wolf still presumably in the area, she went looking for a weapon. Not a rifle because she knows how much you disapprove of guns. Instead she bought a crossbow, arrows, and broadheads from the local sporting goods store, Fairbanks Firearms in Farmington. Then she started practicing with them on your property, probably against your wishes."

"How did you . . . ?"

"There were two things that made me suspicious. The first was that, when Warden Landry and I were visiting Mrs. Stoll, Indigo left ahead of us, and I had the strong impression her purpose was to block us from driving onto your land. It could have been for any number of reasons, of course.

"It was the next day when I began to piece things together. There was straw all over your road that hadn't been there when Landry and I had driven partway in. But I knew you didn't keep livestock. And when you showed me around the place later, I didn't see a single hay bale or even a scarecrow stuffed with cornstalks. Now any archer will tell you that the best targets to use—if you're cheap and don't want to spring for synthetic ones—are hay bales, because you're unlikely to damage your broadheads on the fibers."

Zane stood there like a zombie.

"This was all conjecture on my part. Then yesterday, Warden Landry found a broadhead in the back of Peaslee's truck. Gorman claimed it was planted—which gave me the idea for this little trick with Indigo's car, I have to confess. I asked him where he'd driven that day, and he rattled off a bunch of locations. But one interested me in particular. Peaslee said he visited the Farmington hospital to fight with their accounting department over a billing dispute. And you had told me that Indigo was at a doctor's appointment."

From behind me came a shrill voice: "Shut up, Zane!"

The young man raised his hands in the universal gesture for helplessness. "He already knows!"

Indigo came striding toward us with her hands clenched in tight little balls. Someone inside the house must have spotted us. "What did you tell him?"

"I didn't have to tell him. He's figured it all out." He pointed at the bed of her little Subaru.

She flicked her eyes from the arrow to me. "You planted that there, you fucking asshole. That's entrapment."

"Actually, that arrow belongs to me."

"So what the fucking fuck is this about?"

"I was telling Zane about my theory of how you shot Shadow because you were angry over him killing Little Amos."

Her hand went to her lips, hovered there a moment, then dropped to reveal a curled smile. "What's your evidence?"

"Fingerprints recovered off the bolt the wolf carried inside him for a week. I had them tested by the Maine State Crime Lab."

"I've never been arrested or fingerprinted—unless you stole something of mine to take prints."

"That's not how I conduct investigations, Ms. Mazur."

"You just plant arrows in other people's vehicles."

Zane interrupted before I could respond. "He knows about the hams, Indy."

She came out with the explanation so quickly there was no doubt she had been rehearsing it in her head. "It's true Zane bought those hams. Maybe you're too much of hard-ass to notice, but my man has a big, soft heart. He saw that wolf with an arrow sticking out of him, and he couldn't deal with it being in pain, and he bought those hams to lure the animal in close so he could help it. That's what you told him, Zane, isn't it? Because it's the truth, so help me God."

"I know it's the truth. From the start, I wondered why Shadow ended up where he did, and it was because even though he was dying, he wanted to eat. So I believe you about the hams."

I held up a hand before she could lay into me again. "There's something I need to add here, because it's important. I use the term *wolf* to describe Shadow, but strictly speaking he's what's known as a high-content wolf hybrid. He has gray-wolf and domestic-dog genes in him. He's been in the wild for a few years, but he started life as a pet. He was a puppy who lived in a box in a living room. His original owner fed him dog chow in a plastic bowl. A lot has happened to him since then—and it's clear he has become an accomplished hunter—but some part of him will always be a dog. Which is why, I believe, he sought shelter at a human's house."

Indigo's dreadlocks swung when she cocked her head. "That's touching. But if you know Zane bought the hams to feed an injured animal, why are you still harassing us? Didn't one of you wardens find a broadhead in Peaslee's truck yesterday? He's the logical suspect."

"There's one more thing I need to show you."

From my pocket I removed the copy of a sales receipt from Edmunds' Market. It was dated two days after Shadow killed the donkey. The slip tallied the total for a rack of lamb and a leg of lamb. The purchase had been made on a personal account. The receipt was signed with the name of the holder of that account.

Indigo Mazur.

38

She was only trying to help the Stolls," said Zane, his voice rising. He had never seemed so young as at that moment. "She didn't want him to take any more of their animals."

"Did she tell you what she was planning?"

The question rendered him mute.

"I didn't tell him until afterward," Indigo said. "I knew he'd try to stop me. He thought that wolf—or whatever he is—was innocent. As if that matters."

"He was acting out of instinct!" Zane spoke these words as if he had uttered them to her before, perhaps several times before. How often, I wondered, had they argued about her near-lethal decision?

She turned to me as if we were two adults discussing a naïve child unable to understand us. "What did I tell you about him?"

Her condescension wasn't lost on her boyfriend. "Do you know how hard it was for me to lie for you? I felt like I was betraying everything I believe in."

"Then why did you?"

"Because I love you."

"Oh, Zane. I know you believe that. You're such a sweet, beautiful man." She held out her tattooed wrists to me. "Let's get this over with."

"I'm not going to handcuff you, Ms. Mazur."

She interpreted even my gesture of courtesy to be an insult. "Is it because you don't believe a 'girl' would attack you on the ride to jail?"

I could have told Indigo Mazur that I'd once been stabbed by a "girl" who bore a slight resemblance to her. And that I'd learned a hard but valuable lesson from that experience. Never underestimate the threat even the least outwardly intimidating person can pose to your life.

But I wasn't there to tell them about my brushes with death. "I'm not going to arrest you. I'm not even going to write you a summons, although I could probably come up with a charge that might even stick if the district attorney happened to be feeling generous towards me. But there's no point in punishing you."

"What's your game here?"

"I'm not playing a game. I'm telling you that the State of Maine will not be bringing charges against you, not for luring a domestic dog to a bait pile, not for failing to pursue the animal you wounded, not even for planting a broadhead in Gorman Peaslee's truck when you saw it parked at the Farmington hospital."

"Why not?"

"First, because it's not worth the time of the state employees who would be assigned to a case we might not even win. But second, and most important, because I choose not to."

"What does that mean?"

"It means you're free to go."

"Am I supposed to thank you for being magnanimous?"

I retrieved my crossbow bolt from the back of her Baja. "If you don't get it, you don't get it."

Zane had been stunned into silence by his girlfriend's diminishment of him. Now I saw that he was struggling to ask the question that had pained him from the moment he'd seen the injured animal on Alcohol Mary's mountain.

"How is the wolf dog doing?"

"His name is Shadow, and it looks like he's going to live."

"Can I go see him?"

"What the fuck, Zane?" Indigo said.

"I can take you there if you'd like," I said. "He's in the Pennacook Hospital for Animals, so it's going to take about an hour to get there and another hour back."

"Thank you." Zane turned to his girlfriend, the unspoken question hanging in the air between them.

Her answer was a snort and a shake of the dreads. "Are you crazy? Why would I want to go?"

"Because you . . . ?"

"What?"

She honestly had no clue.

I had felt sorry for Zane before. But Indigo had revealed herself as clearly to him as she ever would. I understood that he had a choice to make that would shape the rest of his life.

What had Dani said to me? "You have all the information you need to make a decision." And now Zane did, too.

When Dr. Holman's pink-haired assistant showed us to the back room of the clinic where they were keeping Shadow, I was surprised to find the wolf on his feet. He still looked hollow eyed and gaunt, and the unevenly shaved spots in his fur gave him a sad, patchwork appearance, but he had been eating heartily, the young woman said, and had showed no signs of aggression to the doctor or herself. He did, however, make a noise that wasn't quite a growl but signaled his displeasure with the three of us gawking at him in his confinement.

"He's even bigger than I realized," said Zane, who held back from the cage as if the animal might have the strength to crash through the bars. "What a specimen!"

"He's inglorious," agreed pink-hair. She cast a glance at me. "Am I using that word right?"

"You are," I lied.

Holman was in surgery, dealing with an unlucky cat whose teeth were being painfully resorbed into her jaws—a condition I had never heard of. The vet promised she would peek in if she got free. But I suspected we wouldn't be seeing her.

"What's going to happen to him?" Zane asked.

I hadn't thought that far ahead. Holman had said Shadow would heal in time, but not completely. If he really had suffered nerve damage, he might never be able to run at top speed. Clearly I wouldn't be releasing him back into the woods to find his female companion— not that I would have. No wolf could dwell safely in this part of Maine, not for the foreseeable future.

Nor could I think of a sanctuary where I might deliver Shadow for safekeeping where he could live out the rest of his days in the company of other wolf dogs. The closest such facility, across the border in New Hampshire, was a compound consisting of acre-size enclosures in the woods. The inmates were fed scraps from a slaughterhouse and had either the same vacant stares or nervous tics I had observed among their human equivalents at the Maine State Prison.

Taking responsibility for the well-being of a creature such as Shadow—unpredictable, dangerous, and wild at heart—was a life commitment of the first order.

"We're still working out the details," I said.

Zane lingered behind me. "When I look at him, I can't decide if he's a dog or a wolf."

"Both. Or neither."

"I wish Indigo had come with us."

"I do, too." I cleared my throat. "I'm going to hang out here a second if that's all right."

I wanted a few more minutes with the wolf now that he didn't have the pall of death hanging over him. I suppose I was curious if he remembered me. We'd only been together a few short days, and that was several years prior. I felt that I was projecting a bond with him that was one-sided and as sentimental as the beliefs I ridiculed when I heard them expressed by animal rights activists.

"I'm not surprised you don't remember me," I said to the wolf.

He stood with his head tucked beneath his shaggy shoulders.

"There's no reason you would, I guess. Considering the crazy life you've led. I wanted to tell you that she's alive. Your female. I'm not sure what I can do to keep her safe, but I am working on it. But you're not going to see her again, bud. I'm sorry about that, but it's for the best."

His yellow eyes didn't blink.

"I'm starting to feel ridiculous now so I guess I'll be on my way. I'm glad to see you looking strong again. I'll never understand how you survived what you survived. But I'll see you again soon."

As I began to turn toward the door, I heard the click of his long nails on the painted concrete. He had approached the bars and had pushed his black nose through them and was sniffing at me with that nasal inquisitiveness all canines possess.

I squatted down on my heels and held out the top of my hand. The bars were too close together for him to bite it off the way the Norse wolf Fenris did to the god Tyr. But I sure as hell wasn't going to extend any fingers.

He continued his loud snuffling. Then he let out a whine. He extended a tongue that was about twice as long as I had anticipated and rubbed my knuckles with it. I fought the primal urge to jerk back my hand. His luminous gaze held me spellbound, unmoving, as if by unspoken command.

Roughly an hour later, I dropped Zane Wilson off at his yurt. The ground fog was still rising from the sublimating snow, but we could see, driving across the field, that no lights were on in the walled tent or any of the outbuildings. Nor was the Baja parked in its usual spot. I wasn't surprised that Indigo had left without explanation, even if Zane seemed both baffled and hurt.

We had been quiet on the drive over the mountains. I had asked him about his search for a new truck, and he'd said some of the urgency was no longer there as Alcohol Mary had, for vague reasons, revoked her offer to apprentice him. My take on Mary Gowdie was that most of the reasons behind her decisions were vague. She was one of those people who, living alone in the woods, have no interest in explaining or justifying themselves to others. But if Zane and Indigo were on the verge of a split—and I wagered they were— he would need a new set of wheels.

"Am I right that Indigo owns this land?"

He was slow to answer. "Her dad does."

It seemed a little cruel to be pushing these revelations on him, but he wasn't a kid even if he possessed a childish innocence. I could have taught a Ph.D. seminar in betrayal. I knew what it felt like to learn that someone you loved, someone you thought you understood inside and out, lacked a hole in the chest where a heart should have been. But Zane was going to have to suffer through his own epiphanies.

He mumbled a goodbye in the back of his throat. Then he

unlatched the door. The air that seeped inside had the damp taste of rain even though a drop hadn't yet fallen.

"Zane?"

He looked back at me, neck bent, with the bone weariness of a man twice his age.

"Take care of yourself."

I didn't envy him.

39

The rain still hadn't started falling as I turned onto the Tantrattle Road. Then the sky burst open, and all the fog that had risen from the softening snowbanks returned to earth with a sudden and terrific weight. The drops that splashed off my windshield were as big as dimes.

I crept along carefully, afraid to outpace my rain-hazed head-lights.

I realized I was about to reenter a cellular dead zone and took the opportunity to check my phone for new messages I had missed. There was only one of consequence. Steve Klesko wanted me to call him back.

He sounded tired. "Billy was at Pegg's house, Mike. We found size-fourteen sneaker prints inside matching the ones he wore at Bolduc. Not to mention his fingerprints all over the mudroom."

After I'd recovered from the bombshell, I said, "But you told me whoever murdered the Peggs tried to make it look like an accident. Why would Billy go to the trouble of trying to conceal the cause of death only to give himself away so clumsily?"

"No offense, but your friend isn't exactly Einstein."

"You said you found all the prints he left in the mudroom?"

"Yep. Why?"

"Wouldn't it make sense for you to have found them near the furnace, or wherever else the killer sabotaged the system?"

"Maybe he was looking for gloves in the mudroom. Maybe he found the gloves. Maybe he removed his shoes. Maybe he left the house without remembering to clean up after himself. The point is Billy Cronk was there."

The call dropped. I put the Scout into park and redialed the detective's number.

I wasted no time asking the question. "Why would he kill Pegg?"

"We'll be sure to ask him when we make the collar."

"He didn't do it, Steve."

But the call had dropped again, and my friend, the detective, hadn't heard my testimony.

None of this made sense. I wasn't going to be of much help if I remained holed up in my vacation cabin. I needed to return to the Midcoast if I was going to intercede—yet again—on behalf of my star-crossed friend.

But a thought came to me as I reached for the shifter.

The phone connection being so sketchy, I texted a message to my self-appointed private investigator, Charley Stevens:

> Do me a favor and check something else. Find out if any guards from Machiasport transferred to the Maine State Prison in the year *before* the shutdown.

If Dawn Richie really was a budding criminal kingpin, she had to have more than one accomplice besides the late CO Mears.

With luck, an answer from Charley would be waiting when I drove back out with my gear.

Before I reached the gate, the beams of my headlights bounced off the reflectors of a parked vehicle. I stomped on the brake and leaned over the wheel. The SUV was big and dark, maybe black, maybe blue. *Definitely* blue. I didn't have to read the license plate to know it spelled out BB544.

Aimee's Tahoe.

How had she known where I was?

The answer smacked me against the side of the head. She had found the topographical map I had left on my kitchen table, I realized. I'd mentioned that I was heading to a remote camp in the woods. She had deciphered the marks I'd made on the map and known exactly where to find me.

The Tahoe was blocking me from driving past.

I pulled my hood over my head and reached behind the seat for a Maglite. In my pocket I always carried a small SureFire, but it was time to bring out the heavy artillery. Made of machined aluminum, the Maglite was as long as my forearm. With six D-cell batteries inside, it weighed three pounds. Those big flashlights used to be standard police issue before the LED revolution. Who needed a baton when you could club a hooligan into submission with your handheld torch?

I ducked under the metal arm of the gate and started up the road following the light. Where there had been potholes, there were now ankle-deep ponds. My Bean boots kept my feet dry, but they offered terrible traction on the slick rocks and skinned tree roots.

Whatever footprints the Cronks had made in the mud had been washed away by the downpour.

I smelled woodsmoke even before I saw the glow from the cabin windows. My heart was pounding beyond the physical exertion of navigating the muddy trail. My anxiety came from not knowing what I would find—whom I would find—when I opened the door.

I switched off my flashlight and mounted the steps to the rebuilt porch. Hopefully Aimee would be expecting me and not have a firearm pointed at the door. Then again, they were running for their lives.

Better to announce myself than to barge in. I rapped on the new door. "It's me, guys! It's Mike!"

The next thing I knew the door had swung open, and Aimee Cronk had her arms around me, her face pressed against my damp coat.

"Thank God!"

Over her head I saw the five Cronklets: two peeking out from a bedroom, two sprawled by the stove, the girl hanging on to the back of her mom's thick leg.

I whispered into Aimee's ear. "Is Billy here?"

She raised her wet face. "We don't know where he is. He said it would be safer that way."

"Safer from whom?"

"Come inside and get warm, and I'll explain." She invited me into the cabin as if she'd built it with her own hands.

Ethan took my coat and hung it on a clothesline over the stove.

Little Emma was charged with unlacing my boots and placing them beside the stove to dry. Aimee had water boiling for tea and cocoa.

We all sat around the picnic table with our steaming mugs while she began her account of the past two days.

The manager of the Happy Clam Motel had watched them check out. He seemed to suspect that they might abscond with a stack of towels, ice buckets, the television remotes, whatever wasn't nailed down.

From there they'd stopped at the grocery store because Aimee would be damned if she didn't pay for her family's food. Plus, she wasn't sure I had the healthiest diet as a bachelor game warden.

But my house in the woods had raised her low-down spirits. Right as they pulled up, Logan had spotted a fox and her kits in the backyard. He was even more thrilled when he found three bloody squirrel tails under the platform bird feeder. Two came from gray squirrels and one came from a red squirrel, declared the ten-year-old aspiring biologist.

The day was pleasant enough. She spoke with their lawyer, who was tracking the pardon and commutation warrants as they made their way from the governor's office to the secretary of state. Once they were certified, the attorney said, Billy would be a free man. He could walk out the front door of the Bolduc Correctional Facility as if the past four years had been a bad dream.

But when Billy called and she passed along this information, he received the news with a strange subdued silence.

"How soon can I get out of here?" he'd asked.

"Maybe today!"

"Who else knows where you are?" He was being vague because all calls made by inmates in Maine prisons are recorded.

"Nobody."

"Not your sister?"

"No."

"And you're sure you weren't followed there?"

"What's going on with you, Billy? Why are you afraid?"

"I'm not afraid."

"Billy."

"I'm antsy over getting out. I'll believe it when I see it, you know?"

"That doesn't explain who you think might be following us."

"It's probably nothing."

The conversation had pricked Aimee's balloon, so to speak. She considered leaving the kids in the care of the oldest and driving back to the prison farm to hear the real reason her husband was acting paranoid. But the last time she'd left Logan in charge, she'd returned home to the final flag of a demolition derby. And it would be foolish to show herself in public if Billy was worried about some unnamed but evidently dangerous person stalking them.

She resolved to get through the afternoon by watching the birds come to the feeder—including the first red-winged blackbird of the season—and waiting for the lawyer to call back with confirmation.

Then Aiden came running inside to tell her that a creepy car had snuck up the driveway. It backed out wicked fast when the bad man behind the wheel saw him there.

"How do you know he was bad?" she asked.

"'Cause he backed out wicked fast."

"Can you describe the car, honey?"

"White with spots."

"Rust spots?"

"Yeah."

"Was it big or small?"

"Real small. Like the smallest car I've ever seen. Well, not as small as a go-cart."

The boy hadn't gotten a look at the driver, other than to notice he was wearing dark glasses, but the appearance of the unidentified man after Billy's warning made Aimee nervous. She told the kids to repack their backpacks and sleeping bags in case she decided they needed to leave in a hurry.

Emma interrupted us. "I gotta go poo-poo."

"Brady, take your sister to the outhouse."

"Mom!"

"And check it for spiders. You know how she hates creepy-crawlies."

Aimee bundled them up and gave them a flashlight. When the kids opened the door, a warm gust of humid air caused the lanterns to flicker. The rain had begun to lighten. It might even have stopped. The sound on the roof was no longer a martial drumbeat but more erratic, as of drops falling from the bare branches to plink like coins off the new shingles.

Aimee returned to her story.

The rest of the afternoon passed without incident, she said. All was calm and quiet—or as calm and quiet as the Cronk household ever got—until the phone rang after she'd put the kids to bed. By then she'd found my topo map and made a game of figuring out where I had gone up-country.

She'd hoped it was the lawyer calling with news, then realized it was almost midnight: too late for such a thing.

Instead she heard her husband's voice on the other end of the line. From the rushing car sounds behind him, she knew at once he wasn't calling from the prison farm.

"You need to get out of there!"

"What? Why? Where are you? What's going on?"

"You need to go someplace no one would ever think to look."

Her stomach had begun to agitate. "Billy, have you . . . escaped?"

"I'm pardoned, ain't I? It's only paperwork keeping me locked up. And it'll be too late if I wait any longer."

She placed no trust in her husband's legal acumen. But what worried her most was the real fear in his voice. "Who are you afraid of?"

"It's a group of renegade COs. They were going to try to kill me tonight before I was released, which is why I had to leave early. When they realize I'm gone, they're gonna come for you. They know I won't talk if they have you as hostages. Please, baby, you need to run and run fast. Tell me where you're going and I'll find a way to catch up."

The cabin on Tantrattle Pond was the first place to leap to her mind. For one thing, she knew I would be there and able to protect them. Second, she didn't figure many people outside of a few wardens knew where I was since it was obvious I was up to my usual mischief.

"And so we shot up here like shit through a goose," she said by way of conclusion.

My mug was empty. "What about Billy?"

"He said he'd find a way to get here."

"Warren is close to a hundred miles from Intervale. And I'm sure his pardon doesn't exonerate him in advance for stealing a car. Oh, shit. What did you do with the topo map I left—?"

Her rebuking smile reminded me she was smarter than I was when it came to the practicalities of life.

So far, I had resisted sharing details of my abbreviated conversation with Detective Klesko. She would agree with me that there was no way on God's earth that her husband would have murdered another man's family to protect himself. But I owed it to her to share the investigators' suspicions and the direness of Billy's situation. I couldn't make my mouth form the words.

"So who are these men who are after us?" she asked. "Do you know any of their names?"

"Are you sure this is a conversation we should have in front of the kids?"

"At this stage, they've gotten the idea that we're kind of in a pickle."

"What I have to tell you is bad, Aimee. Whoever these guys are, they already killed a fellow guard by the name of Tyler Pegg. They made it look like accidental carbon monoxide poisoning. I can't be sure, but I suspect one of them is the CO who allowed Darius Chapman to get loose at the hospital. Letting him 'escape' was a pretense to shoot him before he could trade what he knew for a lighter punishment."

"Is his name Rancid?"

"Rancic."

"That's not what the inmates call him. I thought he and Pegg were friends."

"So did Pegg, I suspect, until Tyler saw what happened at the hospital and began to have doubts about things he'd seen and heard."

"But this Rancid guy ain't the mastermind."

"No," I said. "I don't think he is."

"So who's the big shot running the show?"

I resisted sharing my suspicion about Dawn Richie. It felt premature and raised questions for which I had no answers. "We're going to need to ask Billy, if he ever makes it here."

"When he makes it here. My husband's got his faults and failings, but he's the most motivated individual I've ever met when the spirit moves him."

Just then, I heard a distant blaring noise. I recognized it at once. Someone was leaning on the horn of my Scout, which I had left unlocked in my haste to reach the cabin.

"Who is *that*?" Ethan Cronk asked.

"He sounds *mad*," said Aiden.

I picked up my Maglite from the table and put on my drying jacket, steaming by the fire. I tucked the hem behind the grip of my sidearm so I could get at it quickly. "There's only one way to find out."

40

As I ventured out into the dripping darkness, I was surprised by the duck-like quacks of wood frogs along the shores of the pond. The day's abrupt warmth must have awakened them from their winterlong sleep beneath the mud. Now a few males had begun their annual, awkward songfest. Soon, the bandit-masked frogs would be joined by thousands of lovesick spring peepers, and the nights would become earsplitting.

The fog continued to drift among the trees, obscuring whatever starlight or moonlight might have been above the valley. I chose not to turn on my Maglite. Until I knew who was here and what was going on, I didn't want to give away my position.

The snow was melting fast. The first patches of bare ground showed as impressions around the trunks of the biggest beeches and pines.

I made a path parallel to the drive, close enough that I could see it. I had decent night vision—though nothing like that of Charley or Stacey, who could move like bobcats through the darkness. Nevertheless, I tripped and nearly slipped on the wet leaves and moss-slick rocks.

All the while the horn continued to blare. That this unknown person had entered my own vehicle to summon me was somehow more galling than the obnoxiousness of the sound itself.

Who can it be?

Not Ronette or her husband, checking in on me. They would have done the neighborly thing and walked up the trail.

I hadn't told Zane Wilson where I was staying. Nor did he have a working vehicle of his own.

Gary Pulsifer knew where I'd chosen to pitch camp. In his drink-ing days he might have laid on the horn to summon me. But the new man he'd become seemed above those kinds of adolescent an-tics.

Billy, if he had managed to find his way here, would have been circumspect to say the least. As a former combat soldier, he would have approached the cabin with caution and under the cover of darkness to assess whether someone other than his family and me was waiting for him.

I had a thought that I might have disclosed the information to others, but my memory had a hole in it.

Eventually I drew near enough to the gate to see the looming shape of Aimee's Tahoe. My Scout would be parked behind it. Pre-sumably the vehicle driven by our visitor would be blocking me from backing out. I decided to make a semicircle through a stand of poplars and beeches to approach the interloper from behind.

Just as darkness makes blood appear black, so did the night rob this familiar truck of its redness. Crew cab. Extended bed. Off-road tires. It belonged to Gorman Peaslee: out of jail and out for revenge.

From experience, I knew he possessed an arsenal that extended from slingshots to shotguns to, in all likelihood, modern sporting rifles equipped with bump stocks to make them nearly fully auto-matic weapons. I supposed I should have considered myself grate-ful he hadn't brought along his pack of man-eating Rottermans.

As I snuck up on him from the rear, I could make out that the big man was standing with the driver's door open and his right hand planted on the horn. His left hand gripped the top of the door. So whatever weapon he might be carrying, I would have the drop on him at least.

He seemed to be in shirtsleeves, which struck me as odd consid-ering the chill and dampness.

I pressed the thumb lock on my holster and quietly drew my service-issued SIG P239. I had no qualms about leveling the night sights at his center mass.

"Knock it off with the horn, Gorman."

He tensed immediately and drew himself up to his full height, but while he removed his hand from the horn, he didn't remove it from the inside of my vehicle.

"Bowditch?"

"Don't make a move. I've got a gun aimed at your back."

"Warden Bowditch?" His voice sounded unexpectedly shaky. And a bit too loud.

"I don't appreciate your letting yourself into my vehicle. Let alone putting your greasy hands on it. What are you doing here?"

He just about shouted the next two words. "It's him!"

I didn't feel the bullet where it grazed the side of my head. The sensation was of my hair being lifted as if someone, leaning close to me, had blown breath upon it. Then I heard the gunshot.

The sound triggered my reflexes. I threw myself facedown in the mud.

Gorman was shouting, "He's there! Behind my truck!"

I had no clue where the shooter had stationed himself for the ambush. But my instincts had me crawling on elbows and knees along the passenger side of the Ram. Despite what you might have seen in movies, bullets can easily punch holes through the metal frames of cars and trucks. They might bounce off the engine block or the axle, but you're about as safe hiding behind a motor vehicle as you would be taking shelter behind a sheet of plywood.

For that reason, I scrambled into the woods, where, at least, the trees would provide some camouflage. I had dropped my Maglite, I realized. But the pistol might as well have been super-glued to my hand.

Now I felt a sharp stinging along my scalp. I pressed a muddy palm against my hair, an inch above my left ear, and it came away warm and black with blood. So the shooter wasn't a marksman, at least; he had missed what should have been an easy head shot.

As Gorman continued to shout directions—he had lost sight of me but guessed where I was headed—it dawned on me that he hadn't moved at all. He continued to stand beside the open door of my Scout where I'd first discovered him. It was as if he had been chained there.

Now a bullet shattered against a tree trunk five feet above my head.

So the assassin had night-vision sights on whatever rifle he was using. But at least I had a better sense of his position now. He was firing from the cabin side of the gate and across the parked vehicles. He had expected me to come straight down the road toward the sound of the horn.

My wariness had saved my life—for the moment.

The night scope provided him with an advantage, but he would be cautious about giving himself away because he knew that I was armed as well.

What happened next caught me off guard. Gorman began to run. He took off down the road in the direction of the highway. I followed him with my eyes until I heard the supersonic explosion of a bullet slicing through the air. Gorman stumbled, threw out his arms, then sprawled to the ground. The first round had caught him in the lower abdomen: a poor shot. It required a second round to the back of his shaved head to put him down.

I took the opportunity to make my move. I used a spruce bough to pull myself to my feet and ducked behind the nearest big tree. A moment later I vaulted over a spiky deadfall and came within inches of impaling myself on another, hidden behind the first.

The rifle exploded again.

Like all head wounds, mine hurt like a son of a bitch, and although it wasn't deep, it was gushing blood. I needed to apply pressure to slow the bleeding, but I didn't have a spare hand.

It seemed I was being targeted by a single individual. But Billy had suspected that a larger conspiracy was at work inside the prison. I had to proceed on the assumption that other armed men who wanted to kill me were in the woods.

Predators that hunt in packs behave in predictable ways. They might work together to separate the weakest individual from the herd so they can run it to ground. Or they might drive a prey animal toward a waiting attacker. When they have to overcome a guardian, say a bull moose defending his harem, they keep him occupied while other members of the pack cooperate to separate a vulnerable female from the circle of the male's protection.

These thoughts didn't run through my head in a systematic manner. I was too shaken, too pumped full of adrenaline. Instead I found myself guided by flashes of insight and physical reactions that only made sense in retrospect.

The attackers were here for Aimee and the Cronklets. I was nothing but an obstacle in their way. A dangerous obstacle.

I had to get back to the cabin. They knew I was coming. Why waste time and manpower hunting the woods for me when they would understand I had no choice but to place myself inside their killing zone?

The coldly logical thing to do would be to take Gorman Peaslee's truck and, horn blaring, let them know I was leaving to fetch help. But chances were, they had a truck of their own blockading the road and would know my stratagem couldn't succeed. Nor would they believe I would leave a woman and children to their possible deaths—whether it was the coldly logical move or not.

My SIG had seven rounds in the magazine with another already chambered.

I had two other loaded magazines in my pocket. Twenty-two bullets in all.

Plus an automatic Gerber 06 knife Billy had carried with him across Iraq and Afghanistan, which he had given me as a memento before he went to prison.

Against an unknown number of attackers equipped with rifles outfitted with night-vision technology, those were my armaments.

The forest had grown still again. I listened for footfalls. Leaves rustling. Twigs snapping. My executioner approaching.

Just then, multiple gunshots went off from the direction of the cabin. They sounded almost like firecrackers in the way they exploded one after the other. From a distance I couldn't differentiate them from the rounds that had been fired at Gorman Peaslee and me. But they sounded *different* somehow.

I heard a crash off to my left and realized it was my attacker bulling his way out of the forest. He was daring to leave me unguarded. Maybe he thought he'd wounded me worse than he had.

I took a chance and started after him. Like the cornerback I had been in high school, I took a pursuit angle on the runner.

He was distracted, his attention focused on what was happening ahead of him. For the first time I heard a radio receiver, which he must have had in his ear. As I moved to intercept him, I saw his silhouette. His rifle barrel was hanging down and across his legs so that he kept knocking it with his knees.

When I broke through the cover, I was nearly parallel with him. The sniper was smaller than me, dressed in black tactical clothes and a black knit cap. I hit him with a brutal blindside tackle. I pinned his arms to his body with my own and slammed him hard to the ground. His forehead must have struck against a rock because he went limp when I landed on top of him.

I rose to my knees. He was wearing the rifle—a Bushmaster carbine with a collapsible stock and an Armasight scope—hung around his neck on a bungee sling. None of it was military or law-enforcement issue. Nor was the Taurus revolver he had holstered against his thigh.

I turned him over but didn't recognize his face. He was young with a buzz cut and a neck tattoo I associated with turnkeys. He had lips the color of a night crawler. I doubted he had a military background given his atrocious aim and his clumsiness carrying a loaded rifle.

He was breathing, but I figured his skull was pretty well cracked. If he awoke from his concussion in the next hour, he'd be too busy puking to pose a problem to me. I doubted he would remember his own name.

I relieved the unconscious man of his weapons. I re-holstered my SIG and stuck the Taurus in the back of my pants. Then I pulled the bungee sling over my head and checked to see if a round was in the chamber.

I unclipped the radio from the unconscious man's belt and screwed the earpiece into my own ear. The sound of static was like freezing rain against a windowpane.

My last action was to yank the cap from the killer's head and pull it down over my ears. It wasn't the best disguise, but maybe it would create some confusion if I was spotted and provide me an extra few seconds. The merino helped soak up blood from my wound at least.

When I stared through the scope, the world turned an unreal greenish color, as if I were looking at it through an uncleaned aquarium. With the barrel raised, I began to creep slowly up the drive in the direction of the cabin. I hadn't heard a thing since those popcorn gunshots.

When I crested the rise, I noticed that the door of the cabin was standing open and the windows had gone dark. From the outside it was impossible to tell if the building was occupied or vacant. What did I say about people always underestimating Aimee Cronk?

41

I stepped into the forest on the side of the trail opposite the pond. Not wanting to show a defined profile, I kept to the trees as I would have hunting deer. The Armasight scope was not a thermal imaging model: it didn't show heat signatures. But the other assailants might be better equipped.

The man I'd taken down had the bulked-up physique and lack of training I associated, right or wrongly, with correctional officers. Which made sense. I had to believe that Rancic was here. He seemed to have had tactical training, and after what I'd seen him do to Darius Chapman, he struck me as the kind of stone-cold killer who lived for this sort of stealth operation.

But who is he working with?

At the moment, the question didn't matter.

What I needed to figure out—and fast—was their mission.

It started with neutralizing me. Only once I was off the board would they proceed to the next step. If their goal was to lure Billy out of hiding, they would seek to take Aimee and the kids hostage. I wanted to reassure myself that the Cronklets were needed alive as potential bargaining chips, but knowing the collateral damage they'd been willing to inflict to kill Pegg, I couldn't take the risk.

Those popcorn gunshots I'd heard earlier, the ones that had distracted my pursuer, puzzled me. Aimee had told me she was unarmed. Then I remembered the musty box of birdshot shells Peter Landry had found behind one of the walls.

As a distraction, she'd thrown them into the woodstove, where the gunpowder had combusted and the tiny ball bearings had careened harmlessly around the inside of the cast-iron furnace.

Smart woman, Aimee Cronk.

I heard a rustle to my left and froze. Slowly, I swung the rifle barrel around. I caught a split-second glimpse of an armed man moving into a mass of head-high evergreens. Something about seeing the world through the hazy green of the scope ratcheted up my heartbeat even more.

He was heading toward the outhouse, I realized.

I remembered Emma having asked Aimee if she could use the toilet before we heard the car horn. Had she and her brother returned to the cabin? Or might they be sheltering in place there now?

The evergreens were short, dense balsams that would make perfect Christmas trees in eight months. I could hear boughs being bent and twigs being snapped underfoot. The thicket was too dense. I would have to find a way around it.

Suddenly a man's voice spoke through my earpiece: *"Gamma, come in."*

The person in the trees ahead of me froze.

I carefully set my foot down, heel first, on the sodden fir needles.

"Gamma, this is Alpha. Report."

The voice sounded familiar, but between the whispered tone and the radio distortion I couldn't be sure.

"Beta, this is Alpha. Do you copy?"

"Copy, Alpha." It was another male voice. Again familiar.

"I think Gamma is down."

So now I knew that there had been, at least, three of them to start: Alpha, Beta, and Gamma. Probably only three.

The tree boughs ahead of me swooshed again, then went quiet as if someone was turning around to listen.

"Alpha, this is Beta. I think I'm hearing a radio behind me."

I had turned off the transmitter but must have been close enough to Beta that he'd heard his own transmission come through my earpiece.

"Fuck yeah," said Beta, *"we're compromised. Bowditch has got Gamma's radio. What do you want to do here?"*

Alpha came back, *"I want you to run a drag route. Got it? Then move to radio silence until my say-so."*

"Copy that."

My earpiece went dead as the two men simultaneously turned off their radios.

A drag route in football is when a receiver runs straight over the line of scrimmage, then cuts parallel across the field. What the hell did that mean in this context?

It didn't take me long to find out.

Beta broke from the evergreens on the opposite side of the thicket. Instead of continuing toward the outhouse, he made a ninety-degree change in direction. I couldn't see him through the cover, but my gut told me he was making a run for the backside of the cabin.

So where was Alpha?

Waiting to ambush me, I wagered. He was hoping I would pursue Beta and step out into the open where he would have a clean shot.

As quietly as I could, keeping to the trees, I took three steps in the direction of the dooryard. When I had a bead on the front steps, I knelt down and steadied my rifle barrel by bracing my left elbow against my knee.

From the sounds of things, Alpha and Beta hadn't discovered where the Cronks were. Aimee might have led the kids on a flight into the forest. Or she might have left the door open as misdirection while the family remained hidden inside the building. Sooner or later, someone was going to need to go up those steps—the only way inside the building—and have a look.

These men thought of themselves as the aggressors in this scenario. I needed to flip the script.

How do you defeat an ambush predator? By waiting him out.

Patience, alas, has never been one of my virtues. It was why I preferred stalking deer to sitting in a tree stand. It was why Charley Stevens chided me for giving up too quickly on riffles that held trout.

What I would have given to have Charley with me now.

But no one was likely to come to my rescue tonight. Tantrattle Pond was so far from anything that the shots that killed Peaslee would have been heard only by owls, raccoons, and fishers. The she-wolf. My fellow nocturnal hunters.

Water from the branches above me dripped onto my head and shoulders.

The wood frogs had been joined in their singing by a few spring peepers.

My right quadriceps began to burn.

Then to my left I heard an expulsion of breath. "Fuck it."

Alpha was leaving his place of hiding. If I held still a few seconds more, I might have a shot at him as he approached the cabin door.

One of the hardest lessons you learn in law enforcement is this: sometimes the bad guys get lucky.

"Motherfucker! Son of a bitch!"

The voice had come from behind the cabin where Beta had disappeared.

Alpha drew back into the cover. "What's happening?" he called.

"They're under the fucking cabin! The bitch slashed me with a knife when I squatted down for a look."

I could almost hear the well-oiled wheels turning inside Alpha's head.

"Drag one of them out!"

"Which one?"

"It doesn't matter."

Alpha wasn't going to show himself. Now that he had the advantage, he was willing to wait as long as needed.

There was a thump that sounded like steel hitting bone.

Aimee began to scream. "No! Stop! Let her go!"

Beta emerged around the side of the cabin, clutching little Emma to his chest with one arm while he leveled the carbine at her mother with the other one. Aimee gripped a butcher's knife with both hands. From Beta's hopping limp, it was clear she had slashed him badly across the shin and the forearm he was using to hold his sobbing prisoner.

He was an anonymous man dressed in black tactical clothes and a balaclava. But I thought I recognized his posture of all things: the stiff military straightness with which he carried himself.

One click and I could have put a bullet through Beta's head—assuming the Bushmaster had been sighted in accurately, assuming he didn't flinch, assuming Emma didn't raise an arm in front of his face, assuming all kinds of things I couldn't assume.

And even if I managed to kill him, what then?

Alpha had demonstrated he was willing to execute an innocent mother and daughter for the sake of silencing Tyler Pegg. With a trigger pull of his own, he could shoot Aimee Cronk dead, and he would still have five Cronklets to use as bait to draw their father in for the kill.

"Turn on your radio, Bowditch," he called. "I'm tired of yelling."

I did at the lowest possible volume, afraid that even that setting might give my location away.

Emma continued to cry, and now her brothers were trying to rush to the rescue, too, so that poor Aimee was forced to drop her knife to corral them, lest Beta start shooting.

The littlest boy, Brady, picked up the knife and waved it in the air like a cutlass.

He was Billy Cronk's son, all right.

The whisper in my ear was like the hissing of a snake: "*Mike, you've got to realize that we've got the upper hand here.*"

"Who is this?"

"*You don't know?*" He started to chuckle. "*And all this time I've been assuming you were smart.*"

"Rancic?"

A single laugh came in response.

"I take it that's a no."

"*Throw out your weapons. If you have Crossman's radio, then you must also have his rifle and revolver. Plus your own sidearm of course.*"

I remained motionless.

"*You know I have no problem killing one of those brats.*"

"Please, Mike!" Aimee had managed to keep her boys from rushing to their sister's rescue. They huddled within the comfort of her arms, except bold little Brady, who refused to relinquish his blade.

"*Do you really need a demonstration of my resolve?*"

His resolve. The last occasion I'd heard the strange turn of phrase eluded me. Then the memory arrived with a forceful immediacy. Me sitting at a table in the hospital cafeteria. Him across from me, toying with a salt shaker.

How had I been so blind?

Alpha was Angelo Donato, deputy warden at the Maine State Prison.

42

The man in the black balaclava had to be Donato's right-hand man, Sergeant Hoyt. He displayed the same ramrod posture I'd noticed when we met at the hospital. I should have been able to identify Beta from the stick up his ass alone.

"I have a question for you, Angelo."

Hearing his name, realizing I had belatedly deduced his identity, gave him pause.

"What?"

"When did you start using your own product?"

Every minute I could keep Donato off-balance was a minute when I didn't need to start voluntarily disarming.

He dispensed with the radio: "Just throw out your goddamn guns!"

Hoyt followed his commanding officer's lead by shouting, "Do it, Bowditch!"

Somehow I needed to take both men out before they could harm any of the Cronks. My mind kept attacking the problem, looking for an opening. But every option resulted in one of Billy's family being shot.

"I could see how unhealthy you looked when I saw you at the hospital," I said, playing for time. "When you and I first met—how many years ago was that?—you were as strong as a bull. When did you get hooked on the heroin you were smuggling into the prison?"

"Do you want us to kill them all?" Donato answered. "Keep talking and we will."

"Mike, please!" Aimee said.

"Is that why your wife left you—because of your drug use? I noticed your wedding ring was missing. She took the kids, right? I remember you have kids."

"Hoyt," said Donato. "Shoot the boy."

Aimee rose from her crouch. "No!"

The prison guard dropped the girl to the ground, and then, to everyone's surprise, Brady Cronk lunged with the knife at Hoyt's wounded shin. The man found it impossible to get the barrel of his carbine in the right position to take a shot without firing into his own leg. He stumbled away from the boy berserker.

I never formed a plan. It all happened too quickly for me to apply my rational mind to the unfolding events. I think I intended to shoot Hoyt, who stood fully exposed in the scope.

But before I could squeeze the trigger, the strangest thing happened. In that eerie-green circle of my scope, I saw Hoyt arch his back sharply, almost as if he'd received an electrical shock. His masked face lifted toward the hazy sky and he lost his grip on his rifle, which swung and danced on its bungee sling.

Then his head dropped in amazement and confusion.

An arrow was sticking through his chest. The broadhead had pierced his back and ribs and was protruding through the soft tissue beside his sternum. He pressed a hand to the strange object that had impaled him and only succeeded in puncturing his palm on its razor edges.

Seconds later, he was dead.

I turned toward the spot I had last heard Donato's voice and began squeezing off rounds.

I had expected to receive fire in return, but Alpha was a combat veteran of Afghanistan and not prone to dumb panic. The moment he saw Hoyt collapse, he must have realized that he was outnumbered. Worse, he didn't have a clue who had fired the arrow or where the archer was hiding.

I was pretty sure I knew. But I didn't want to get my hopes up.

I swung the scope around for a peek at the cabin and found, to my relief, that Aimee and the kids had scooted under cover.

Donato must have had an escape vehicle stashed somewhere. He would be making for it now. The truck would have to be parked far enough down the Tantrattle Road that I hadn't seen it from the gate.

I gambled that the men had all ridden in together, except for whoever had guarded their sacrificial lamb, Peaslee. I wasn't sure how Gorman could have known where I was holed up, but he was a local with all kinds of connections, and it didn't matter who'd told him.

A bullet ricocheted off the trunk above my head. Then another, ripping loose scales from the pine.

Donato had somehow circled around behind me.

I rolled over and over, trying to get the tree between us again.

For all my time stalking game and the tactical training I received each year, I had only been in a few firefights. Compared to a war fighter such as Donato, I was out of my depth. Pride had always been the chief of my vices, and now it was going to get me killed.

Except that Donato had other plans than to finish me. Maybe he feared the archer was too close.

I heard his heavy footsteps as he sprinted down the trail.

Those two shots had been suppressive fire; he'd needed a moment of me ducking my head to get past.

Leaves and pine needles stuck to my muddy clothes. Blood had plastered the knit cap to my head wound. I clawed my way to my feet.

I followed Donato down the trail. My pace was brisk: a jog not a run. I made sure to pause and scan the woods ahead in case my target had stepped off the path to attempt another ambush.

There were multiple sets of bootprints heading into the camp, but only one set heading out. From the depth and the heaviness of the toe marks, I could tell that Angelo Donato was running all out.

I picked up speed.

Suddenly I heard a single gunshot ahead.

I stopped short, raised my rifle. I became a Cyclops; my one eye was the scope.

Careful, careful.

Even before I reached the place where I'd knocked Crossman cold, I could guess what I would find. Donato had executed his unconscious collaborator. One less witness who might testify against him.

A moment later I heard a metallic screech. Donato, unable to vault the gate, had swung his legs over. He was opening his lead on me. I picked up my pace.

Once he got past my Scout, and Peaslee's Ram, it would be a straight shot to his vehicle if it was hidden where I expected it to be hidden.

I had yanked the earpiece out of my ear minutes ago. But the pigtail wire was still attached to my body. When the radio crackled, I fumbled to push the receiver in place again. What I heard was a long scream.

Then groans, labored breaths, curses.

I advanced carefully, hearing only Donato's side of the conversation, the words he could barely spit out.

"I should have known."

Something unintelligible muttered in response.

"Fucking fool. She played you. She played everyone."

Something more. Through the earpiece it sounded less like human speech and more like the grunt of some beast.

"Do it!"

The microphone picked up the thump of the arrow as it pierced Donato's throat. There was some gurgling, then a crash, then a long stretch of nothing.

I trotted forward, but I was farther behind than I'd realized.

Because, before I could reach the gate, another man spoke through the radio. *"Do you read me, Mike?"* said Billy Cronk.

I fumbled to turn off the muting function. "I'm here."

"Are they all OK?"

"Yeah, they're safe, Billy."

"Thank you."

"Donato?"

"He won't be getting up again."

"I'm coming down."

"I need to see Aimee and the kids. I'll meet you halfway."

He did.

43

Billy was still dressed in his prison blues, still wearing his size-fourteen sneakers. The crossbow was the one I had purchased at Fairbanks Firearms. He'd found it inside my Scout when he'd arrived and grabbed it as the only lethal weapon available.

"How did you get ahead of him?" I asked.

"You kept running toward where he was. I ran toward where he was going to be."

Billy's long blond hair hung loose about his shoulders. His cheeks were scratched from fighting his way through the underbrush. But his eyes were clear and bright. He seemed recharged.

"So you cut through the woods to get in front of him?"

"Barely did so. He was a fast mother."

"I have so many questions, Billy."

"I need to see my family first. You're a smart guy, though. You'll find a few answers down the road. We'll be up at the cabin waiting for whatever comes next. It looks like a cozy place."

"It is."

He left me with the crossbow and a set of car keys. Then he strode up the trail, his broad shoulders visible for less than a minute before the fog dissolved his silhouette.

I continued downhill until I came to Donato's lifeless body. I inspected the corpse. One crossbow bolt had pierced his lung. The other had split his Adam's apple with the accuracy of William Tell.

Under his black jacket and shirt, Donato had been wearing a Class III ballistic vest not unlike the one I wore when on duty. Hoyt had probably been wearing similar protection. Irony of ironies: Kevlar vests, being woven of superfibers, are exceptionally effective at stopping blunt objects, including bullet slugs, from penetrating them. They do less well against pointed weapons and are nearly useless against blades. A broadhead arrow fired by a crossbow with even a moderate draw weight was just the thing to have stopped these armored men.

Standing over his cooling body, I recalled Donato's last words. "She played you. She played everyone."

He must have meant Dawn Richie. But how had she fooled anyone when she'd come within inches of having had her throat slashed?

I placed the crossbow in the back seat of my Scout and, this time, locked the doors.

The key fob Billy had handed me had a button you could push to remotely unlock the vehicle. I pressed it and heard a tinny beep ahead.

Maybe a hundred yards down the road I found the Land Rover Defender in which Donato and his men had driven into the forest. Parked behind it, bumper to bumper, was a white Honda Fit that had seen better days. The car looked to be half the size of the sport utility.

I could understand why Aiden Cronk, seeing the subcompact turn in my driveway, had described it as "Real small. Like the smallest car I've ever seen."

The registration clipped to the driver's visor was in the name of Tyler Pegg. What was it that he knew that had cost him his life—that it was Donato who hired the two prisoners to assassinate Dawn Richie before she ratted him out to his superiors?

Seeing the car answered one question, at least.

Billy must have hiked from the Bolduc Correctional Facility to the Peggs' house, hoping to catch a ride with the one guard he considered trustworthy. Or maybe he had intended to "borrow" the vehicle.

According to Klesko, the fingerprint and footprint evidence showed that Billy had never gotten farther into the house than the mudroom, where, presumably, he'd found the keys he needed to abscond with the clown-size Honda. He might have arrived while the Peggs were slowly expiring from carbon monoxide or after they were dead. Because the gas is odorless, and he was there so briefly, he might never have noticed anything was amiss. He might still believe that Tyler Pegg was alive. That would be hard news for me to break to him.

I didn't consider it to be disturbing the crime scene to back the stolen car down the road until I could get a cell phone signal.

Charley had tried calling me eleven times before he broke down and left me a voice mail with the big secret he had dug up and had hoped to spring on me "in person."

"Sometimes I wonder if I taught you too well, young feller. You were right to have me check the transfers out of Machiasport in the months prior to the closing. Turns out that one foresighted guard managed to find work at the Maine State Prison six months before Sergeant Richie made the leap. You might recognize his name: Novak Rancic. I'd call that quite the coincidence, wouldn't you?"

I met Steve Klesko and his detectives, along with the chief medical examiner and technicians from the Evidence Response Team, halfway along the Tantrattle Road. I hadn't minded waiting alone, listening to the birds awaken in the predawn darkness: first a cardinal, then the robins. I figured the Cronks could use every second together as a temporarily reunited family. I also needed time to get my story straight.

Because I would be damned to hell before I gave evidence that might send Billy Cronk back to prison.

Let the Warden Service fire me.

If the attorney general offered me immunity, and I still refused to testify, I was more than willing to go to jail to protect my friend.

While I'd been waiting for the first responders to arrive, I returned Charley's call and told him the actions I was prepared to take if need be.

"Are you sure you're willing to pay that price?" the old man had asked. He had been a prisoner of war in Vietnam and knew something about the toll incarceration took upon the mind as well as the body. "Are you willing to trade your own freedom for your friend's?"

"In a heartbeat."

"It won't matter if they have evidence that he committed felonies beyond those for which he was pardoned."

"Then Billy and I can share a cell."

"I'm proud of you, Mike."

As it turned out, Charley had congratulated me on my brave decision too soon.

Within minutes of his arrival, Klesko had presented me with a cell phone and asked me to look at the image displayed. The screen showed a document affixed with the state seal. The detective directed me to the last paragraph:

> WHEREFORE, upon full consideration of the facts previously stated, I do hereby grant William James Cronk a FULL AND FREE PARDON respecting all such offenses of which all are to take notice.

The Penguin's florid signature followed.

"He commuted the sentence, too," added Klesko.

"When did this come through?"

"The same night Billy walked out of Bolduc."

"So was he free to go or not?"

"Do you want the technical answer or—never mind. In light of what you told us, I wouldn't expect pushback from the governor for Billy jumping the gun."

"What about the attorney general, though? Isn't it up to Hildreth to determine whether the statutes were followed?"

"Hildreth has enough to worry about. It's in everyone's best interest for your friend Cronk to disappear from the news. The deputy warden of the Maine State Prison orchestrated a conspiracy resulting in multiple homicides and the attempted murder of Cronk's wife and kids. There isn't a politician on earth who's going to say the man was wrong to protect his family after having demonstrated his heroism—especially with an election looming."

"In other words?"

"I'm not a lawyer, but I have it on good authority that if Cronk tells the truth about everything he did and why he did it, he's going home a free man before the night is over."

I didn't bother to mention to him that the Cronks were basically homeless.

* * *

"Why don't they stay at the camp?" Ronette Landry suggested.

I had returned to the cordon at the base of the road after having walked the state police detectives through the crime scene. The clouds above the mountains were swirled red and gold from the rising sun.

"Stay here?" I said.

"Unless it would be too traumatic after what happened."

"One thing I can say about the Cronks is that they are a resilient family. I'm sure they'd be delighted to accept. I honestly can't think of a better place for Billy to reenter the outside world. Are you sure the colonel will go along with this, though?"

"I think it will depend on who asks him."

Meaning not me.

However happy I might be, I still hadn't clawed my way out of the hole I'd dug on Maquoit Island and probably wouldn't find myself back in the good graces of my superiors until that case went to trial and we secured a conviction. Nor would Billy's brave actions redound to my benefit. If anything, my presence at this homicide scene would serve as yet another reminder to my enemies in the department that I had an unerring instinct for finding the nearest tar pit.

"I keep wondering how Peaslee got pulled into this," I said.

"After he was released from jail, he went around cursing your name to anyone who would listen. He wanted to know everything about you so he could destroy your life. Word must have gotten back to Donato or one of his men that Gorman knew where you were. From there it was just a matter of making a phone call."

I could imagine a choleric Gorman Peaslee arranging to meet with the deputy warden of the Maine State Prison who shared his hatred for me and had made a pact over the phone to collaborate with him in taking me down. Gorman must have left his house expecting to exact his revenge. Instead the bullying blowhard had gone to his death.

Another state police cruiser rolled up, a Ford Interceptor SUV. I recognized the driver.

Despite the predawn hour, Dani emerged from her cruiser wearing her shades and broad-brimmed campaign hat.

"I'll give you two a minute," whispered Ronette.

I dug my hands into my pockets and affected a loose posture so it would look as if Dani and I were having a casual conversation. "You made record time."

"It's the advantage of driving a vehicle that scares people into slowing down and moving over. What's under that bandage?" Her tone was businesslike, a little brusque.

"A scratch."

"Any other injuries?"

"My pride took a blow."

"It needed one."

"Ouch."

"Can I speak with you a minute, Warden Bowditch?"

Lots of people were around. It was hard finding a private niche, but we did behind the Intervale Volunteer Fire Department's pumper.

She removed her sunglasses. Her ever-changing gray eyes had gone as soft as the lifting fog. "Thank you for not dying tonight."

"I did my best." I resisted the urge to embrace her. "Listen, I'm sorry I've been so preoccupied."

"No, I get it. Maybe I've been pushing things too fast. We both have busy, complicated careers."

"Dangerous, too."

"Dangerous, too."

Furtively I took hold of her hand. It was as much contact as I dared. It wouldn't be good for either of us if rumors of our romance started making the rounds.

"Last night, back at the cabin, hanging out with Aimee and the kids, I kept thinking how lucky Billy is. In spite of everything, I was envious of my friend, the fugitive."

"What are you trying to say?"

"I wondered if you wanted to follow me back over the mountains to Pennacook."

She seemed startled. "You want to meet my family?"

"That didn't come out the way I meant. Sure, I'd like to meet your family. But maybe not today—"

"So what did you mean, Mike?"

"I wondered if you wanted to meet Shadow. He's doing really

well, Dr. Holman says. I need to figure out what happens next with him."

And with you.

She offered me a suspicious smile. "You want me to meet your wolf?"

I raised her small, strong hand to my lips and kissed it. "It's probably not what you were expecting."

"No. But it's a start."

44

Eleven days had passed, and back on the Midcoast, you had to squint to see that spring was actually happening.

Sometimes I think the only way to understand the season would be to point a time-lapse camera at a frozen bog and watch the ice melt; then a purple-green spear would begin poking through the mud, growing to resemble one of those face-eating alien pods until it finally exploded into full luminescent leafiness. The skunk cabbage: Maine's unsung herald of springtime.

In truth there were other indications that the hemisphere was beginning to tilt toward the sun again. A heretofore unknown to me bed of crocuses and daffodils turned the sunny side of my house purple and yellow. The first palm warbler of the year alighted on my porch, bobbed his tail three times, and continued on his migration north.

Charley and Ora flew down for the big day. I picked them up at the boat launch over on Pitcher Pond, where the old pilot had managed to set down his Cessna with the precision of a duck landing in a swimming pool. Now we were watching Billy finish the last touches on the acre-and-a-half pen he'd built in the woods on my property. The sea air coming up the river was cool, but the sun was strong, and Billy had his shirt off. His golden hair and beard shone as if forged from precious metal, and he'd built up a serious sweat.

"I know how jealous you can get, Charley," said Ora Stevens from her wheelchair. "But if I were fifty years younger, I would be all aquiver watching that beautiful man."

"What's the word I'm searching for?" said her husband. *"Har-umph?"*

The wiry, wizened man was wearing his usual uniform of green Dickies, green button-down shirt, and green ball cap with the insignia of the Maine Warden Service Association.

His beautiful snowy-haired wife had on a jade sweater that matched her eyes. As usual she kept a wool blanket draped over her paralyzed legs. Only her white tennis shoes peeked out.

It was hard for me to meet Ora's green gaze without thinking of their daughter.

"Have you heard from Stacey lately?"

"Last week," said her mother. "Her work has been hard. Two panthers were hit by cars in Florida in the past month. They put up signs and fences and other barriers, but it's simply a math problem: too many people want to live where the cats do."

"At least she's met someone," said Charley.

Ora gripped his hand as a signal to shut up.

Maybe he had meant those words to sting. Maybe he hadn't. I knew he was still heartbroken that their beloved daughter and their surrogate son had broken up.

But I was with Dani Tate now, and the Stevenses knew it, even if their absent daughter haunted this otherwise celebratory scene.

Dani's nonattendance had a more prosaic explanation. This was one of the days of the month that she spent at the Cumberland County Courthouse testifying in criminal cases in which she had been the arresting officer. The Department of Public Safety didn't give troopers days off for housewarming parties.

"What's Kathy's ETA?" Charley asked after a long pause.

"She should be here anytime now."

"What's this I've heard about her finding someone, too?" asked Ora, ever curious.

"He's a mystery man is all I can tell you. But I think he's someone she met doing one of her K9 rescue-and-recovery seminars. The one thing we can be confident about is he isn't a cat man."

"I'll pry the details out of her," Ora said. "Don't you worry."

"She means it," said Charley.

"I know she does."

I had turned to Kathy Frost to help me map out the dimensions of the pen. The enclosure was made of ten-foot-high steel posts and a chain-link fence that stretched between them. The wire apron extended five feet into the ground. We'd been forced to dig a trench around the entire enclosure and fill it with cement to keep my new lodger from digging his way out his first night in residence.

"I hope those foxes you mentioned aren't denned up in there, too," said Charley.

"I tracked them. They're holed up down by the river. But I doubt they'll stick around when they get wind of the new tenant."

"What about your human neighbors?"

"I went around telling them they might soon hear howling. I said they shouldn't be alarmed. But I watched a lot of faces go white."

"It's good you don't have anyone living right nearby," said Ora.

"For now," I said.

The Stevenses weren't going to settle for an enigmatic comment.

"That shack down the road, the one with the family plot in the front yard that no one would buy," I said. "I bought it."

"Bless your heart, Mike Bowditch," said Ora, who was so emotionally intelligent she needed no further explanation.

Her husband, however, required a more forthright response. "You're giving that dump to the Cronks?"

"In exchange for their fixing it up, I'll credit them as making payments toward the principal. Aimee is uncomfortable with anything that feels like a handout, but I'm trying to make it as fair as I can. It'll be nice having them nearby. The Cronklets are eager to help me with Shadow."

Ora winked at me. "As long as they don't get eaten."

"You bought that house?" said Charley Stevens in amazement that may or may not have been mock. "I seem to remember a time, not so long ago, when you made a church mouse look wealthy."

"At the rate I'm spending my inheritance I'll be a mouse again soon enough."

"Can you two men excuse me for a moment?" said Ora.

"Do you need a hand, Boss?" said Charley.

"Thank you, but I should be all right."

After she'd wheeled herself through the sliding door, leaving her husband and me alone on the porch, the old man leaned against the rail.

"So Billy's in the free and clear."

"That's what his lawyer tells us. He won't even be considered a felon for the purposes of voting or owning a firearm."

"I didn't want to vote for the damned Penguin in his reelection bid, but now I have to, I guess."

"That's what I said!"

"Ora accuses us of being cut from the same black cloth."

A clanging came from the yard where Billy was testing the double set of doors. He'd joked about how, as a former prisoner, he should get into the fencing business, given what he'd learned on the inside.

I glanced at the sliding door in case Ora was coming out. "No one must be happier about what happened to Donato and his co-conspirators than Dawn Richie. Now everyone knows how corrupt things were inside the prison. The state will be desperate to settle her lawsuit."

"She'll have a long wait before she sees any money, I wager," said Charley. "And who knows what might yet happen to upset her best-laid plans."

"Getting stabbed has worked out pretty well for her so far. First she arranged to secure a transfer for herself and Rancic out of Machiasport before the governor closed it. Then she started rumors about exposing Donato, causing him to miscalculate and overreact."

"I was convinced Rancic was Donato's stooge," said Charley.

"Me, too. Instead he was just another of Richie's puppy dogs. Loyal to the end."

"We'll see about that."

From that comment I could tell he was itching to tell me a secret. "What have you heard, Charley?"

"The DEA has taken an interest in the recent goings-on at the prison."

Unlike the local authorities, the Feds could not be ignored, slighted, or shrugged off. Their arrival on the scene offered the first faint glimmer that Dawn Richie and Novak Rancic might yet get their comeuppance. First though, the agents would need to find a wedge to drive between them. Richie seemed unlikely to succumb, but Rancic was a cocky bastard, quick to action, and a man could always hope.

A hundred feet away, Billy had paused to wipe off the perspiration and quench his thirst with a pint of Foster's lager.

What was unusual about the pen was that Kathy had told us to build it in a stand of birches, popples, and cedars. Shadow, she said, would want cover where he could conceal himself from watchful eyes. On my behalf she had contacted wolf biologists and operators of wolf dog sanctuaries in the United States and Canada, and she'd come back with a warning. Even though Shadow had been raised in a human home, his years as an apex predator in the wild had changed him in ways no one could predict—and wolf dogs were already notorious for being dangerously erratic. Hard as it was to accept, I might never be able to enter that pen in safety.

As he always did, Charley was reading my mind.

"How sure are you he won't rip out your throat someday when you're in there rubbing his chin?"

"There are worse ways to go."

"That's true. He could always disembowel you and eat you alive." Charley paused as Ora wheeled herself back out onto the porch. "Even with your warden buddies giving you carcasses, your pet-food bill is going to be higher than most folks' mortgages."

"Kathy knows the owner of a slaughterhouse who can cut me a deal on offal."

"Welcome to your glamorous new life," said my old friend with a slap on the shoulders.

"There's Kathy now," said Ora, leaning forward in her chair.

Sure enough, a Nissan Xterra SUV was idling down the drive, the slowness being deliberate so that the Cronklets could run along behind in excited expectation. I had warned them against shouting lest they disturb Kathy's passenger.

Charley and I carried Ora in her wheelchair down the porch stairs (I needed to hire Billy to build me a ramp) and we all convened beside the open gate.

Kathy swung down out of her vehicle, looking years younger than the last time we'd seen each other in person. She'd lost her spleen to a gunshot and still carried pellets inside her that threatened to work their way to her heart. But in that moment, standing in a beam of sunlight, she seemed to be the freckled, sandy-haired, former college basketball star I remembered from my first day as a game warden.

"Thanks for handling the transport," I said.

"Lizzie Holman sent along some meds you're going to need to put in his food. She thinks he's past the point of infection but wants to be safe. Don't be surprised if she stops in for a visit the next time she's on the Midcoast."

"Can we see him now?" asked little Emma.

"In a minute, honey," said Kathy. "Did your uncle Mike already talk to you about how Shadow isn't the same as other dogs you've met before?"

Emma's brother Aiden answered on behalf of all the Cronklets: "He said we have to tie our shoelaces and can't wear anything made out of fur or have any dangly things hanging off us. And we have to be calm and quiet."

"What about your hands?"

"Keep them away from the wolf!"

"Sounds like Uncle Mike has done a good job with the safety course." Kathy turned to Billy and me. "I'm going to let the stud muffins carry his kennel out of the vehicle. That animal is a heavy son of a gun."

Aimee came strolling down the drive at last, her cheek still bruised from where Hoyt had hit her with the butt of his rifle, and looking worried in a mother-hen fashion. "Kids, stay out of their way. OK?"

"Don't yell, Mom," her son Brady said.

"Right. Sorry."

Holman had given Shadow a tranquilizer for the road, but when Kathy opened the lift gate on the Xterra, he let out a terrific snarl from inside the enormous carrier in which he was imprisoned. The Cronklets scattered. Little Emma went running for the safety of her mother's arms.

Billy and I took hold of opposite ends of the plastic crate and lifted with our legs. The animal shifted position inside, pressing his butt to my end so he was facing the cage door, ready to attack or escape. We carried him through the gate and set the box down about ten feet in.

"Now what?" Billy asked.

"You get out of here. He's not going to be happy when I open the door."

"I wouldn't be so sure of that." I understood Billy was talking about his own recent experience, except that in this case Shadow was merely being released from one small cell into a larger jail.

I'd thawed a deer haunch and left it on a raised ledge I thought the wolf might claim as a throne since it offered such a sweeping view of the surroundings. With luck he'd catch wind of the meat and make a dash for it. Kathy had said it was more likely he would sprint around the entire perimeter of the enclosure looking for an exit he would never find.

"Hold the gate for me so I can get out fast," I said.

"Will do."

I waited until Billy was clear, then I lifted the rod that held the crate door shut. I wasn't planning on opening it for him; he'd find he could push it ajar himself. But I was caught off guard when he charged out mere seconds after I'd lifted the bolt.

I stumbled backward, ended up catching my foot on something, and sat down hard on the ground.

The wolf turned, the black ruff along his shoulders raised, fangs exposed. He still had that raggedy appearance from where the shaved skin for the bandages had been and where the hair was growing back. But his gold eyes were as hard as metal, and they were filled with an emotion I hesitate to name; but if I had to, I would call it grievance. He knew that he was my prisoner, and I was his jailer. His intelligent gaze seemed to announce that, whatever expectations I might've had about this arrangement, he would never submit, never again be a pet, would always remain wild at heart. He was no more mine than I was his.

"Mike?" said Kathy, the warning audible in her tone.

I heard the fence door swing on its hinges. It had to be Billy, coming to my aid.

I made my voice a hard whisper. "Nobody else come in."

Shadow let out a growl that sent mice scampering up my spine.

Using the strength of my legs, I rose to my feet with my arms low in a posture of surrender, pacification, call it what you will. "Keep cool, buddy. I'm not going to hurt you."

Another, louder growl. So much for the fond memories of the quality time we'd spent together in the animal hospital. So much for my fanciful notions that this creature and I had some special rapport.

Slowly, slowly I backed toward the gate.

As I got close, I heard the door turn on its hinges and felt Billy's big hands on my shoulders, and the next thing I knew I was standing outside on jelly legs while Kathy clicked a padlock.

The wolf trotted off to devour the remains of the dead deer.

"That was needlessly exciting," Kathy said.

Everyone laughed, but all I could hear was my heart trying to break free of my rib cage. My life would never be the same, I realized. Why do we always come to these recognitions too late?

Author's Note

While the title of the first part of this book, "A Civil Death," is explained in the text, the others might require some explanation. "All Stories Are About Wolves" is taken from an often-quoted piece of dialogue by Margaret Atwood from her novel *The Blind Assassin*:

> All stories are about wolves. All worth repeating, that is. Anything else is sentimental drivel.
>
> All of them?
>
> Sure, he says. Think about it. There's escaping from the wolves, fighting the wolves, capturing the wolves, taming the wolves. Being thrown to the wolves, or throwing others to the wolves so the wolves will eat them instead of you. Running with the wolf pack. Turning into a wolf. Best of all, turning into the head wolf. No other decent stories exist.

Similarly, the title of Part 3 of this book, "The Wild, Cruel Beast," also comes from a quotation, albeit a lesser-known one, by the Swedish humanist Axel Munthe: "The wild, cruel beast is not behind the bars of the cage. He is in front of it."

Sharp-eyed readers will recognize another quotation in the book, this one on page 230. As Mike drifts off to sleep, he recalls these words: "I was settled. Nothing could touch me. It was a good place to camp." The line comes from Ernest Hemingway's "Big Two-Hearted River," one of Mike's favorite stories—and mine.

Among the resources that assisted me in the writing of this novel were the memoir *Life Behind Bars: Eight Hours at a Time* by former Maine State Prison guard Robert Reilly and the extensive reporting of Lance Tapley on the Maine corrections system. I am also grateful to Sergeant Lance Mitchell, Sheriff Tim Carroll, and Chief Deputy Patrick Polky of the Knox County's Sheriff's Department for enduring my many questions about police procedure. That said, the inmates and officers in this book are entirely fictional, as are all the other characters in *Almost Midnight*.

For insight into wolf behavior and the passions these inscrutable animals evoke, I would recommend *American Wolf: A True Story of Survival and Obsession in the West* by Nate Blakeslee and *The Wisdom of Wolves: Lessons from the Sawtooth Pack* by Jim Dutcher and Jamie Dutcher.

I am grateful to Joshua Lincoln DVM for answering my questions about veterinary surgery and hope he will forgive the poetic license I took in filtering Shadow's medical treatment through Mike's emotionally blurred lens.

As always, I appreciate the help and forbearance of the Maine Warden Service and the Department of Inland Fisheries and Wildlife.

I would also like to thank the excellent team at Minotaur Books, including Charles Spicer, David Rotstein, Sarah Melnyk, Joseph Brosnan, Paul Hochman, Kelley Ragland, and Andrew Martin. And I would be remiss if I didn't acknowledge my insightful agent, Ann Rittenberg, who has made all of my books better.

My family remains a source of strength and support. I can't imagine doing any of this without your love. Kristen, you give me more than I can ever repay.